Sharp Shooter

Tara Sharp Book One

Sharp Shooter

Marianne Delacourt

deadlines

To the real Smitty, with love.
And to Nicci Whitehouse, my beloved sister.

by *deadlines*

www.twelfthplanetpress.com

This edition published by Deadlines, May 2016
First published in Australia in 2009 by Allen & Unwin.
Copyright © 2009 by Marianne Delacourt

National Library of Australia Cataloguing-in-Publication entry

Creator: Delacourt, Marianne, author. Title: Sharp shooter / Marianne de
Pierres. ISBN: 9781922101297 (paperback) Series: Delacourt, Marianne.
Tara Sharp ; 1. Subjects: Telepathy--Fiction Job offers--Fiction. Lawyers--
Fiction. Organized crime--Fiction. Dewey Number: A823.4

Chapter 1

I stared across the desk at the psychiatrist and tried not to fiddle.

Betsy Waller was a school friend of my mother's, whom I'd known since I was a kid. A no-nonsense type of shrink. Her office was polished floorboards and cherry veneer clean, her leather chair bigger than my bed. Certificates smothered the walls.

She'd been asking me questions for nearly an hour, and by the way her forehead was now wrinkling, I could see she'd reached her verdict.

Tara is nuts. Or, maybe, *Tara is NUTS.*

She closed her folder, slipped her Brendan O'Keefe spectacles up onto her head, and peered at me. 'Tara, I will only say this once so please heed me. You are NOT, as you call it, "nuts". You are, however, possessed of a … talent. You have an extraordinary sensitivity and overdeveloped emotional intelligence.'

'But how do I stop it?' I moaned. 'I mean, it's ruining

my life. I just got sacked because of it. I can't have a normal conversation with anyone. I know when they're lying. I see auras around things. Your pen …'

Bets twiddled the sleek, gold Parker between her fingers. 'What about it?'

'It's glowing orange. Like you.'

'Me? *I* have an orange aura?'

I nodded. 'Subtle, though. Like autumn leaves—not a carrot.'

She managed a weak smile. 'Well that's a relief. But what does it … mean?'

'People transfer their stronger emotions onto their possessions sometimes. Is the pen a gift from someone you really care about?'

Betsy flushed and dropped the pen onto her blotter.

'The auras aren't just colours either, Bets, they have texture and shape. They tell me about the person: if they're happy or miserable. Hell, I think I even know when some people are going to die.'

Bets pursed her lips at that and did an admirable job of NOT looking at her hands to see if they were glowing orange.

'I don't normally do this, understand?' she said at last. 'But I've known you since you were little and I've been in this game for many years. The longer I'm in it, the less convinced I am that we live in as scientifically rational a world as we'd like to think.'

I gave a mock-gasp. 'You've turned New Ager.'

She laughed at that, and slid the O'Keefe's back down into their normal position on the bridge of her prominent nose. 'Perhaps.'

Silence ensued as she wrote something on a piece of paper and slid it across the desk. 'I know a fellow who might be able to help you.'

I read it aloud—'Hara's Body Language Inc.' I looked back at her helplessly then read on. 'A body language and *psychic* business?'

'That's right, dear.' She bent her head back to her work. 'Say hello to your parents for me.'

Dismissed, I wandered to the door, dazed. It wasn't at all what I'd expected. A script for something perhaps, or the six months of counselling my parents had urged on me and offered to pay for but—

'Tara?'

I stopped and turned back towards her hopefully. 'Yes?'

'Don't mention this to anyone. Understand?' she said, a whiff of anxiety evident beneath her professional mask. Her deep orange aura flickered too.

I forced myself to smile. 'Sure, Bets.'

'Good girl.'

I left Bets' office and drove Mona, my beloved Holden Monaro, home along Stirling Highway, past the designer furniture shops and real estate offices.

I love Perth. My city is a woman with so many moods

and angles: dazzling, conceited, sheltered, and sometimes downright stuffy. As I turned off the highway towards my parents' house in Eucalyptus Grove and drove along a quieter road, she felt a tad disapproving, like she was saying, 'Get your act together, Tara.'

Since I'd been sacked from my last job, I'd had to move into my parents' converted garage until I could afford to rent again.

Unemployed and living back at home. Looooser!

I parked the car on the curb outside number 25 Lilac Street and walked down the side of the house to my flat, thinking about my empty bank balance and my lack of job prospects. Staving off the beginnings of a good bawl, I made myself a black tea.

My flat comprised an all-in-one kitchenette, sitting room and bedroom. Toilet and shower were outside, across a bricked patio. Not ideal, but better than returning to my childhood bedroom and having to observe my mother's insane rules on … everything.

After I'd finished the tea, I took a deep breath and rang the number Bets had given me.

'You come over tonight, Ms Sharp,' said Mr Hara, after I'd explained who I was and how Bets had recommended I contact him.

'Err, I guess so?' I was a bit taken aback at the speedy invitation. Still, it wasn't like I had anything else to do. 'What time?'

'After dark. You come to the back. Knock twice. Soft

knock … '

'You got touchy neighbours?' I asked.

'No. My wife is a jealous woman. She doesn't like me talking with females alone.'

I laughed, a little nervously. Mr Hara sounded a bit trippy. What was Bets thinking? And how had she come across him? I hoped he wasn't a former patient of hers. 'Errr … well … maybe—'

'Maaa. Maaa.' His laugh was like the sound of a newborn lamb. 'Kidding! Come at 7PM. I'll be waiting for you.'

'Mr Hara?'

'Yes, Ms Sharp?'

'Why am I coming to see you, exactly?' I know that sounded silly but I wasn't really sure why Bets had referred me to him.

Mr Hara gave the lamb laugh again. 'Well … if you're any good, maybe I'll give you a job.'

The magic words.

Chapter 2

After hanging up, I sat for a bit. What had I just agreed to do, on the faintest sniff of a job? My life felt so out of control at the moment. No one in their late twenties should be as 'between' everything as me. Between jobs. Between homes. Between boyfriends. The only thing that seemed to be on track in my life was my psychic abilities. Kooky was flourishing. Oh, joy!

I pulled on some joggers and scrambled around in my sports bag for my basketball. I did my best thinking when I was shooting hoops, so I headed out to the small square of asphalt in the very back corner of my parents' backyard.

Dad had put the hoop up for me years ago. It was an old-style ring with no 'give'. The clunky, wooden backboard had lost most of its paint, but I still loved it. In my rep days I'd shoot a couple of hundred baskets a day, and practise my post work around the chalk-lined keyway.

The last few years, it had become my meditation place—even when I wasn't living at home. Some people escape to the water when they need time out, others do the whole yoga thing, or sex, or mind-altering substances, or whatever. For me it's always been hoops. The day after my last boyfriend, Pascal, cleared off with our housemate, I spent hours right here, doing nothing but shooting and rebounding.

I chose free throws today, toeing the chalk-worn line for a hundred shots. By the time I'd finished I was sweaty and hungry, so I grabbed a quick shower and went to look in my second-hand fridge. Cheese, chocolate biscuits and some dried-out mandarin segments.

The chocolate biscuits and I retired to my second-hand couch, and I rang Martin Longbok—aka Bok—one of my two best mates. Smitty, my other best friend—Jane Smith-Evans, aka Smitty—would be picking kids up from school right now; her next window to chat wouldn't fall until after the acid hour when she'd fed the meerkats, and gargled down three quarters of a bottle of wine.

I didn't wait to do the *rah, rah, rah* pleasantries with Bok, but plunged straight in when he answered. 'I need a bodyguard. Bets wants me to see some dodgy guy who runs a body language and psychic's business.'

Bok knows everything about me, including my thing with auras. Truth is, though, he isn't much good as a bodyguard. Bok is a shade heavier than an eating disorder, has a cute button nose and long, silky, straight black hair most girls would kill for. We've been friends since prep when he used to sit behind me in class and hit me with his ruler. I put up with it for weeks, and then one day when the teacher stepped out of the room I pushed him off his chair and watched as he fell flat on his skinny, pretty arse.

We could have become lifelong enemies from that moment, but the truth is I liked his aura. I could see auras, even then, and Longbok's was a fresh and lively aqua-blue colour.

When I put out my hand to pull him up, he took it.

Our *thing*—our pattern—had been in place ever since. Longbok needled and wheedled, and occasionally pushed me too far. When that happened I resorted to physical violence. After that, he'd back off for a while and remain sweet just long enough for me to remember why I liked him, before the process started again.

Even when my parents decided I was exhibiting concerning signs of aggression, and switched me from a snobby non-denominational school to a snobby convent—which is where I met Smitty—Bok and I stayed in touch. He helped me pass my language subjects, coached me on fashion, and came to watch me play basketball. In return, I kept a few bullies off his back, and regularly told him how gorgeous he was.

University was the same. We hung out together for mutual benefit and because we filled in each other's gaps. He could be smooth and effective when I got plain angry and objectionable. He counselled me against dating dropkicks, and I watched his back at clubs when he got hassled by gay-bashers.

Not that Bok was strictly gay. He'd jumped the fence a couple of times: firstly, falling in love with his burly ethics tutor, and when that went wrong, casting his net wider to catch a kinky girl who was financing her medical degree by working part-time as an erotic dancer.

When we entered the workforce, we lost contact for a while. I ran the gamut of boring administrative jobs. An arts degree, private schooling and parental contacts made it easy to step into upmarket legal and finance firms. Bok took his journalism degree and tried to cut it in Sydney in the fashion magazine publishing industry. But all that history eventually drew us back together after Bok decided that fashion was muckier than toe jam, and not half as pretty.

He headed back home to Perth's warmer climes with a wardrobe full of designer freebies that kept him looking sharp at interviews. With his Sydney credentials, it wasn't too long before he snagged a job setting up an exciting new glossy magazine. Managing Publisher was his title. It came with a swishy salary, promised bonuses, and a swag of Louis Vuitton luggage. He moved into a refurbished apartment in Swanbourne, a stone's throw from all the most expensive boutiques.

We ran into each other outside Kimmy Koo's pizza parlour in Euccy Grove. I was wearing a tank top, shorts and thongs, and had a vegetarian with chorizo in my hands. He was clutching a Johnny Depp movie against his Ben Sherman t-shirt. His artfully distressed jeans were tight and crisp. But despite the immaculate grooming, his beautiful blue aura was shrunken and as pale as bun icing, and I knew straightaway he was miserable, so I asked him over right there and then.

We sat up all night talking, about the old days mostly. The crazy things we'd done and how we'd helped each other out. By the early morning, his aura was bouncing blue again.

Since then it has been business as usual between us.

'Alright, dahl,' he agreed. 'I'll come to Mr Hara's weirdo studio with you, but only to make sure he's not a slave trader. Then I'm out of there. Savvy?'

Chapter 3

I picked Bok up outside his trendy Swanbourne apartment block just on dark. This time he wore a black silk Kujo shirt and Ralph Lauren pants.

I had on a tank top, trackie daks and runners.

He cringed when he saw my clothes but didn't say anything.

Mr Hara's house was easy enough to find—a half-duplex right next to the train line. The western suburbs are the wealthiest part of Perth but they have a darker side. Along one section of the train line are pockets of less appealing real estate.

It made for an interesting mix of lifestyles: billion-dollar properties only a couple of streets from the other kind. There was a fair bit of theft in the rich quarter because of it, but surprisingly less than you'd imagine.

I'd never had any problem in Crocker Street, but then it wasn't a place I hung out in. You could get beaten up there for knocking on the wrong door, yet it was unlikely you'd get shot or knifed for your runners. Well not mine anyway.

Hara's was right on the railway line a few blocks from Crocker Street.

I knocked on the back door like he'd instructed, and a huge Italian lady with a soup ladle in her hand banged the fly-wire open and looked me up and down.

'M-Mr Hara h-here?' I asked.

'You want see my husband? Why you come to the back door? You think this a chop shop? You think I make love pills in my kitchen? Maybe I use your bones for soup for being so rude.'

'But, … he—'

Bok shouldered me aside and dipped his finger into her dripping ladle.

'Aaah, *bella zuppa*,' he sighed, and the woman's ferocious glare dissolved into a beaming smile.

'You Italian?' she asked.

Bok nodded and put his finger to his lips. 'But my papa don't know.'

She laughed and stepped to one side. 'Come inside. I fix you a bowl.'

Bok gave me a smirk as he waltzed on in. As I went to follow, she stepped in front of me. 'You go to the front door. Knock like a decent girl.'

I stomped back through the duplex's neat little yard, vowing never to take Bok with me anywhere again.

A male face peered around the corner of the front door.

'Hai?'

'Mr Hara?'

'Hai.'

'I'm Tara Sharp,' I said. 'I went to the back door like you said and your ... wife—'

Mr Hara threw the door open wide and gave a perfect little bow. He was a petite, smooth-skinned over-fifty gentleman. His aura was canary yellow laced with purple flecks. When he straightened, I could see he'd been laughing silently.

'Mrs Hara is as gentle as a kitty, but you are frightened of her. You did not read her properly, unlike your friend who is eating my dinner. Perhaps he is the one with the abilities. Hai?'

I felt myself blushing and my competitive streak reared.

'Or perhaps Mrs Hara prefers men to women,' I replied tartly.

His expression became very still, blank almost, and I wondered if I'd just ended our very short acquaintance.

We stood there in silence for much *much* longer than I was comfortable with, before he finally spoke.

'You are quite right. Mrs Hara does prefer men, especially those who like her cooking,' he said, then gave another bow and gestured for me to enter.

I felt a wave of relief. But as I turned to walk down the common-wall corridor of the Hara's half-duplex, his aura produced more purple speckles, and a little voice in my head started chattering. Had Mr Hara just cleverly manipulated me through my competitive nature?

A headache nibbled at my temples and I stopped mid stride.

Mr Hara bumped into me. 'Missy?'

I grappled with a moment of panic. This type of second-guessing people's motives because their auras were changing was exactly what was making me nuts. *I had to do something about it.*

I took a decisive step forward into Hara's tiny sitting room.

Chapter 4

The sitting room was only sparsely furnished—two old armchairs and an expensive LCD TV perched on a sideboard—apart from shelves and *shelves* of ghastly, luminously glazed china. I could just imagine my mother's reaction, and it made me want to giggle. The Queen of Wedgewood and Royal Doulton would be appalled.

Mr Hara jogged my elbow. 'You like Wembley Ware?' he asked.

I opened my mouth and shut it again. How could anyone like anything so kitsch? How could anyone *ask* anyone if they liked anything so kitsch?

'Very nice,' I squeaked.

Mr Hara walked along the shelves telling me about the collection of lurid frogs, gross open-mouthed fish, toadstools complete with gnomes, tomatoes and lettuce leaves, reclining kangaroos and a sinister black cat's head...

'Have you been collecting long?' I asked politely,

hoping my aura wasn't showing my distaste.

'Not me. Mrs Hara. I buy her one for every birthday. Still many, many pieces to go,' he said. He grinned at me, like he knew what I was thinking. 'You want to get on her good side? You find the marron or the platypus plate.'

'I'll remember that,' I said, dumping it straight into my mental rubbish bin.

Mr Hara finished his loop of the shelves and pointed me to a chair before settling into the other one. 'You're a bad liar, Missy Sharp. Now you tell me what you see. What colour am I?'

His question surprised me but I answered it without thinking. 'Your aura is yellow with some purple specks through it. I've never seen anything like it before.'

He raised an eyebrow. 'What else?'

'What do you mean "what else"?'

'Eliz'beth sent you here for a reason.'

It took me a moment to realise he was talking about Bets. 'I ... err ... read too much into things. I see into conversations. See energy between people—I mean really *see* it.' I hung my head. It sounded too kooky to say 'psychic'.

Before he could reply, Mrs Hara bustled into the room with soup on a tray, which she placed on her husband's lap before tucking a napkin under his chin. She left without giving me a glance.

Mr Hara picked up the spoon and slurped down a mouthful. 'So, Missy. What did you see then?'

'Your wife brought you soup and ignored me.'

He blew on the spoonful. 'What did you *really* see? What colour's her aura?'

'It's mottled,' I said. 'Purple and grey.'

'What else?'

I mused on the way Mrs Hara walked, the way she'd put the tray down. 'She loves you, but...'

Mr Hara leaned forward. 'Yes?'

I blushed. I didn't want to say what I'd really seen. I hesitated, trying to think of a way to put it. 'But she treats you more like a child. Not a husband.'

I waited for his face to crease in annoyance, or for him to throw his soup at me. Instead he said, 'You're not a psychic, Missy. But you've got BIG empathy. Off the scale. You come and learn with me here. Maybe you use it, instead of it using you.'

'I don't want to use it. I just want it to go away.'

'Can't hide from what you are. You learn things, and get better at it,' he said. 'You know about kinesics and proxemics?'

I shook my head. 'Are they fungal infections?' I said with a straight face.

He did his lamb laugh, then put his soup spoon down and leaned forward out of his chair until I could feel his breath.

'This is proxemics. People got four distances: intimate, personal, social, public. You gotta know which one to use, but you also gotta know why other people choose one or other. We've got another way to say it … *propinquity*.'

'Well, I got another way to say it too. How about, *Get your face out of my face*.'

He lamb-laughed again, then leaned back into his chair and resumed his noisy soup slurping.

'One thing you gotta know first is what culture you're dealing with. You've got an Italian like Mrs Hara, she likes to stand close. You got some Swedes, you've gotta stand on the other side of the room if you wanna have a conversation. If you got a half and half then you've gotta problem.'

'So you're saying body language is all about a person's culture?'

'No, no, no. I say you've gotta watch out for that. Sometimes the rules change.' His face got a peculiar sort of intensity when he said 'rules change', like he was listening for a winning number. 'Some stuff you just know,' he added, tapping his finger to his temple. 'But you can learn as well. Makes the difference between being kooky and being rich.'

My stomach fluttered. Rich? I'd settle for solvent.

'You study with me, learn enough, you can start your own business.' This time he slid his fingertips together like he was rustling dollar notes.

'But…' I looked around. I guess Wembley Ware tickles some collectors' fancy, but other than that, Mr Hara's home was less than modest.

He read my thoughts instantly. 'You think this all we

got? This just for the tax guy. Mrs Hara owns a chalet in Hokkaido and an apartment in Sydney. Keeps them in her name.'

I stared at him, flabbergasted. I mean, *really,* could I … *should* I, believe the strange little man?

Doubt crept back in to my mind as I watched his aura dance around his body. I didn't know what it was trying to tell me, so I fell back on the estimation of the straightest person I knew, Bets. Surely she wouldn't stitch me up with a whacko.

'But how do I repay you for your teaching time? I-I'm unemployed and utterly broke,' I said, honestly.

'I run a business. Sometimes there's too much work for me. You do one job for free. We call it squits. You do it good, then I give you more work, cut you in.'

'Cut me in?'

'Percentage.'

'How much percentage?'

'Thirty. Plus expenses.'

It sounded fair. But then I'd never been a good judge of those things. I once answered a 'make three hundred dollars a day from the comfort of your own home' ad. The job turned out to be phone selling an abdominal exerciser—the Ab Fab. It cost me four hundred dollars in sales training, and I never sold a single damn one.

But Mr Hara didn't appear to be hiding any upfront costs, so I stayed, and talked, agreeing in the end to become his student.

Much later, as I drove us home, Bok relived his gastronomic evening.

'She's the most amazing cook, T. Really. After the soup, there was gnocchi, veal, artichoke tart, and for dessert there was vanilla gel—'

'Shut up,' I interrupted.

I had a headache from hunger pangs and from listening to Mr Hara's peculiar Aussie-Amero-Italio-Japanese accent. Bok's swooning wasn't helping one little bit. If he hadn't been doing me a favour in the first place I would've dumped him on the roadside and left him to walk home. Thankfully, he fell into a food coma when we reached the highway, and I had the rest of the drive home to reflect on the strange direction my life had just taken.

Chapter 5

My classes with Mr Hara started the next week.

To my annoyance, when I arrived, Bok was there drinking miso and eating meatballs. I ignored his jaunty wave as Mr Hara led me through the kitchen—part of the desensitising process for Mrs Hara.

Thankfully our lesson wasn't in the sitting room with the spooky Wembley Ware. Instead, Mr Hara led me to a tiny office at the front of the house crammed with books and curling certificates blue-tacked to the wall, proclaiming his martial arts expertise in aikido, kendo, jujitsu and karate. It was a comfy room, and I set myself the task of being a model student.

'Here, you like chocolate biscuits, Missy?' said Mr Hara, pulling a packet of Tim Tams from between two large hardbacks, and offering me one.

Chocolate! 'Yum,' I said, and took one.

He settled into an old studded-leather swivel chair and helped himself to several more. 'Mrs Hara not like me eating this. Says it makes me fat,' he said and rubbed his muscled belly.

I choked down an envious sigh. I had a good metabolism, but not *that* good.

'Now you tell me some stuff first,' he said. 'Then I teach you.'

'Tell you what?' I asked, getting comfortable on a dilapidated two-seater so that I could suck the chocolate coating off my second Tim Tam.

'How you lose your job?'

'I punched my boss.'

He stopped munching for a moment, 'Yes, tell more please.'

'Well, it was complicated. I worked with this guy … and we both worked for an advertising consultant. Every time our boss walked into our office this colleague of mine's aura shrank so small it almost disappeared. He was *terrified* of her. We never talked about it, but I could see. Anyway, this one time, I forgot to take my gym shoes after work and had to go back to get them. And I heard him in her office.' I licked my chocolate-stained lips to calm my rising embarrassment. 'He was screaming as if he was being tortured. Before I knew it, I'd run in and smacked her in the face. Knocked the whip right out of her hand.' The memory burned the back of my eyeballs.

Mr Hara began chewing with intensity again; eyes wide, as if he'd reached an exciting part in a movie.

'See, he was tied upside down in her chair—naked

bum in the air. Only it was consensual.' I rolled my eyes. 'Who'd have thought it? The next day she called me in, said she no longer needed two assistants and told me to clear out my desk. I could have argued it, I guess, but I didn't want to stay after that.'

To his credit Mr Hara didn't laugh, or call me an idiot like Bok had. 'Sure, sure. You just gotta learn to read this stuff better.'

'How?'

'Little bit experience, lotta bit of learning.'

He talked on and on then, about proxemics and gestures, until I started to twitch.

'You getting cuckoo,' he said, finally. 'Go sleep on it and come back soon.'

I filled in the time until my next class with Mr Hara by meeting Bok for coffee, and catching up with Smitty. Bok was on a salary so he paid for the vanilla slices, and Smitty was always good for a chicken and mayo sandwich if I turned up around midday.

Dearest Smitty. Married. Kids. Well adjusted. Everything Bok and I were not. Smitty's husband, Henry Evans, was an overworked GP and one of my favourite people—except when it came to me and Smitty.

Henry, or Henny as Smitts affectionately called him, had gone to one of Perth's most elite boys' schools and Smitty had gone to the nearby girls' equivalent with *moi*.

We all caught the same bus home from school and later, uni, until Henny bought his first car, a Holden Statesman, and then we drove with him. His mum still lived in the next street, two houses down from Smitty's.

Henny knew every scrape and best-forgotten incident Smitty, Bok and I had ever been involved in—which was fine until the day he and Smitts got married. The day she said 'Yes, I do,' he started to say 'No, you don't go out with Tara to nightclubs.' 'No, you don't go paragliding.' 'No, you don't...' Blah, blah, blah.

His burgeoning domineering attitude had got right up my nose until Bok persuaded me it was a natural rite of passage, and that Henny would come to his senses when he realised he wasn't having any fun.

Smitty had taken the road of least resistance at first. Then she and Henny had their first kid, which pretty much wiped her out for most things anyway. To make it worse, she had twins a couple of years later. Everything had been chaotically hunky dory for them, until Claire—the oldest—developed Crohn's disease. Claire was gorgeous, like a young, olive-skinned Cate Blanchett. But the pain, exhaustion and hospitalisations she'd endured could be glimpsed in the hollows beneath her cheekbones and the dark shadows under her eyes.

The all-round difficulty of having a chronically ill child, took its own kind of toll on the entire family. I couldn't begin to understand it, but I loved Smitty for hanging tough.

I babysat for her occasionally now that the kids were

older and I wasn't so afraid of dropping them. For her part, she always supported me whenever I went left field, including this time.

'Mr Hara sounds like a hoot,' she told me. 'I say go for it.'

At my next class, I smuggled a packet of mint slices past Mrs Hara, who was making osso bucco, and Bok, who appeared to be her chief taster with much ecstatic eye-rolling and lip-smacking. Crawler.

Mr H and I settled into the office to watch some YouTube clips that captured micro-expressions and micro-rhythms.

By the end of the mint slices, we had well and truly bonded. He told me his rule of thumb for auras. 'Bright and light is good. Excepting white. White very bad. Dark colours bad too. And dark spots.'

Dark spots. I'd had some ex-boyfriends with those.

He pulled a chart from his drawer. It was laminated, like a bookmark, and had an explanation of what each colour meant. 'You keep this while you learn. Most people have layers of colours, like rainbow. Usually one colour is most strong though. Some have just one colour, with flashes of others. Like me. I flash purple.'

'What does that mean?'

'You check.'

I scanned down one side of the chart. Bright yellow

meant a cheerful, free spirit. The other side of the card was lined with symbols. The speckled symbol meant dominant surges. Then I checked back with the colours. Purple meant strongly spiritual. 'So you're basically a free spirit with surges of spirituality.'

'Hai. Now, that man you worked with, you remember his aura?'

I did—skinny little thing that it was. 'Pink with … I'd guess you'd call them swirls.'

I glanced down at the chart again. Pink was a healthy balance between spiritual and material. Swirls meant uncontrolled emotions. 'I don't get it. His aura was balanced, but raging at the same time.'

'Some things do that to a person,' said Mr Hara, then he reached up to his bookcase and pulled out a book, which he handed to me.

I sagged. It weighed only a little less than Mona's engine.

'Sex is one,' he said.

'So I should have read his aura as "horny" not scared!'

Mr Hara smiled and nodded. 'All in here. Many, many subtleties, Missy. My chart is just the start—learning to crawl. You take this home and study, then you can learn to walk. You get good like me, you run fast.'

Running fast. I liked the sound of that.

'Hoshi?' Mrs Hara stood at the door with a steaming hot bowl of soupy veal.

We both looked guilty.

'What is this?' she said, her ferocious gaze fixed on the gap left by Mr Hara's book. A gap now filled by empty chocolate wrappers, no longer compressed by the book's great weight.

Her fifty-kilo death stare fell to the book, me and the empty packet of mint slices balanced on my knee—in that order. 'You!' she lifted one hefty arm and pointed. 'You poison my husband!'

I opened my mouth and it stayed open. I had nothing.

'Bella,' soothed Mr Hara, and began speaking to her in loving, pacifying Italian. At least that's what I was hoping as I beat it down the corridor, collected Bok, and ran out into the blessedly Mrs-Hara-free night air.

Chapter 6

For three months Mrs Hara ran spot 'choc' checks on us, creeping silently into the room while Hoshi deluged me with everything a person could want to know about kinesics. He had formal titles for things, like *Affect Display* and *Illustrators*, which simply meant ways of showing emotion and reinforcing verbal messages.

Each class, he made me read his and Mrs Hara's aura, until I knew way more about them than I wanted to. Mrs Hara endured the aura reading with unmartyred hostility. She still wasn't speaking to me, and when Hoshi escorted me through the kitchen, just stopped short of frisking me, though I could see that it was on her mind.

While Bok put on weight eating homemade gnocchi, I learned the aura colour chart off by heart, and began to familiarise myself with the meanings of the streaks and swirls and spots and blotches. Mr Hara also taught me how to categorise people's behaviour when they were talking. There were eight identifying factors, he said, including olfactory (how they smell to each other) and thermal (body heat!), as well as the obvious ones such as eye contact and body-contact distance.

I practised observing the things I learned from him on everyone in my life, particularly my parents, Bok and Smitty.

Smitts promptly told me if I was going to treat her like a guinea pig then I had to babysit once a week for her while she went to Pilates.

Grumblingly, I agreed. But in actual fact, babysitting the Evans clan was one of the highlights of my life, and—the way my love life was—possibly the closest I'd ever get to having a family. The boys, Jo and Xavier, were little blond bundles of naughtiness. Their older sister, Claire, was ... Claire—mature and serene, as kids with chronic illnesses often are. That is, of course, until she had a good old eight-going-on-nine-year-old hissy fit.

The Evans' lived in a mostly renovated, stylishly decorated thirties cottage in Mosman Park—the next suburb along from Euccy Grove.

'When are you going to do some real exercise?' I shouted after Smitts, as she ran for the door on the evening of her first class.

'Kids are fed. Your dinner's on a plate in the fridge. Don't let Bones in. If he sheds on the new Persian rug Henny'll have a coronary.'

The door slammed.

'The cat got sick on it last week. Henry nearly cried,'

said Claire coolly.

'You mean "Dad",' I corrected.

'Whatever,' she said, and picked her schoolbag up off the floor. 'I'm going to do homework.'

This was, of course, code for 'I'm going to Snapchat my friends'. I'd give her half an hour before I started hassling.

That left me with the boys. Xave was plugged into his PlayStation, Joe was mucking around at the breakfast bar on Smitty's iPad.

I headed for the fridge, thinking that the next generation of kids will be born with USB ports and scroll-wheels in their fingertips.

The microwave had ten seconds left on the timer when I felt a tap on my thigh.

'What's up, Joe?' I hunkered down to his level.

'Got a problem,' said the quieter of the twins.

'Hang on a tick.' I grabbed my plate and a fork and slid down onto the floor so we could talk eye to eye. Beef in black bean sauce and coconut rice. Yum! 'Shoot,' I said.

'Jamie Snell pushes me.'

'How come?' I shovelled in some food and waited. Joe often took a while to think things through.

''Cos she can.'

'You told the teacher?' I asked.

Joe shrugged. Then nodded.

'Told your mum and dad?'

More shrugging. More nodding.

'What did they say?'

'Mummy says jus' ignore her. Says she's just a tenshun seeker.'

'What about Xavier?'

'He's in d'udda class.'

Smitts had made sure the twins were separated so Joe didn't live in Xavier's shadow.

'What would you like to do about it, Joe?'

'Mummy told Daddy that you punch as good as a man.'

I followed his line of thought. 'You wanna know how to punch?'

A great big grin broke over his serious little face.

'Now hang on a minute, Joe. I just asked. I didn't say I'd show you.'

He grabbed my little finger and held on. 'Pleeeaaassse, Aunty T.'

He delivered it with such heartfelt need that I was sold. The kid had to be able to defend himself.

I jerked my head. 'Outside. And don't tell Mum and Dad. Deal?'

He wagged my little finger up and down.

We adjourned to the porch so no one could see us, and I instructed Joe on the art of a good punch. His plump little fingers made a fierce fist while he practised.

We were having a grand old time, swinging and dodging, when I heard an ungodly screech. I tore back into the family room with Joe hot on my heels.

Claire was standing in the middle room, holding one foot in the air. Bones was under the table looking sheepish.

'You left the door open and the dog got in,' Joe kindly pointed out.

'Claire's standing in poo!' shrieked Xavier with delight. He ditched the PS3 and before I knew it, he and Joe were doing a war-dance around her. Bones joined in, barking and jumping.

Claire began to howl.

Instead of swinging into action like any half-decent mother would do, paralysis took control of me. Then I started to laugh. I was standing there, tears streaming down my face, when Henny walked into the room.

'What in the—'

The twins' war-dance came to an abrupt halt. Joe bumped into Xave. Xave turned around and pushed him. Joe responded with a perfect roundhouse. Xave fell to the floor, wailing.

Henry snatched Xave up and jammed a packet of frozen peas on his eye. Then he turned to me without a flicker of hesitation. 'Tara!'

I dived for the scotch decanter and poured him a large one. While he downed it, I got about cleaning up the worst of the poo.

By the time Smitty got home, Henny was three sheets to the wind, listening to AC/DC on the stereo while I poured over the Yellow Pages in the vain hope of finding a 24-hour carpet cleaner.

Smitty listened patiently to several renditions of events, then sent me home with a promise to never help Joe out with problems at school again.

I headed home feeling wronged, and sank my free time into reading Hoshi Hara's *Kinesics* book from cover to cover.

On the last evening of my allotted twelve-week course with Mr Hara, he produced a slightly grease-stained Level One certificate to authenticate my graduation.

I felt like I'd won an ironwoman competition as he presented it to me. I turned it over in my hands like I was examining a precious jewel. 'What's the black stripe for?' I asked, thinking perhaps I'd earned a black belt in proxemics.

'Ink run out on printer,' he said.

'Oh.'

'You OK now, Missy. You got basics. Just remember to think first. Examine all the possibilities. You can't have too much information.'

We parted with a bow and he promised to call me when he had a job for me to pay off my tuition.

The very next day I placed two advertisements. The first offered group sessions to: *Improve Your Social Skills—learn to read those around you in four weeks.* The second was for *The Tara Sharp Kinesics and Paralanguage Consultancy* as *specialising in communication analysis and relationship dynamics.*

After a week, I got three enrolments for the *Improve Your Social Skills* group sessions: Wallace Grominsky,

Harvey T. and Enid Bell. Real people—I couldn't believe it.

But that was all.

We conducted our first meeting in my flat, which I quickly converted to a meeting room by whipping a fake tapestry screen (courtesy of the local op shop) in front of my bed, throwing all my clothes behind it, and dropping a couple of cushions on the floor in front of the couch.

My new students shuffled in shyly within a few minutes of each other. I did an introduction thing and then got them to talk a little about themselves.

Harvey (he refused to give us his full name or talk about his job!) was a sweet, shy, weedy type with coeliac disease. He said he liked reptiles and owned six different species of gecko. Harvey looked like he rarely saw the light of day—and even that was from behind brick-thick prescription sunnies.

Enid Bell offered to go next. She was a self-professed potato chip junkie who managed a health food store in the city. She batted her eyes at Harvey, and her bosoms heaved as she admitted to wanting to meet someone and fall in love. 'The trouble is,' she said, 'I say things when I get mad. Bad things. Real bad sometimes. And I get mad easily. Guys get turned off.'

The last one was Wal—Wallace Grominsky. He had a short wrestler's build and long, ginger hair that he wore in an untidy plait. It took me less than a minute to work out that he was crazy. Psychiatrist Betsy might have put it down to a neglected childhood, but I was inclined to go with substance abuse.

Something—maybe the slightly disconnected look in his eyes, or the way he kept nodding off mid-sentence—told me I should turn him away from Social Skills Class. But I needed the money.

Wal told us his hobby was weapons, and that he worked as a part-time roadie for a bunch of local bands.

'Usually, Deadspeaker and The Lead Slippers,' he said. 'Prefer Metal meself but I'll work with most any. 'Cept them cabaret acts. Anyway, it's hard to meet chicks when you work nights.'

We did some preliminary stuff, goal setting and problem sharing, and I sent Wal and Harvey away to practise some ice breakers. To Enid, I assigned Mr Hara's simple technique called Count and Think to help her keep her cool.

After Los Trios left to wreak havoc on their unsuspecting peers, I sat on my office desk—the couch—and wondered what the hell I was doing. Their meagre course fees would take care of my phone credit, petrol and board, but my visions of a chateau in France and tickets to the NBA finals evaporated.

I must have dozed off because my phone's ring jerked me awake. I checked the caller ID; a private number.

Just for the hell of it I answered in my poshest girl's school voice. 'Tara Sharp Consultancy. Tara Sharp speaking.'

'Hello It's Lloyd, honey—'

'Actually, I prefer to be addressed as *Ms Sharp*.'

'No … that is … I mean … Honey is my name. *Mr Honey*. I'd like to meet you to discuss a … err … a … possible job.'

'Oh,' I said. 'Let me check my diary, Mr Honey.' I took a calming breath and counted to ten. 'Oh … how fortunate. I have a cancellation late this afternoon. Do you live north of the river?'

'Yes, Ms Sharp,' he said, in a 'who didn't?' manner?

'Then let's say we meet at Latte Ole on Broadway in Nedlands at 5PM,' I suggested.

'Yes … um … that would be suitable. I'll wait at the table next to the door.'

'Fine. Until then.'

'Yes, Ms Sharp. Until then—'

I hung up quickly to give the impression I was busy, and hopped around the office with excitement.

OMG, a client! My first client, my first client… What if he hates me on sight? Or wants me to read his sex slave's body language? What if—

'Tar-ah!'

Crap!

The female part of the joint parent entity I thought of as *JoBob* peeked in the window of the garage.

Don't get me wrong, I love my mother to death, but did God have to give her such a la-di-da voice and a Gestapo-esque attitude to manners? She was the mistress of the wounded look and delicate sensibility. Plus, she seemed to have forgotten that I'd lived away from home for ten years and was only back here to *regroup*.

Yes, that's what I was doing—*regrouping*.

'Yeah? Here.'

'You mean "yes", don't you, darling? Dad and I are off for a day out with the Wobbies. Will you please walk the birds?'

The Wobbies were JoBob's oldest friends, secret allies from BC (Before Children *and* Christ). Mabel and Arthur Walker-Robertson were two priceless peas in a pod with a jointly wicked sense of humour. In fact, I'd never quite worked out how they hooked up with straight-laced JoBob.

'I can't, Mum. I've got to … err … meet Longbok.'

'Must you spend so much time with that scrawny Martin creature?'

'Yes, Joanna.' She hated me using her first name. It robbed her of parental power.

'You have some odd friends, Tara,' she continued, heedless of my obvious irritation. 'I do wish you would spend your time with some decent young people, like Phillip Dewar and his crowd.'

There it was. That name! *Phillip Dewar*. I stifled the gag reflex with practised ease. Did she know, I wondered, that Phillip Dewar was a blossoming alcoholic? 'Don't you think I'm a little too old for you to be trying to choose my friends, Joanna?'

She released a martyred sigh. 'The birds need to be walked before dark. Tara, I ask so little from you, the least you can do is this one small thing. I mean, we are providing you with a roof over your head…'

I tuned out about there. Joanna, the Mistress of Blackmail.

When I came out of my trance, she'd disappeared from the window frame like the vampire you couldn't see in the mirror, and my phone was ringing again. I picked up the receiver and did it straight this time. 'Tara Sharp Paralanguage Agency. Tara Sharp speaking.'

'Missy?'

'Mr Hara.' I broke into a smile. I hadn't heard from him since the day he'd handed me my certificate.

'Gotta job for you.'

'Great. I'll come over. Be good to catch up again.' I meant it. I kinda missed our chocolate-smuggling game. And other than Bok (not counting Bets), Mr H was the only person in the world who knew about my 'thing'. I hadn't even told Smitty about the really weird stuff. As far as Smitts was concerned I was flaky and lovable. I was just, well, TARA.

'Not catching up, sorry. Mrs Hara wants to ski.' He gave an unhappy sigh. 'We're going to Hokkaido for two weeks. Taxi's coming soon.'

'Um, well have fun. So what's the job?'

'Not sure. No time to check it out yet. You go to Klintoff building on Satin Beach at 6PM today. Ask for

Mr Delgado.'

I checked the clock—2PM. It wouldn't be a problem making my five o'clock appointment and getting to Delgado by six.

'Fine.'

There was a pause before Mr Hara signed off. 'Only take the work if it's alright. This job came through a friend of Mrs Hara. Not sure if it's OK.'

Mrs Hara? Alarm bells tinkled in my head but I silenced them with well-practised ease. 'Sure,' I said airily and hung up.

I bounced over to the kitchenette and got down to making a triple-decker sandwich: salami, cream cheese and pickle. A pretty damn tough ask when your kitchen consists of a bar fridge, a cupboard pretending to be a pantry, an electric fry pan and a sink.

Sandwich and I returned to the office-couch and I scrabbled underneath the pile of clothes for my second-most-prized possession: my laptop. Taking care to drop the crumbs on the floor not my keyboard, I spent the afternoon doing one of the things that Mr Hara had drummed into me—research. *You can't have too much information.*

Today, though, Google failed me, and I was forced to think outside the screen.

I did some wall staring while I waited for inspiration to strike.

Chapter 7

It came by way of the human web. The great thing about living in a smallish city is that everything and everyone are connected—if you dig a bit. I remembered that my accountant, Garth Wilmot, had kept an office in Klintoff House until they put the rent up and told him he had to have gold-plated toilet-roll holders. Poor old Garth had retired to a less plush suite on the railway side where the rent was much better, though the security screens had cost him a fortune.

Klintoff House was one of the few high-rises along the western suburbs beach strip. Somehow the owners of the building had snuck their plans through council when no one was looking. These days you couldn't build anything over three storeys that hadn't been vetted by every blue rinser, white-shirt, and Louis Vuitton-toting kindy mum in the council. They wanted *ambience* on their morning jog along the beach, not the brash and trash that came with the high rise development of places like the Gold

Coast glitter strip in the Eastern States. I suppose money in plain brown envelopes solved many a problem!

I searched on the building name and came up with Klintoff's table of residents, which included three law firms, two accountants, one judge, a cardiologist and an import–export business front office. I didn't figure Delgado to be old enough for a judge or anal enough for an accountant. Cardiologist seemed unlikely too. That left lawyer or import–export manager. Lawyer would be my pick.

This time, my search picked on a *Pietro* Delgado, a solicitor who'd represented some dubious cases for known criminals. I began to get a bad feeling, so I rang Garth.

'Hi Tara.'

I didn't need my newly acquired paralanguage prowess to know he sounded tired and peeved. Garth and I had dated for a while—well before he went bald and got a designer-beer belly. He'd wanted to marry me until he found out that I had no ability whatsoever to keep to a budget. His love seemed to go stone cold as he realised just how fiscally challenged I was. Meanwhile, *I* realised that I couldn't bear to spend the rest of my life toting up how much I'd saved by using supermarket petrol vouchers.

Our break-up was amicable enough for us to remain friends, but niggly enough that we could only handle each other in small doses. I relied on him for 'sensible advice'. And occasionally, he called me when he needed a hot date for the Accountants Annual Ball or a financier's dinner.

'Bad day?' I commiserated.

'Some prick broke in here last night, took my computer and all my reams of A4 paper. Why the fuck would someone want A4 paper?'

'Umm … beats me. What about your new security screens? Didn't they work?'

He sighed. 'Cleaner left the front door unlocked.'

I laughed. I shouldn't have but Garth had that sort of bad luck all the time. Maybe he'd been born under a ladder.

'I might have known you'd be sympathetic,' he said dryly. 'What do you want?'

I cut straight to it. Like Bok, Garth and I didn't need to beat around the bush. 'Did you ever come across a solicitor named Pietro or Peter Delgado when you were in the Klintoff building?'

'Pete Delgado! You don't want to be dating him, T.'

'I'm not dating him, stupid,' I snapped. I didn't need Garth being protective. Hell, I weighed five kilos more than him and could run his pants off.

'Then why are you asking?'

'Never mind that. Tell me what you know.'

'He works for Positoni & Kizzick.'

I knew that should mean something to me but it didn't. 'Eh?'

'They handle all the Johnny Vogue cases.'

'Oh.' My stomach flipped. Johnny Vogue was our wee city's supremo crime lord. His real name was John Viaspa, but in our fair nation we don't handle formal or complete names too well.

'Don't you read the papers?' he asked.

'Only the sport.'

'Well I'm telling you, T. Stay clear of that one. He's a slime ball, and I've heard his wife is as dangerous as a cut snake. Listen, I've got to go. Cops are here about the break-in. Take care.' Then he gave a chuckle.

'What?'

'I'm looking out the window and guess who one of the boys-in-blue is? Whitey. I'll give him your regards.'

'Ugh!' I said and hung up.

Greg Whiteman's sister and I had gone to school together. I met Greg—Whitey—when I was fifteen, and harboured a *huge* secret crush on him until I was seventeen. When we finally went out on a date, I discovered he was vain, stupid and the worst kind of lecher. Right after he'd bought my first drink he'd leaned in close. 'Tara,' he'd said. 'You wanna go back to my place for a root?'

My latent western suburbs sensibilities were so offended that I washed his face with my vodka cooler. I stopped short of kneeing him in the nuts because you never know when you might need to know a cop, but these days the sight of him brought bile to my mouth.

Unfortunately, Whitey seemed to like my hostile treatment. He badgered me endlessly after that. I ignored his calls until they eventually tapered off when he got married to a girl from my school.

Garth knew the story. He also knew Whitey and his sister. Good old Garth. Never one not to rub something in.

I stared at the wall above my bed, my thoughts flittering about. So Peter Delgado was a bad boy's lawyer. I wondered if that was as dangerous and mob-ish as it sounded. I mean this was Perth, *Aw-stray-yah,* not Soho, or Washington DC. Surely organised crime in my fair city meant a few cartons of ecstasy tablets, the odd shipment of hashish and a backroom ice lab here and there, maybe even some horse-race fixing. (Perth's New Year's Day racing carnival was always a big event, for me anyway—lost my shoes on more than one occasion after an afternoon in the Moët tent). How bad could it be?

I could just hear Smitty's answer to that question. *Could anyone be more gullible than you, T? Remember the time you thought a girl in your aerobics class kept running to the toilet because she had giardia when she was actually bulimic?*

Prickles of indecision ran tag across my skin. Garth had sounded serious enough, and despite what I'd said to him, I *had* seen Johnny Vogue in the paper. Often. Perth's crime lord 'owned' the nightclub stretch of the city. The seedier parts of Northbridge were populated by pimps, dance clubs, kebab shops and sex studios. And Johnny Vogue ran the lot.

I hadn't been up to Little Perth since scoring a bout of oyster poisoning from Hot Cockles.

To meet Delgado, or not to meet?

I checked the clock: half an hour till my appointment with Mr Honey and I hadn't even showered. I slapped the blinds shut and stripped off. Grabbing a towel from somewhere on the couch, I tumbled in and out of the shower. Then I dashed back to my bedroom and squeezed into my best black pants and a gauzy, silk-sleeved top that hid my biceps. I shoed-up in high heels but immediately kicked them off in favour of flats—just in case I had to run away from Mr Honey or Peter Delgado.

Shoving my phone and a key card in a mini sling purse, I drew on some eyeliner.

Hair up or down?

In, I decided. Don't want to look unkempt. Or worse, sexy. That got me sniggering out loud as I jumped into Mona and sped in the direction of Latte Ole.

The sniggering *almost* kept the worries at bay. What if I couldn't find Mr Honey? What did someone like Delgado want? What if…?

Tara, when will you ever learn that your impulsiveness always gets you into trouble?

Did I mention that my Joanna implant was also an echo machine? You'd think by twenty-six years of age I'd have shrugged off some of my parental programming, but when you have no job, no long-term partner, and you're living in your parents' garage … well…

Aunty Lavilla had nailed it. 'Tara,' she'd said to me recently over a bottle of pinot grigio and some sweet chilli philly, 'I love you to death but you are the most curious creature. So adolescent one moment, and so switched on and mature the next. Couth and refined in one breath; positively raucous in another. It's like two people inhabit that scone of yours.'

From anyone else I would have been mortally offended, *violently* offended even, but Liv was one of my favourite people in the world. She dripped expensive jewellery, loved the odd chemically induced mind-altering experience, and supported some of her more extravagant habits by selling her artwork to large corporations for a shit-load of money. Who'd have thought Joanna could have a sister who was so improper and creative and out there?

Thank God for Liv and her penthouse!

Chapter 8

I swerved Mona into a tight space near the café with practised ease. Monaros are a *statement* car and I'd wanted one since I could burp and say 'gimmee'. That didn't change as I grew up and all my girlfriends got Mercedes sports and BMW Roadsters from their daddies. I fancied big cars—Pontiacs, Cadillacs and SUVs—but ever one to embrace my national identity, Holdens were my true love.

In the end JoBob gave up trying to dissuade me from spending my entire bank balance on a restored, gunmetal-grey 1973 HQ LS Monaro, complete with original doeskin vinyl roof, Corvette rocker covers and a 350 air-cleaner, but insisted I go to an advanced driving school. When my initial blood-rush at the possibility of being the first woman to race at an Indy faded, I actually learned some good shit. I could corner pretty fast and skid in the wet like a veteran. Not to mention being hell-on-wheels in a straight line.

Latte Ole was in full swing—5PM was cusp time, when the patrons switched from short blacks and shortbreads to Hahns and beer nuts. This meant I had to find Mr Honey before things got too rowdy.

Two crowds: a bunch of uniformed bank Johnnies and Janes were knocking back Brass Monkeys and looking pretty loose already; and a large birthday group which had taken over the mid-section of tables and chairs, with waiters racing jugs of beer and glasses out to them. Their psychic energies blended in to a hazy rainbow of colours.

There were two tables next to the door. A plump, nerdy IT type with a sharp and shiny cobalt aura tucked into a large plate of steak and chips ... *there* he was: a middle-aged bald guy whose eyes skittered between the numerous bare, suntanned midriffs. His aura was pancake flat and the colour of custard.

Aaah ... don't you love a quiet perv.

Not.

I stepped confidently towards his table and thrust out my hand. 'Spotted you!'

A fierce glare met my bald introduction. 'Who the h-hell are y-you?' the man spluttered.

His reaction gave me such a fright that I stepped back and accidentally knocked into the waiter. A chocolate sundae slid right off his tray into the plump IT man's lap.

Thrown off balance, I followed it.

Mr IT blinked through his whisky-tumbler-thick glasses and bit his bottom lip as the ice-cream seeped through the crotch of his pants.

'Jeez,' he groaned.

I scrambled off him, nuts and strawberry topping clinging to the arse of my pants, and made dabbing gestures at the mess with his serviette.

'So sorry,' I cried. 'Soooo sorry. So incredibly ... I beg your pardon,' before I realised I was wiping a strange man's crotch. I dropped the serviette on the waiter's tray and ran to the toilet.

When I emerged a short time later shaken but crushed-nut free, I glanced around. Mr IT had a fresh sundae sitting in front of him, though he looked like he'd lost his appetite. With my bag strategically slung to hide my stained butt, I forced myself across the room.

The IT guy stared up at me with fear in his bug-keeper-magnified eyes.

'Mr Honey?' I whispered. 'I'm terribly, terribly sorry to say this, but I'm Tara Sharp.'

He swallowed hard as I sat down opposite him.

'I don't normally fall into my clients' laps. Mostly I just tap-dance on their tables,' I said with a rush.

My weak attempt at humour just seemed to confuse him more, so I reached into my purse and brought out a small notebook and pen. 'Now, tell me, how can I help you?'

'I ... I ... I...'

'It's alright,' I said soothingly. 'These things can be difficult to talk about. Take your time.'

He began to fold his napkin as if getting up to leave.

I cast around desperately for a hook. 'Let *me* tell *you* instead,' I said, guessing wildly. 'You've just been promoted into a great job and your girlfriend wants to get married. That would be OK, because you love her, but you don't know if she's only interested in your money.'

Mr Honey's jaw dropped and the napkin fluttered from his fingers to shroud the remnants of his chocolate sundae.

'Oh, and she doesn't like you eating meat or eating dessert. She thinks you should work out more.'

'How ... how...'

'I made a terrible fool of myself a moment ago, Mr Honey. But believe me, I do know people. On the phone I picked you as bald. I got that wrong; you've got a great head of hair.'

Mr Honey's incredulous expression blossomed into a full-blown smile. 'Y-you think so? Th-thanks.'

Bingo!

'That is amazing, Ms Sharp,' he continued. 'How could you know all that from looking at me?'

I smiled, then tapped the side of my nose. 'Secrets of the trade. Now tell me more about yourself.'

Mr Honey's first name was Lloyd, and he wanted me to meet his girlfriend and suss out her true feelings.

My guess had been intuitive. Not just pure luck. He was nerdy, but well-dressed enough not to be friendless. He was eating guiltily, like he wasn't normally allowed to do it. He wore a trendy friendship ring and an expensive Omega watch. Smart + rich geek = hot babe.

Lloyd and I ran a few scenarios as to how I might meet his intended: everything from a double-date to a fabricated work encounter. In the end we devised a plan. I'd go to a bar she drank at on Saturday evenings with her girlfriends. Apparently when she'd had a skinful she would call him and he'd pick her up. I'd be at the next table, he'd pretend I was a long-lost friend, we'd meet, chat for a few minutes, and I would earn my three hundred dollars by making a judgement on how she acted towards him. He'd email her photo to me later on tonight.

I was pretty happy with how things were going in my new profession.

Chapter 9

Thirty minutes and three coffees later, I was still busting to go to the toilet, but was running late for my appointment with Peter Delgado.

I whipped Mona out of her snug parking spot without losing any paint and sped down the beach road, weaving through the speed chicanes like a slalom skier on speed. Mona wasn't a brilliant car on corners but made up for it with grunt. I knew I was being an eco-savage owning an eight-cylinder car, but I tried to make up for it with green shopping bags and friendly cleaning fluids.

Ahem ... by not cleaning, actually!

The car behind me tooted, and I realised I was still stopped at the crosswalk. I accelerated hard for three blocks, causing mobs of beach-goers to give me hot, sandy, indignant stares. I waved at them. Hot, indignant stares didn't work on me. This was my town and my suburb.

The Klintoff car park was chockers, so I had to park Mona around the corner and up the hill. That gave me time to brush my hair and re-lippy in private. But by the time I'd run down the hill and caught the beachfront gale head-on, my good work was all undone. My plan to enter the foyer looking groomed and pimped had turned into panic-at-the-disco. Crossing my legs, I did a quick directory search.

Positoni & Kizzick—6th floor.

By the time the lift reached the fifth, my need for a toilet became dire. As soon as the door opened, I plunged down the corridor looking for the little lady silhouette.

The restroom was sandwiched between two plushly appointed law firms. I skittled into it, found the last cubicle and let flow. Just as Niagara Falls had nearly abated, I heard the door open. Two women made their way into the first two cubicles.

'What happened with Pete?' asked one.

The other giggled. 'He took me back to his place.'

'What? Was his wife away?'

'No. He's got a flat in the city. Beautiful view of the river. Said if we got regular he might set me up in there.'

'You're crazy. What if she finds out?'

'She won't. He's cute and he's got connections,' said Giggler.

'Johnny Vogue?'

'Don't knock it. Johnny Vogue takes his people to the Caribbean every year for a holiday. I always wanted to go there.'

I sat as quiet as a mouse, not even daring to pull my

pants up.

'What was he like?' asked Giggler's friend.

'Delgado?'

'No, the fricking prime minister, idiot.'

Giggler hesitated. 'He's … active. You know. Staying power.'

'Must be those olives.'

'Or the little blue pills.'

'*He uses Viagra?*'

I held my breath waiting for her to answer. This was too damn delicious for words.

'Well who doesn't?'

My phone began to ring. I fumbled in my jeans pocket to stop it and it fell out on the floor. *Bugger.*

'Shit,' whispered Giggler to her friend, followed by two quick flushes and clanging doors. I yanked my knickers and pants up together, and tried to zip them with one hand. The knickers got caught in the zip but by the time I'd disentangled and opened the door, Giggler and her friend had bolted.

And my damn phone had started ringing again.

'Yes,' I snapped into it.

'Tara Sharp, how the hell are you?' said a vaguely familiar male voice.

I washed my free hand and dried it on the luxury-thick towels. 'Who is this?'

'Don't you know me?'

I fished the brush out of my bag and raked it through

my hair, pulling faces at myself in the mirror. 'No. And I don't have time—'

'It's Whitey.'

'Whitey? Greg Whitehead?' I swung the bathroom door open and stepped out into the corridor.

'The one and only,' said the cocky voice.

'What do you want? And how did you get my phone number?'

'Fat boy gave it to me.'

'Garth?' My voice raised an octave.

'He said you'd asked after me and that you were in some type of escort business these days. I thought we might hook up. I can pay.'

'E-escort. H-hook up?' I could barely say the words. Garth would be lucky to ever add another column of figures when I got through with him.

'So do you still want to sleep with me?' asked Whitey.

'What?' I was dumbfounded. 'You're married. You only got married last year.'

'So?'

I'd worked up a real head of steam now. I planted my feet and squared my shoulders. '*So?* Listen to me you slimy dirtbag,' I spat into the phone. 'Let's get something very clear. If you were doused in petrol, I'd be the one to light the match. If you were starving, I'd steal your last scrap of food. I wouldn't sleep with you if we were trapped in a Viagra factory together.' I slammed the phone shut and stamped my foot in fury.

A man in his late thirties with jet-black hair and sly good looks encapsulated in a Zegna pinstripe, stood in the open doorway of Positoni & Kizzick. Fearing he might have heard the end of my call, a flush of embarrassment started somewhere around my bra line and radiated out to every extremity, until I was glowing hotter than Kimmy Koo's pizza oven. I wanted to run back into the toilet and dampen my burning cheeks but faint heart never won a lady a business contract, and I wasn't going to let another two-timing bastard bung the superior act on me.

I held out my hand without hesitation. 'Peter Delgado, I'm guessing from what the girls in the Ladies were just saying. I'm Tara Sharp, here to represent Mr Hara.'

He hesitated then met my handshake. His hand was firm enough but ice-cube cold, and his aura was murky brown and slippery. He stood back and held the door open.

I waltzed into Positoni & Kizzick, past the receptionist, who buried her streaked extensions in a filing cabinet. Was she the Giggler?

I didn't get time to test my theory as Delgado shepherded me into a corner office with a great view over Satin Beach. Not bad for someone who didn't even have his name on the brass plate at the door.

I perched on a Queen Anne-style Chesterfield without waiting to be asked and crossed my legs in my best private girls' school manner. The studs were cool against my back and I suppressed a little shiver of pleasure. Sitting on fine furniture was nearly as good as sex.

Delgado stepped past the matching Queen Anne and stood near the desk. 'I have a job that requires discretion, Ms Sharp.'

Listen for pitch quality, said the Mr-Hara-in-my-head. *Voice qualifiers. Over-loud means lotsa intensity.* 'May I ask what the nature of your job might be?'

There was a pause.

I filled it with, 'You understand that I also need to screen for the appropriate kind of business.'

'I work in the corporate world, Ms Sharp, and I need a person to gain the confidence of a high-profile individual and acquire certain information about them. Who, when and what, are details that I will divulge when *I* have screened *you*.'

I should have said no right then. It sounded dodgy, and he was intense and arrogant in one sentence. But curiosity, a powerful need to prove myself to Mr Hara and a competitive nature were stronger hooks. *Of course I was suitable.*

He moved behind his desk. The slight flush on his olive skin and his need to put distance between us told me that he was off balance still. But as soon as he sat down and steepled his fingers I knew he was moving back into control mode.

'I am what I need to be at any given time, Mr Delgado,' I countered. 'When discretion is needed you won't even notice I'm there.' I smiled and kept my posture deliberately relaxed but not too open. A man like Delgado might misinterpret that as a come-on.

He placed one hand over his mouth and rubbed his chin. Not a good sign.

My foot started to jiggle before I could stop it. I was blowing it.

His eyes were drawn to the movement but continued up past my ankle and along the length of my leg to my thigh. 'Do you wear high heels, Ms Sharp?'

'Not when I'm running,' I quipped.

'You run?' His eyebrows rose into a surprised peak.

'I used to,' I said. 'Until I switched codes.'

'To?'

'Basketball. State player until I was nineteen. I couldn't choose between it and athletics.' I sighed. I wasn't above bragging if I needed to. And I needed to do *something*.

Delgado's face relaxed and he smiled—if you could call it that. 'Well, Ms Sharp, Mr Hara recommended you, and you do have certain attributes that lend themselves to the nature of this job.' He rose and walked to the door. 'You'll be given a retainer once I've run a background check on you. I'll be in touch.'

A background check? Why the—

He handed me a card. 'This has my private number. Do not share it with anyone. Terms are as per Mr Hara's usual rates with a thousand-dollar bonus if the job is exemplary,' he finished.

A thousand-dollar bonus. Yikes! Maybe Mr Hara

would let me keep the bonus. After all, that hadn't been mentioned. 'Fabulous,' said I.

Then I left in my most serene, lady-like manner.

Out in reception Giggler was talking to an attractive but sullen-looking woman wearing dangerously high stilettos. Giggler whispered something to her as I walked past, but I didn't catch it over the blood still pounding in my ears.

Chapter 10

Once outside the Klintoff House foyer, I sprinted up the hill to my car, whooping. A thousand smackeroonies! On the way home I stopped at Perky's Pies and the newsagents for two caramel tarts and a copy of *Sports Today*, to celebrate.

By the time I got home it was dark, I had twenty cents left, and I was on more than just a sugar high.

As I walked down JoBob's empty, darkened driveway I heard a mass of screeching and fluttering. *Crap!* I'd forgotten to walk the birds and they were killing each other.

JoBob's birds were native pink and grey galahs with the mischievous cunning of bored three-year-olds. They beaked everything, including each other, to bits, and they loved their 'out' time. Normally JoBob walked the birds up and down the driveway and onto their perfectly manicured lawn, first thing in the morning and around drinkies time in the late afternoon; unless of course they went out and then it was left to me.

There were only a couple of dead-set rules with the galahs. Don't forget to feed and water them (doh!), and don't take them out in the dark because they were likely to disappear into a bush or under a hedge never to be seen again.

When I reached the cage, I poked my finger in between the bars, and made clicking noises. Hoo, the little sook, scrambled over to me for a scratch, but Brains was cranky and gave me her best side. I walked around to the other end of the cage—which I could have lived in, it was so damn big—and stuck my finger closer to her. Brains whipped her head around quicker than a brown snake and bit me.

'Owww. You cranky old bag.' I snatched my finger back and reached into my bag for some caramel tart crumbs as a peace offering.

As I dragged the wrapper out and dangled the bag before Brains, I remembered a call I wanted to make. I dialled Garth.

Brains relented and came closer. I returned to the front of the cage and opened the door. Brains followed me around there, as my now *least* favourite accountant answered his phone.

'Garth here.'

'Loser!'

'Who is this?'

'Work it out, dirt bag,' I growled.

Silence.

I jiggled the bag at Brains. She crept closer, but Hoo, the greedy guts, overtook her. He climbed right over her back and plunged his head inside the bag.

'Stop it, you bad boy!' I cried.

'Tara? Tara, is that you?'

I tried to pull the bag out of the cage, but Hoo came with it, ripping at the paper with vehemence.

'Of course it's me. The one who works as a *paid escort*.'

Garth began to laugh. 'He didn't really call you, did he?'

I thought about how I would reply as I did battle with Hoo. Then Brains came from nowhere, jumped onto my wrist, nipped it and climbed out of the gate onto the top of the cage.

'Shit!' I said into the phone. I dropped the paper bag and it crashed to the cage floor with Hoo inside it.

'No need to get so mad,' said Garth. 'I didn't think he'd really follow up. It was a joke. And I didn't say you were a paid escort. I said you knew a lot about body language these days. He made the wrong connection. Tara?'

'Sorry baby. Are you alright?' I crooned down at Hoo.

Hoo emerged from the bag and fluffed his feathers in a huff.

'Tara! You're talking nonsense. Are you drunk?'

'Of course I'm not drunk,' I snapped. 'It's only seven o'clock.' I swung the cage door shut, and began to make clicking noises with my tongue to woo Brains.

She was having none of it and scampered to the back edge of the cage.

I climbed up onto the lip of the spill tray to try to reach her. JoBob would have me taxidermied if I lost Brains. Unfortunately, it wasn't as strong as it looked, and it buckled under my weight. I crashed through it and Brains took fright.

Even with her clipped wings she could fly a few metres. She fluttered down to the driveway and then scuttled over to the neighbour's hedge.

I began to croon and click again but Brains was well and truly spooked. A car tooted out on the street, and she was gone into the hedge like a rat down a drain.

'Shit! Bugger! Shit!' I yelped.

'Tara! Get a grip of yourself. You sound deranged.'

'Grrr!' was all I could manage before I snapped the phone shut and plunged after Brains.

My chase took me through Mr Jameson's garden and down the back lane. Every time I got within an arm's length of Brains, she'd flip her wings. It was like chasing paper in the wind. Our little dance continued to the end of JoBob's back lane and into another. And another. My crooning started to give way to growling-like noises.

When a dog from a high-walled backyard began to howl like crazy, Brains' snipped wings beat frantically and she sailed up over a galvanised-steel fence.

I peered through the fence into the grounds of a Euccy

Grove mansion. There was a TV glow somewhere in the house and a dim back porch light on, but that was all. Surely they wouldn't notice if I just snuck in and grabbed my bird. I mean if I went to the front door and asked, I'd lose sight of Brains and then...

I could see her in the porch glow now, poor silly bird, sitting halfway up a small jam tree, shivering. I went to hitch a leg up, but my pants were too tight to climb it. Without stopping to think, I stripped them off and shimmied over the fence in my knickers.

I crept up to the tree and put my finger out. Brains jumped on, ran up my arm to my shoulder and cuddled into my neck.

'Sook,' I chastised.

Now I had to get back over the fence with her on my shoulder. I was halfway through that delicate manoeuvre when I heard noises—screams and the slamming of doors. A back screen on the next-door mansion crashed open, and a house alarm began squalling. All the neighbourhood dogs set off in chorus, as a figure hurtled out into the night.

Burglar!

With Brains on my shoulder, and the fence peaks jabbing into my soft bits, I jumped down into the alley and dialled 000. I told the cop operator where I was and what was happening. 'Take down my mobile number. I'll try and watch where he goes.'

She started to say something about my personal safety, but I hung up.

The burglar headed in the opposite way down the alley from me, and veered left. I figured his getaway car must be in the next lane, so I took a shortcut alongside Professor Evans' orchid house—the way I used to go when I was wagging school.

Brains hopped around on my shoulder, not happy at the speed I was moving, so I coaxed her onto my hand and slipped her inside my shirt. She raked her claws along my bare skin in complaint.

'Shush!' I paused to uproot a weed, which I poked in the vicinity of her beak. She latched onto it and settled into crunching as I pelted through into the next lane.

A small white car was parked up against a fence but there was no sign of the burglar.

My phone rang. 'Yes?'

'This is Constable Bligh of the Eucalyptus Grove police. Did you call in a burglary sighting?' said a formal voice.

'Yes. I think I've found the getaway car. Where are you?'

'Violet Street,' said the cop.

'Take the back lane. The car's halfway along. He's not here yet. He might have got lost getting back to it.'

'Stay out of sight, Miss—'

'Yeah, yeah.' I hung up and crouched down behind the bumper of the white car.

Moments later I heard the rasp of laboured breathing. I peeked around the bumper. The burglar had climbed over someone's fence and was running towards the car.

If he got out of the laneway before the cops arrived, he'd get away. The cops were close. I just had to delay him for a minute.

I opened my shirt and popped Brains down on the ground. She was still beaking her weed. Poor darling was starving.

As the burglar passed the boot, I blindsided him. Not just a girlie push, but a full-scale knees-and-ankles rugby league tackle worthy of State of Origin.

We grappled as headlights flooded the lane and police cars bore down on us from either end.

'Get off!' shouted the figure, lashing out at me with his fists and feet.

I took one in the eye and screamed.

Brains screeched and flew at him, pecking the burglar's face like she was a trained killer.

I dropped a knee into what I hoped was the region of his groin but only caught his thigh.

'Freeze,' bellowed a cop voice.

A spotlight fixed on us, but the guy was still flailing at Brains, who was doing a pro-boxer's job of evading him and still getting in a nip.

'Stop it! Stop it!' he cried.

'Sit still,' I snarled. 'She'll keep attacking while you jump around like that.'

He swiped at her again and this time I kicked him hard in the nuts. He went limp and Brains settled on his chest where she dropped a dirty dollop.

The cops from one car ran up. One of them shooed Brains away and rolled the guy over. In the cop's torchlight I could see the burglar's face: low forehead, thick curly hair, and a pained expression. Not a face I'd forget on account of the vicious look he was giving me as he cupped his balls. 'I'll get you for this, bitch.'

The other cop helped me up, as the burglar was cuffed and dragged off to the car.

'The people you meet in a dark alley,' said my cop.

I stared at him. His voice sounded unhappily familiar. 'Wh-Whitey? Is that you?'

'Tara Sharp, where are your pants?' he replied. 'And what were you doing chasing burglars?'

'I wasn't,' I declared hotly. 'I was chasing my bird. She got out of her cage and flew into someone's backyard.' I pointed at the mansions beyond. 'I had to take my pants off to climb the fence and catch her.'

'So you were trespassing then?' I heard a catch of laughter in his voice.

'I was on a fence. This guy came bolting out from next door.'

'What do you reckon, Tony? Shall we cuff her?'

Tony—the other cop—flashed his torch around the backyard. 'I reckon so. Girls in underwear can be hazardous.'

I felt a hot flush of anger. Men were all the same.

'Down boys,' said a female voice. The cops from the other car had joined our merry little group. One of them was a woman. 'What's your name, love?' she asked.

'Tara,' I said.

'That your bird there?'

Everyone stared at Brains. She was sitting huddled in the midst of our feet.

'Yes.' I bent over and made friendly sounds. If Brains decided to pull another running-away stunt now, they'd never believe me. But Brains—bless her beak—waddled over to sit on my hand. She was looking sleepy. I lifted her onto my shoulder. She click-clicked in my ear and then purred.

'Can I please go home?' I asked. 'I need to put her in her cage.' *Before JoBob finds out.*

''Fraid not, Tara.' The woman reached over and scratched Brains on the crest. The bird let her do it without ruffling a feather. She liked women more than men. 'You'll have to come to the station and make a statement.'

'Then can I please go and get my pants.'

'Don't get dressed on my account,' said Whitey. He and his sidekick burst out laughing.

Chapter 11

The Euccy Grove cop shop was a fifties brick and tile with a concrete parking lot out the front and a rose garden at the side. At night, in winter, with only the station floodlights on, the rose garden looked like grotesque sculptures.

It turned out that the perp—whose name was Sam Barbaro—had taken fright when an occupant disturbed him, and fled into the night.

The female cop, Fiona Bligh, took my statement and then said Brains and I could go home.

'Any chance of a ride?' I asked. 'I don't have my purse with me. Prefer not to ring my parents.'

Bligh glanced around. 'Well, we're not supposed to, but … under the circumstances … alright.' She turned to her partner, 'Bill, find a towel for the seat. That bird is a crap machine.'

'All birds are crap machines,' I said, scratching Brains under the chin. 'But she's also a hero.'

Bill and Fiona agreed on that count.

They drove me home and promised to drop some peanuts around when they had a chance.

I returned Brains to a very grateful and slightly frantic Hoo, fed them both and staggered off to bed.

It seemed I'd just laid my head on the pillow when JoBob's voice perforated my dreams. I sat up floundering as I fought off a nightmare involving Whitey and his tentacle fingers.

JoBob was at the sliding door, rattling the handle for all it was worth.

I pulled some jeans on under my knee-length tee, stumbled over and flicked the lock open. 'Wassa panic,' I mumbled, unhappily. I had pins and needles in one arm and a crappy taste in my mouth.

Joanna was clutching the daily paper, which she thrust under my nose. 'Tara Mary Sharp, explain *page two*.'

I took the paper and retreated to my couch where I spread it open. The headline read '*One Bird in the Hand…*' with a subheader, *Childhood sweethearts reunited to foil robbery*. Alongside the article were photos of Whitey in his cop uniform, wearing a smarmy smile, and me, taken at Bok's birthday party the previous summer. I had on a strapless top and looked like I could easily do ten rounds with Anthony Mundine.

My heart lurched as I skim read the lead-in. *Eucalyptus Grove socialite and one-time state athlete, Tara Sharp, was reunited with her former boyfriend, Constable Greg Whitehead, as they foiled a robbery on an aged woman living in Ms Sharp's home suburb.*

What about the bird, was all I could think!

My phone rang and I fished it out of my jeans automatically. 'Tara Sharp.'

'Keep your hands off my husband!'

'Excuse me?'

'My husband. Keep away from him,' she screamed before hanging up.

I sat in stunned silence, with Joanna doing the hands-on-hips, furrowed brow, and where-did-I-go-wrong thing across the room.

The phone rang again. I snatched it open. 'Listen here, who the hell—'

'Ms Sharp?'

I recognised the cool, arrogant voice and choked off my tirade.

'This is Peter Delgado.'

'Yes,' I squeaked. 'When and where?' I listened to the address he gave me. 'I'll be there.'

I snapped the phone shut and the room was suddenly very quiet.

'I'm waiting, Tara.' Joanna stopped short of toe-tapping but I could see it was on her mind.

'It's nothing, mother, just a blatant example of sensationalist journalism,' I said, before launching into an amended version of events, leaving out the part about taking my pants off.

'I can't believe you let Brains out of her cage at night. Poor darling, I'd better go and see if she's alright,' she humphed, and pattered off.

I sighed and slumped back on my couch. What a start to the day.

'Ahem.'

I glanced up at the door and realised that the other half of the JoBob entity was still there.

'Dad? Come in.'

My father, Robert—known to everyone as Bob—was the gentlest of gentlemen with a quiet sense of humour that he kept well hidden from Mum. As a kid I'd thought him invincible and heroic. Now I realised he was just a nice man married to a very dominating woman. I think I loved him more for that. He was so real.

He shuffled forward in his dressing gown and tartan slippers. My father wouldn't be seen dead in a pair of thongs.

'Tara, you know I don't like to interfere. You're a grown woman with a life of your own. But I'm worried about this new line of work you've taken up. If you need money…' he started, his face turning pink with embarrassment.

I felt guilty and I wasn't sure why. 'You know what I'm doing? I've been deliberately vague.'

'I haven't said anything to your mother, of course, but I was in here unblocking the sink and your phone rang.'

'You answered my phone?'

'I thought it might be important. Tara, what are these group sessions?'

For the second time that morning I was speechless. When the shock of what my father was inferring wore off, I began to giggle. The giggle turned into a laugh and the laugh into a guffaw until I was hee-hawing in a most unladylike fashion.

Dad stood silent, nonplussed.

When I could catch my breath I explained what the classes were about.

Relief lifted thirty years from his face.

I got up and came around the desk to give him a hug. Then I told him about my paralanguage business. 'I was keeping it quiet from you until I earned some money. I thought you'd think I was being flaky and irresponsible.'

He sighed and gave me a quick squeeze. 'I would have lent you the money.'

'I know,' I said. 'But I didn't want you to.'

There was a pause and the moment passed. He stepped away awkwardly. 'Just as long as you're alright then.'

I smiled. 'I'm right. I gotta go, Dad. Work, y'know.'

Chapter 12

Peter Delgado had given me the address of a party in Claremont, the next suburb to Euccy Grove. Claremont was wall-to-wall millionaires without the welfare housing contingent to keep its nose up in the air about.

I'd been told to be there by 9PM sharp. *In high heels.*

My gut feeling about the high-heels emphasis wasn't good, but, with only twenty cents to my name, the lure of a retainer and the possibility of a thousand-dollar bonus meant I could ignore a few little client foibles.

As I slid and wriggled into my newest LBD (two years old, on sale at Rucci's), I called Mr Hara and left a message. 'Hi Mr H, it's Tara. The client is in the bag and I start work tonight at the usual rate. Will let you know how it goes, but nothing to worry about. Hope Mrs H is ripping up the ski slopes.'

As I eased Mona out onto the highway and took a right at Bayview Terrace, I tried to imagine Mrs Hara skiing. For some reason I conjured a picture of her with her head and body buried in the snow, legs poking up in the air. I tried to change it—God knows, the woman could probably read my mind from Japan—but it wouldn't go away. Thick, varicose-veined legs waving in the air.

Blech.

As I turned left into Victoria Avenue though, the street was its own distraction. 'Millionaires' Row' they called it. Palatial houses and smug apartments that looked out onto a contented, yacht-strewn river. Some of the houses had their own little piers which looked as picturesque at night as they did in the daytime.

The address Peter Delgado had given me was both palatial and had its own jetty. I drove up past the house and turned right, parking Mona outside a block of luxury apartments. As I walked back I saw Mercs, Porsches and Beamers sweeping up into the white-gravel driveway.

Fortunately my LBD and black strappy heels were simple enough to be invisible. *You can't go wrong in black. You can't go wrong in black*, I told myself all the way to the gate.

I waited there for the car congestion to clear, then clattered up the front path and rang the doorbell.

A butler answered.

Butler! Yikes! Lots of my friends' parents had had expensive houses, but none of them had a butler.

I told him my name and he checked his list and asked for ID. Satisfied that I was who I said I was, he stood aside, making a sweeping motion with his hand. 'The ballroom is the first door on the left. Do you have anything you would like to check in, mademoiselle?'

'Uuh?' I said. 'Like what?'

'A coat. We also have a no weapons policy.'

I shook my head dumbly. I mean I'd been brought up properly, Joanna had seen to that, but no one had ever asked me if I'd like to check in a weapon with my coat.

For Chrissake, this was Perth!

'Enjoy your evening, Miss Sharp,' he intoned, then dipped his head to hide the kind of superior grin reserved for people who had gravy stains on their shirt, or sauce on their chin.

I make a point of standing tall when I'm nervous, so as I entered the ballroom I was ram-rod straight. This put me close on six feet four in my high heels, something I was ordinarily comfortable with ... though not when every head of a hundred-plus Party Elegant swivelled in my direction and stared.

The staring was not because of my beautiful posture, not even because I was the tallest person there (because I wasn't—there were a couple of absolute giants), but because everyone else was dressed in white.

Peter Delgado appeared from nowhere, an expensively dressed woman with straight, dark hair clutching his arm. The woman's aura was wintery blue and lumpy, and an unattractive sneer lifted her top lip back from her teeth.

'Good evening, Ms Sharp. This is my wife, Carlotta.'

Ah, the cut-snake lady. I smiled and held out my hand,

despite remembering Garth's description of her. 'Pleased to meet you.'

The woman declined my handshake and shot her husband a searching look.

'Get me a drink, will you?' Delgado told her.

She flicked her hair over her shoulder and walked away through the crowd without a backward glance. It was the height of her killer heels that jogged my memory. She'd been standing at Delgado's reception the other day.

'What the hell are you wearing?' Delgado said to me between gritted teeth. 'It's a "white" party.'

'You told me to wear heels,' I gritted back. 'Nothing about the colour of my clothes.'

'Francine rang you.'

Francine? The Giggler? 'You mean your PA?'

He nodded and swung me into a position so that his body partly obscured mine. Over his shoulder I could see people going back to their conversations. Show over.

'Yes,' he hissed.

'Well maybe you'd better get yourself a new PA with an IQ higher than her boob measurement, 'cos that one clearly can't understand plain English. She never contacted me,' I said, furious, then I shook him off me and tried to think of something else to talk about. 'Nice house. Who owns it?'

'Mr Viaspa.'

I swallowed. 'Johnny Vogue?'

Delgado looked me in the eye. 'You do know who he

is, don't you, Ms Sharp?'

I glanced around at all the people. The white suits and gowns made their auras sharper. It was like stepping out into the centre of a very bright rainbow. I screwed up my eyes and searched the room until I located the face I'd seen in the newspapers. 'Skinny dude over there with the big nose and the mullet, standing in between the gladiators and sucking down the Corona—'

'I'm sure he'd be flattered by the description,' said Delgado dryly. 'There's Nick. I'm going to introduce you. Now do your thing, Ms Sharp.'

'What thing?'

'Do what it takes to get close to him, then dig around in his private life. I want to know everything you can find out. Especially, the state of his finances.' He slipped a white envelope into my hand. 'Here's your retainer.'

I peeked inside and saw five crisp hundred-dollar bills. 'Um, thanks,' I said, stuffing it in my bag.

I didn't have time to ask anything else before my prey responded to Delgado's wave and came over.

I looked up. I had to. The guy was close to seven foot and built like an athlete who'd only gone the teensiest bit to seed by the way his suit hugged his massive frame. He had the face of a boy, an attractive one at that, and there was something familiar about that face…

Dark 'n' delish is how Bok would have described him. I suddenly wished Bok was here with me to poke fun at the beautiful people and tell me I looked hot in my LBD.

'Delgado,' nodded the giant, holding his fingers out for a slap, homey style. Though his smile was in place and perfectly pleasant, his gorgeous, creamy caramel aura shrank to a mere silhouette as he touched hands with Delgado.

'Nick Tozzi, meet Tara Sharp.'

I held out my hand for a traditional man-shake. When we touched, his aura expanded warmly, engulfing Delgado's sludge-brown shadow. I almost jumped back, which would have looked flaky, because for all intents and purposes he was wearing a smile and just politely shaking my hand.

He caught my slight wince and loosened his grip.

I grabbed his hand harder, not wanting him to think I wasn't up for a decent handshake, and succeeded in making his eyes widen in the way a person does when they are getting a Mason's secret shake—or a come-on. Imagining *he* was thinking the latter, I dropped his hand an instant later.

This was getting off to a bad start, and Delgado was creeping me out with his intense eyeballing, so I resorted to my default male conversation topic. Sport.

'Hi, Nick,' I said. 'You look like you might have spent time at the back of the scrum.'

He broke into a wide grin. 'I was just thinking the same thing about you.'

A girl could take offence at that kind of comment, but strangely it felt more like a compliment. I laughed. 'That's no way to speak to a girl who's wearing spiky heels.'

His eyes quickly dropped to my shoes then took a very slow trip back to my face via my legs, hips and chest. 'Why? Will you take it out on me?' His smile was more boyish this time.

I couldn't help it, I laughed again. We were already flirting inside our first fifty words to each other. I hadn't had that happen in a long time.

'I'll be right back, Nick,' said Delgado, slapping him on the back.

'Sure, Peter,' he said, his aura shrinking when Delgado touched him, then growing as soon as he looked back at me.

Flattering really, I guess, but then I noticed something I'd missed before. There was a spot of darkness like a bruise in his lovely caramel aura. Something was wrong in his life.

'So what *is* your sport, Nick?' I asked, truly curious now.

'Basketball.'

'Seriously? Errr … what I mean is … you look—'

He interrupted before I could bury myself. 'I played college in the States. Got invited to NBA tryouts and didn't make it.' His smile faded a bit then.

'Shame. But then not really. That's more than most players even dream about,' I said brightly, while I racked my brains. Who was this guy? I knew most of the ex-players around town, but Nick was maybe ten or fifteen years older than me. I'd probably been wearing water wings when he was a contender.

He shrugged. 'I decided to come back home to play the Aussie league but things had changed here a lot. I was the last of the big, slow centres. They're all my size now, but *quick* as well. I got sick of training harder than everyone else just to match up. Running up sand hills when you're my weight…'

I nodded in sympathy. 'Yeah, there are some things some bodies are not meant to do.'

'Your body looks like it's pretty versatile,' he said, looking me up and down again with a bald-faced appreciation that should have got me hopping mad. But he had a way about him, a slight goofiness that took the sting out of it. And a longing, like he hadn't been with a girl in a while. But that couldn't be right.

'So what do you do now?' I asked.

'When I quit playing I missed it so much, I kinda went out and…' He glanced at the wall and then the ceiling.

'And what?' I asked suspiciously.

'Bought the team.'

It took a few seconds for what he'd said to sink in. 'You mean the Western Thunder?'

He nodded and I wondered if the flush creeping up his neck was embarrassment or annoyance.

I bit my lip. 'You're Nick Tozzi, owner of the Western Thunder.' I had to say it out loud just to be sure I got it right.

'Yeah,' he said mildly. 'Sounds like I should apologise?'

I shook my head. 'No. But I think I'll go home now and crawl under my bed.'

'Why?'

'I can't believe I didn't know who you were. You look different on TV,' I finished lamely.

To my relief, I saw Peter Delgado shouldering his way back to us with a couple of drinks in his hand. Not so shiny was the ship sailing in his wake, Johnny Vogue.

'I mean I'm not just a fan, I used to play,' I babbled on.

Delgado was sliding towards us as quick and determined as a snake after a rat.

'I know,' Nick said softly. 'I remember you.'

Chapter 13

Delgado stopped in front of us and thrust a drink into my hand, insinuating his way in between Nick and me with his oily manner. 'Nick. You know John?'

Johnny Viaspa stepped into the middle of our cosy little tête-à-tête, splitting it like an arrow through an apple. Heads were turning our way again—a ripple of interest: Nick Tozzi and Johnny Vogue?

Where the sheer size and energy of Nick's aura had me stepping back, Johnny Vogue's made my skin crawl. It was stained yellow, the colour of pus.

'Tozzi,' said Viaspa.

'Yeah. Fancy.'

The air was so thick with conflicting charges that I felt a rush of nervousness. As usual it got me opening my mouth. 'I'm Tara,' I said.

Johnny Vogue mustn't have heard me. There wasn't even a twitch, or a flicker in my direction.

'Tara Sharp!' I said louder.

Nothing again.

'I think the lady is speaking to you,' said Nick.

Vogue turned his head ever so slightly and our eyes made contact. It wasn't an experience I ever wanted to repeat again. I'd felt bad karma with people before; I mean, Peter Delgado had enough. But no karma was even worse. There was a guy one time at uni, a friend of Bok's. The three of us hung out for a few months but I always found it uncomfortable because Tikki had no aura. Thing is, he died not so long after in a car accident. If I see people without auras these days, I don't make friends.

That wasn't Johnny Vogue, though. What he was carrying around was diseased. I could see the black blotches in it. Even as his pinned-out eyes held mine, I was aware of his aura flaking: sloughing small bits onto the furniture, and the floor, and my clothes. It made me want to run home and stand under a hot shower for a few hours.

Satisfied that he'd quelled me, he turned back to Nick. Not a word had passed between us, just a look and a whole lot of karmic buffeting.

'How's that team of yours going? Heard the recession's hit you hard.'

'The Thunder is doing just fine,' said Nick, flushing.

The words they were exchanging were civil, pleasant even. Delgado was smiling, Nick was smiling, and Johnny Vogue had his mouth set in a way that could have been a smile. But their auras were conducting a private war and

I felt like my head was sticking too far out of the bunker.

Fortunately, diversion came in the form of a tall, slim blonde leaning against the entrance to the ballroom.

It wasn't just our happy group that paused to ogle her either. This girl was a room-stopper. I mean she wasn't beautiful, she was *beautiful*. And the dress! A hugging, low-scooped white tunic embroidered with Swarovski diamonds. Her 'D' cup looked natural but couldn't have been—nobody could be *that* slim with breasts so big, it's just not physiologically possible. I mean, you can't just order your fat to stay in that one place. Her hair was like her legs, long and honey coloured, and her face was the kind of perfection that made you breathe deep. I couldn't even be jealous; you gotta bow before a goddess when you see one.

'Wow!' I muttered under my breath. 'A fallen angel.'

'You've met my wife before, have you?' asked Nick Tozzi.

I hadn't. But I'd seen her alright. Antonia Falk. Her family were big-time mining magnates. Capital 'L' loaded. Somewhere along the track I'd missed the fact that she'd hooked up with Nick Tozzi. Probably happened when I was four-wheel driving that toad, Pascal, around Cape York so he could see real live crocodiles. Shoulda fed him to them.

'Nicky?' the angel tittered, then swiped a drink from the hovering waiter's tray. She staggered a little, clearly stoned.

Nick Tozzi crossed the space between them in two giant strides and they spoke some quiet, tense words to each other. Their auras mingled uneasily, her fire-red psychic energy bleeding into his, diluting the caramel colour, as he took her arm and directed her back out the door.

I felt a little deflated as I watched them go. Of course he'd be married, I told myself. Only married men know how to flirt like that. Still, it had been fun for a few moments.

I glanced back at Johnny Vogue. He was watching them too—his eyes glazed with preoccupation. And it didn't look like it was *Nick* Tozzi he was thinking about. Then his cell phone rang, and he and his unhealthy aura disappeared through another door to answer it.

'Gotta go to the Ladies!' I announced, and dashed off to the loo before Delgado could pin me.

The bathroom was nearly as grand as the ballroom—green and black marble, and a vase of fresh-cut flowers the size of King's Park. I washed my hot face in the gleaming hand basin and patted it dry with a fresh, white hand towel from the pile the maid was restocking. Garth had been right about Peter Delgado, and I tried to think of a discreet way of begging off the job. I ended up deciding to cut and run instead. I'd mail his retainer back to him.

Scooting out of the toilet, I headed deeper into the house looking for a back exit. But as I rushed past an impressive living room the sound of Johnny Vogue's muffled voice stopped me in my tracks. It was coming from the patio outside the French doors. Unable to quell my curiosity, I sidled up to the curtains and turned the handle of the door, opening it just a crack.

'—find a way to bring the arsehole down. Tozzi won't get away from me this time, even if I have to plant coke up his arse. Give it six months and he'll be ruined. She'll come begging.' He paused. 'Yeah. See you at the Bunka warehouse on Monda—'

OMG.

'Ms Sharp?' Peter Delgado's cold fingers grabbed my elbow.

'Oops!' I let go of the handle. 'There you are. I was on my way back from the loo and I must have taken a wrong turn. Then I heard a voice and I was about to ask for directions.' My excuse sounded ridiculously lame.

He stepped past me and pushed open one of the French doors. He and Johnny Vogue exchanged looks. Vogue slipped his phone into his pocket then inclined his head in an abrupt semi-nod which could have meant anything.

Delgado grabbed my arm and steered me back towards the ballroom. I didn't like the way his fingers were digging into my flesh. His face had lost all the colour it had gained from ogling Nick Tozzi's wife, and was now a furious kind of white.

'Look,' I said, trying to pull my arm away. 'I'm not sure I'm the right person for this job you have in mind.'

'Well, I'd think twice before making a decision like that. What did you just hear, Ms Sharp?'

'When?' I asked dumbly, as we re-entered the ballroom.

His fingers dug deeper. 'Don't bullshit me.'

'N-nothing,' I said. 'Nothing. Just a muffled voice.'

'Well, I would stick to that story if I was you.'

I felt sick. Delgado knew I'd overheard something I shouldn't have. And now the arsehole was *threatening* me. For the second time this evening I wished Bok was with me. He knew how to handle even the most practised slime balls. Hell, the fashion industry teemed with them.

Chapter 14

I was spared answering Delgado because an explosion of uniformed police suddenly piled in the doors, one of them holding the leash of a sniffer dog. A couple of the party-goers tried to bail out the windows but there were more cops waiting outside with torches and tasers.

I saw Delgado reach into his pocket and dump a dozen or so capsules into the drip tray of the ice statue. With his other hand he lifted his phone to his ear. From the few words he uttered, I guessed that Johnny Vogue had managed to get clear of the fracas.

When he hung up, a few seconds later, his mouth settled into a grim line. I didn't need to have ESP to know he was trying to figure out who'd tipped off the cops.

I searched above the heads of the milling crowd but couldn't see Nick Tozzi. Lucky for him, he'd left before the cops arrived, and taken his wife with him.

A cop stood up on a chair and told everyone to *quieten down!* He then explained that it was a raid—doh!—and that each person would be searched for illegal substances. No one was allowed to move unless instructed to do so. The search would proceed as quickly and painlessly as possible—but no attempts to evade the search would be tolerated.

Sweat ran down the inside of my LBD. I didn't take drugs, I didn't have any drugs on me, and yet I felt as guilty as hell. Maybe it was because I was standing next to a gangster's lawyer.

The cops had told us not to move so I was stuck there. The best I could do was turn away from Delgado and study the ice statue, pretending we were accidentally caught next to each other, and I didn't know him.

I wondered how many others were trying that one.

The cops worked their way through the crowd while the sniffer dog ran around the room. When the dog stopped beside me I thought I might faint. It flung its paws up on the ice statue table and began to yelp. In a flash I was surrounded by cops.

Not only that, but the water around the ice statue was slowly turning blue.

One of the cops produced a vial and scooped up some of the coloured icy water. 'Could be trail mix,' he said, holding it up to the light and peering at it.

Trail mix? What in fuck's name was that? I glanced behind me. Delgado had taken advantage of the surge of cops around me and slipped further back.

'Identification please, Miss.'

I jumped. *Dammit!* The cop was talking to me. I fiddled in my clutch purse and found my driver's licence.

'Step this way, Ms Sharp,' he said, after looking at it.

Two cops escorted me back to the entrance hall and then into a side room. They told me to stand in the centre of the room and that they'd be searching me as soon as female police officers were present.

One of them closed the door and leaned casually against it while the other walked around me in small circles. I felt like puking, and sweat was running down my legs into my shoes. Being caught with my pants off by Whitey was one thing, but being in a drug raid in Millionaires' Row was quite another. I wondered if JoBob would put up my bail money. Or if Bok would stop laughing long enough to visit me in the clink.

'You like a few party drugs, Ms Sharp?' said the circler. He was average height—i.e. smaller than me—but solid and muscular, with lips set in sneer mode.

I shook my head. 'No.'

'How do you explain that you just happened to be the closest to a puddle of trail mix then?'

'I can't help where I was standing, and I've never heard of *trail mix*.' I said it as honestly as I felt it, trying to hold back the irritation that was swinging in counterweight to my fear.

'MDMA and Viagra. Ground up and mixed. Everything you could want for a night out,' said the door cop.

'If you're a guy,' I said.

'"*If* you're a guy. *If* you're a guy"! What about "*If* you're a *drug dealer*"?' The circler raised his voice to a shade less than a shout. 'You're the one who's in trouble here, Ms Sharp, so I suggest you start with the truth.'

Belligerence began to well up. I knew I should stay cool and sweet and do the *Yes sir, no sir* thing, but my mouth had its own ideas. 'Why don't you stop wasting your time on an honest citizen and get back in there and find the real crims.'

'Upright citizens don't come to parties on Coke Road,' said door cop.

Coke Road. Great!

Door cop left his posse and came to join the Circler. I felt like a drowning swimmer between two sharks.

'Everything alright, fellas?' came a female voice, halting the sharks. Constable Fiona Bligh had entered the room and was standing with her arms crossed and a hard expression on her face.

'Took your time, Bligh,' said the Sneer.

'Sarge needs you two out on the driveway. Barnes and Lund will be here in a minute to assist me with this search.'

The sharks exchanged looks and left.

Bligh unfolded her arms and slipped a knapsack off her shoulders. Her immaculate bun was dishevelled and she was sweating slightly herself. 'What on earth are you doing here, Tara?'

I swallowed. 'Bad luck I think. And ... well I can *tell* you, I wish I wasn't.'

'You walk under a ladder or something?' She took a box out of her knapsack and pulled some rubber gloves from it. 'If not, you want to think seriously about staying in at night for a while. Sorry, but I'm going to have to do this.'

Another person entered the room. 'Tara Sharp?'

'Hi Bill,' I said. 'Please tell me Whitey's not here.'

'He's out in the wagon,' said Bill Barnes.

'Come on, let's get on with it,' said Bligh, kind of tetchy. 'Bill, send Constable Lund in.'

Another female cop took Bill's place while Bligh did a perfunctory frisk. She didn't poke too hard anywhere, and afterwards, Bill returned and ran an explosive's detector over me.

'Thought you were looking for drugs?'

'Terrorism's a big thing these days.'

'Me. A terrorist? You've got to be kidding.'

'Bill!' Bligh's voice held a stern warning note as if he'd said too much. She began rifling through my handbag and pulled out the white dollar-filled envelope. 'Explanation?'

'Just got paid,' I said truthfully. 'I can give you my client's name. Haven't had time to bank it.'

'Cash, Tara? Hope you're going to declare it.'

'Of course. My accountant is anal. He never lets me slip up on details.'

She sighed. 'Ms Sharp, you're free to go home. However, officers may call on you again for further questioning.'

I nodded meekly and went to follow Bill Barnes out of the room.

'And Tara?' I stopped at Bligh's stern voice and let the door close behind Bill, leaving Bligh and me alone. 'I'm surprised to find you here. I hope you're not thinking of keeping the wrong company,' she said.

'You know I don't take drugs.'

'I've only got your word for that. And things can snowball when you get seen in the wrong places. You don't want to run into Cravich and Blake again.'

'The sharks?'

She nodded.

I sighed. 'OK. Thanks.'

She gave a small grin then. 'The wagon's on the south side of the road. If you turn right out of the gates Whitey won't even know you've been here.'

'Won't he read the reports?'

Bligh walked passed me and opened the door. 'Whitey? Read? When hell freezes over.'

Chapter 15

I rang Bok as soon as I got home and told him the whole story, including the part about Peter Delgado working for Johnny Vogue.

He was kind and sweet and comforting. Not. Actually, he told me what an idiot I was.

'Johnny Vogue, T! What were you *thinking*?'

'I didn't know the job was for him.'

'Did you ask who it was for?'

'Delgado isn't the kind of man you ask anything.' Besides, I was deaf because the words retainer and BONUS were ringing in my ears.

He made an exasperated noise. 'I hereby put you on probation. You're not to go out without Smitty or me until this whole drug stuff has cooled.'

Smitty knew every damn person in the western suburbs, and their pedigree—legacy from her time as a Silver Chain Nurse doing home visits. No one quite like a grandmother to blab the family secrets. Smitts wouldn't be happy that

I'd been to a party at Johnny Vogue's house.

'How long will that be?' I asked miserably.

'Let me see … in the papers tomorrow, and then again in a few days when they lay charges, and then again when they go to court, and then—'

'In that case,' I interrupted huffily, 'you'd better cancel your plans for tomorrow night. I have another job.'

'But it's Saturday night.'

'You made the rules. Saturday is date night for Smitty, so she won't be able to come.' Married couples had to do that sort of thing or they never got to have sex—or so Smitty said.

He took forever to reply, and I thought I'd cracked him with the 'Saturday night' thing. But he stumbled over the finishing line with a long-suffering sigh, muttering something like, 'For the good of all' and then louder, 'What time shall I pick you up?'

'Six PM. We're just going to Club Eighteen. Don't overdress.'

I hung up and stared at the ceiling. It was 1AM and my mind was a whirl. Nick Tozzi seemed like a nice bloke. Who was I kidding? He seemed a lot more than that. But he was married to a princess, and Johnny Vogue wanted to bring them down.

If I was a decent sort I'd contact Nick Tozzi and tell him what I'd heard. If I was smart, I'd lay low and hope Tozzi, Delgado and Johnny Vogue all forgot they'd met me.

Well … I already knew I wasn't having a 'smart' night.

I rolled out of bed and stumbled over clothes to the couch where I burrowed for my laptop under two sets of bras and a pair of worn-recently running shorts.

Crap. Must do some washing tomorrow.

As I waited for it to boot up, I thought about Fiona Bligh. Cravich and Blake hadn't had pure thoughts on their mind. Her intervention had saved me something unpleasant—of that I was sure. I owed her, despite the scolding.

I typed 'Nick Tozzi' into Google and got nearly half a million hits. It didn't take long to confirm he'd married Antonia Falk.

My JoBob implant went off. *'You know, Tara, there were five original families in Perth: the Falks, the Poyntons, the Lathlains, the Shentons and the Dewars (*uggh Phillip Dewar!*). You really should be nicer to young Phil...'*

Those five families were still Perth's royalty—other than the odd rock star or actor who'd been ripened under the sun on Cottesloe Beach and sent off to ferment in Hollywood.

Google also told me that Antonia and Nick had been married for two years, had no kids, and took their holidays in either Mauritius or Vegas. Antonia had been to prep school in Connecticut, uni at the Sorbonne and dropped out to model for a couple of years. Her modelling portfolio included a Victoria's Secret catalogue cover.

I stopped reading then. *Victoria's Secret* for crying out loud! That capped an already disturbing evening.

I hit the kill button and rummaged through my bedside table for eye mask, ear plugs and tablets I usually reserved for migraines. Next thing I was out cold.

The following morning was nearly afternoon, and I woke up feeling sluggish and pissed off. For a start I'd slept through my Saturday pick-up basketball game at the local courts, and secondly, I only had an hour and a half before 'Social Skills Class' with Los Trios.

I threw on cut-off tracks and a singlet and shuffled out the door to the gym, knowing I couldn't handle Los Trios with my head full of cotton balls.

Rather Be Dead? was the quaint name for a boutique gym tucked in a cul-de-sac that ran up near the highway. It was way too expensive for a girl with no income, but it was close to Lilac Street, and I'd been going there for several years and found the habit hard to break. Dad had bailed out my addiction with a twelve-month membership for my birthday. I had ten months to go. Surely I'd have some steady income by then!

The RBD kiosk sold killer muesli slice and freshly squeezed fruit juices, and Craigo, the lead gym instructor, was a shade over perfect: a sweet, patient man with SAS-type conditioning and a bundle of boyfriends. When he wasn't strutting his stuff on the exercise mat he was on the phone arranging dates.

He waved to me as I walked in. I waved back and

stopped to read the noticeboard in the hope he wouldn't offer himself as a work-out partner.

Other than a flyer for an upcoming triathlon, the results of a raffle, and a photo of the fifties-plus fitness fundraiser team, not much else was happening around the traps. I had a bit of a snigger at the three rows of portly middle-aged men and then slunk into the weights room and commandeered the rowing machine.

Forty minutes later, I was back home with a clearer head and relief that blood might actually be flowing through my veins. I showered, dressed and ate dry toast while I shovelled all the clothes off the couch and onto my bed and pulled the screen across. That left me a few minutes to re-read my notes from the previous sessions.

Los Trios arrived together, having met outside on the footpath. I'd told them it was better that way—much less inclined to send JoBob off on a 'prowler alert'.

Enid and Harvey dutifully sat on their allotted cushions but Wal sprawled onto the couch leaving me a sliver of cushion on which to park my bum. I thought about telling him to move but he was showing far too much white around the eyes today for unnecessary conflict.

'Hi guys,' I said. 'Let's start with our homework. Ladies first, Enid?'

'Lady!' Wal snorted like a feral pig and laughed so hard he farted. The smell rose like a tornado, catching Enid and Harvey front-on. Harvey somersaulted backwards and ran to the door, gagging. Enid turned bright red from both the insult and from holding her breath.

I leaped for the ceiling fan and switched it on turbo. When the stink had passed and we'd composed ourselves, I turned it off.

'Come on back, Harvey. Crisis over.' I resumed my postage stamp-sized seat and motioned for him to sit on his pillow. He returned reluctantly, casting Wal annoyed looks through his unwashed fringe.

'Wal,' I said. 'How do you think you made Enid feel with that comment?'

Wal shrugged, and slouched down further, forcing me up onto the arm of the couch.

'Now Enid? How did you go with Count and Think?'

'Well, I'm doing it right now,' she said, glaring at Wal. 'So I suppose it's working.'

'Err … great,' I said brightly. 'What about at work though?'

She ran her plump fingers through her shoulder-length brown hair and yanked the front of her bustier into place. Enid was a very well-endowed young woman poured into a silk bodice and velvet skirt.

Harvey goggled as the mountain of flesh rose, threatened to overflow and then settled. Even Wal was temporarily riveted.

'OK. On Tuesday, Amy, my junior, stacked a whole box of slippery elm packets where the psyllium should be. I wanted to call her a "stupid mother-fucking cunt", but I did the Count and Think thing, and instead I said, "Was your mother taking a bath in lead-based paint when she was pregnant with you?"'

'That's good,' I managed to choke out.

Harvey clapped. 'Bravo, Enid.'

'Harvey? How about you next?'

Harvey dropped his head shyly so that all I could see was the sprinkle of dandruff along his hair part. He fumbled in his shirt pocket for his iPhone. 'I wrote the list of things I could say to ask a girl out, like you told me to do. And I've been practising them.'

'Great.' Harvey was so earnest he kinda tugged at my heartstrings. I also wanted to give him a lecture on personal hygiene. 'Go ahead. Let's hear them.'

'OK. *I've been watching you for a while and I can't take my eyes off you,*' he recited.

I cleared my throat. 'Not bad but could be creepy. What else have you got?'

He peeped up at me from under his lashes then hurriedly dropped his eyes again. '*I think about you when I beat the meat,*' he whispered.

I blinked. 'What?! No, never mind. Ahmmm...'

To my towering relief the phone rang. I leaped up and grabbed it from my bag. 'Just keep practising on Enid while I take this call.' I dived out the door and took some deep gulps before answering.

'Thank you, thank you, *thank* you, whoever you are.'

'My pleasure, Ms Sharp,' said a deep, unbelievably sexy voice.

A bolt of excitement shot down through my belly and out through my toes. *Nick Tozzi*. 'Whoever this is, I can explain,' I squeaked.

Tozzi laughed. 'I'm sure you can.'

I thought for a split second about continuing to act coy and tossed it. 'Hi Nick, how did you get my number?'

'Your mother—Joanna is it?—gave it to me. What a sweet lady. And so helpful.'

'Isn't she,' I replied through gritted teeth.

'I apologise for calling you out of the blue after such a brief acquaintance, but I was wondering if you'd have breakfast with me—'

My heart bounced.

'—I want to ask your opinion about something a little sensitive.'

'Is this about Johnny Vogue?' I asked.

There was a longish silence while *he* decided whether to be coy or not. Like me, he opted for the straightforward approach. 'Yes,' he said, finally.

I liked straightforward.

'Actually, I was thinking about calling you,' I said.

'Oh?'

'Same reason.'

'Oh.' He sounded vaguely disappointed, though I might have been imagining it. 'Well, how's tomorrow morning? Seven-ish?'

Seven-ish? Crap, how could I look good at seven-ish? 'Fine,' I said.

'My PA will text you the details.'

'The personal touch, huh?'

He laughed again. 'You're a straight shooter, aren't you, Ms Sharp.'

'It's Tara, remember?' I said. 'See you tomorrow.'

After I hung up, I hopped up and down on the spot. It was only business, but I was going to see Nick Tozzi again. What would I wear? I needed to ring Bok right away for a wardrobe consultation.

Bok.

I groaned aloud. I was on probation. Surely Bok wouldn't want to come to breakfast too? Maybe I just wouldn't tell him. But then my clothes wouldn't be right. I weighed up the pros and cons. Call me shallow, but having Bok hovering around me during breakfast with Nick was definitely coming in lighter than messing up my wardrobe choice and Bok finding out after the fact. Having a best friend in fashion was exacting. I'd ring him as soon as Los Trios had gone. Maybe we could fit in a shopping trip this afternoon.

In high spirits I waltzed back inside … and stopped dead.

Wal was stretched out on the couch, asleep. I mean 'comatose' asleep. He had to be! Otherwise he would've had a ringside seat to Harvey and Enid going at it hammer and tongs. Obviously one of Harvey's pick-up lines had nailed it.

I averted my eyes from the disturbing vision of Enid,

bosoms escaping from her bodice, sitting astride a much smaller, punier Harvey, and dashed in to get my handbag and computer.

'Pull the door across when you leave,' I shouted, and bolted.

Chapter 16

By the time I got to Mona I was gagging and laughing at the same time. After collapsing into the front seat, I waited until the wave of hysteria passed then tried to calm down and call Bok. He wasn't picking up, so I scraped some muffin crumbs off the passenger seat and tossed them to the magpies, who spent their lives waiting patiently near my car for just that very thing to happen.

Birds seem to know when you're a bird person. Some high-frequency message must go out from tree to tree, species to species, until the entire bird population of the world is alerted to the fact that you're good for food. Maggies, galahs, corellas, lorikeets, willie wagtails and even crows seemed to know when the passenger seat of Mona was littered with last night's pizza, or the morning's croissant.

I watched the maggies squabbling over the crumbs and thought for a moment. I shouldn't be leaving Los Trios alone in my flat but I simply could *not* go back in there.

Another wave of giggling swept over me.

I tried Bok again. Still no pick-up, so I dialled Smitty.

'Hi Smitts, can you spare me an hour?'

'Hello darling. Do you need bail?'

'Very funny. I've got a breakfast appointment tomorrow morning and I have to look good. Can you meet me at The Jam Factory?'

'Hang on. I thought Bok had you on probation.'

'He does.' I sighed. 'He'll be coming with me tomorrow.'

Smitty let out a breath. 'Oh, that's a relief. Saturday is Triple F at our house.'

'Pardonnez?'

'Footy, food-shopping and fifteen-minute fuck.'

'Phew! Too much information, Smitts. Anyway I thought you went out Saturday nights to get in the mood.'

'No, we do it *before* we go out because we're always too tired when we get home.'

'Oh.'

'Is it anyone I know?' she added. Smitty could change topic quicker than a grasshopper on crack.

'Errr … I'll tell you if you come and help me pick out something hot to wear.'

'I'll just check with Henny.' While she explained my dire need to her beloved, I clipped on my seatbelt and started the car.

I heard a muffled, 'Don't be ridiculous, darling, Tara won't land me in jail,' before she came back on and said, 'Henny sends his love. I'll see you there in ten minutes.'

'Sweet.' I hung up and drove Mona out onto the street past an older model blue BMW driving the other way.

As I turned right onto the highway, my musings got interrupted by something in my rear-view mirror. The blue BMW had turned around and was following me. To check I wasn't imagining things, I turned right at Queenslea Drive and took a long, winding loop back to Latte Ole and the Richview shopping strip. The car stayed with me. Not close enough to recognise the driver, but not trying really hard to go unnoticed either.

I parked underneath the David Jones department store. The Beamer drove past me and went on to the lower basement level. Maybe I'd been mistaken, I thought, as I rode the escalator into the shopping complex. This whole Johnny Vogue/Nick Tozzi thing had me edgy, and the Harvey/Enid affair had me plain hysterical.

I tried to calm myself before I saw Smitts. Like Bok, she could pick up on my moods even quicker than she could switch topics.

Chapter 17

Richview shops comprised one multi-storey centre with a whole lot of ground-level boutiques and cafés sprinkled around the outside of it. The exclusive shopping area was bordered by the railway line on one side and the highway on the other. In summer, the 'Rich' centre was packed with people taking advantage of the airconditioning, but the rest of the year most shoppers liked to use the alfresco eateries around the outside. Mostly the boutiques were mortgage-your-house expensive, but a couple of factory-direct stores had survived from the early days—a bit like Euccy Grove's welfare housing.

The factory directs were on the very top level where the architect and builders had had a communication breakdown and forgotten to put in windows. The owners had tried to sue, but in the end it was easier to drop the rent. The Jam Factory had been there as long as I could remember—give or take a few name and radical decor changes. These days it was techno-punk and minimalist.

'T!' a tiny figure barrelled into me and latched around my waist.

I patted the silky, Orica-styled hair with affection. When we were younger it had been wild and messy. Just like her. 'Hi Smitty.'

She let go and stepped back to give me a quick appraisal. 'What's wrong? Your eyelid is twitching again. Last time that happened, you'd just found out that Mr Mauritius was bashing the pants off that slutty boarder of yours.'

She was right. When Pascal left me my eyelid had twitched for three weeks. Smitts, bless her tiny designer socks, had brought me a pair of sunnies to hide the tic—mine were lost—and a reflexology session at a day spa.

While we burrowed through the racks I told her about Enid and Harvey, and by the time I'd picked out a few items to try on, she was crying with laughter.

'I'd better not tell Henny,' she hiccupped. 'I'll be banned from visiting you.'

I laughed and disappeared into the change-room to fight my way into a striped tube-dress.

Smitty stuck her head around the curtain. 'I can't give proper advice until I know who it is.'

'Nick Tozzi,' I mouthed, so the shop assistants couldn't hear. Richview was a VERY small shopping world. 'He was at Johnny Vogue's party.'

'Nick Tozzi,' she mouthed. 'OMG. You mean Antonia Falk's shag?'

'Husband,' I corrected. 'And how many times have I

told you it's totally un-cool to *speak* in acronyms.'

'Well it's damn useful,' Smitty retorted. 'And you can't wear that to breakfast with a Tozzi. You look like a $1000-a-night girl.'

I looked in the mirror. 'You mean an expensive hooker?'

'More mid-range tart.' She pointed to the white halter dress I'd grabbed as a maybe. 'Try that one.'

With a sigh I peeled out of the tube and put on the halter.

'Perfect,' she said. 'Elegant and sexy.'

'I always feel like a princess in white, and not in a good way,' I said.

'Quit whining. I've only got half an hour left. Let's grab a coffee.' She closed the curtain.

Smitty's deadlines were to the second, so I hurried. Just as I got my head and one arm through my t-shirt, I heard a female voice.

'Jane Evans, is that you?'

'I'm sorry,' said Smitty in her most frigid tone. 'I'm afraid I've…'

'June Whitehead nee Barry.'

Who in the hell said 'nee'?

'June Barry,' Smitty repeated loudly and slowly. 'From school. Oh, yes, you married Whitey.'

'Yes, I did,' said the voice, 'and you can tell that friend of yours to keep right away from my man. She's here with you, isn't she?'

All my instincts wanted me to stride out half naked

and thump June Whitehead *nee* Barry in her big gob, but Smitty was cool as a cucumber.

'I don't have the slightest idea who you're talking about. But I do think you should go home and take your tablets, dear.'

The shop girls tittered.

'Tara Sharp is who I'm talking about! That bitch is sniffing around my Greg.'

'Oh you poor deluded thing,' said Smitty with sugary sympathy. 'I'll let you in on a secret. Tara Sharp wouldn't bang Whitey if he was wrapped in hundred-dollar bills. The man's a fugly idiot. Besides, she's dating a Tozzi.'

I'm what?!

June made some snorting sounds that sounded like 'rich bitch' before stomping away.

After enough time had passed, I peeked around the curtain. 'Is the coast clear?'

Smitty's cheeks were as red as a fire hydrant. Her hands were planted firmly on her hips. 'Appalling,' she said, channelling our mothers. 'The manners some people don't have.'

The shop girls stared at us goggle-eyed. I could almost feel the wheels of the rumour mill start to spin, so I resorted to my cure-all. 'Let's eat.'

I paid for the dress with the last of my Social Skills Class money, and hoped Smitty would cover the bill for the cake.

We got the last table downstairs in the brasserie. I

ordered a pot of tea for two, and two vanilla slices. Smitty was the vanilla slice queen.

'Honestly,' she said, sucking custard out from between the pastry. 'Some people should be drowned at birth.'

I squashed my custard out and picked off the globs with my fingers. 'Why did you say I was dating a Tozzi?'

Smitty took a sip of tea. 'Well you are. Tomorrow morning.'

'It's a work meeting with a very married Tozzi. And I don't need another deranged woman claiming I'm after her husband.'

'What do you mean?'

'I got an anonymous abusive call the other day. Something similar.'

'It was probably June Barry.'

I studied my glob of custard and sighed. 'Probably was.'

'Now where were we? Ah, Nick Tozzi.'

'Smitts, I am not dating him.'

'Pooh,' said Smitty. 'His marriage is never going to last.'

I might have rubbed my hands together with glee if my fingers hadn't been sticky with custard—Smitty was always good for the dirt. 'Do tell,' I ordered.

'Antonia's a major coke addict. She managed to hide it until after the wedding though. But I hear she's back to her old tricks.'

I thought about Nick's reaction when he'd seen his wife

at the Coke Road party. Smitty's gossip explained a lot.

'So why doesn't she do rehab?' I asked.

Smitts took delicate bites of the leftover pastry bits. 'Who knows? She's supposed to have picked up the habit when she was modelling overseas. Good way to stay thin. Anyway, it's your turn. Tell *me* everything.' she glanced at her watch. 'And do it in fifteen minutes.'

I launched into a point-form version of how I ran into Whitey, his phone call asking me to have an affair, and the now-infamous party where I'd met Nick Tozzi.

Smitty listened with complete attention, sipping the last of her tea. When I finished, she sighed. 'Your life is so much more interesting than mine, T.'

'I don't know that "interesting" is quite the word, Smitts. I mean, Bok's got me on probation. Besides, you've got a husband and kids who adore you, not to mention enough money to take holidays. I've got … Brains, Hoo and JoBob, and I just spent my savings on a white dress.'

'Is that your sneaky way of saying that I'm paying for afternoon tea?'

I tried for an offended look. 'Well, considering that I'm your entertainment, I think it's only fair.'

She reached into her handbag and pulled out her wallet. 'Tara Sharp,' she said sternly. 'Will you ever grow up?'

Chapter 18

I couldn't get Nick Tozzi off my mind all the way home. Was his marriage really as bad as Smitty had said? I mean, I'm not one to wish a divorce on *anybody*. Still, it'd be a shame to see such a good man go to waste.

As I pulled in to my local garage to fill up Mona, I noticed a blue BMW cruise past. Blue BMWs are like Smiths in the phone directory around here, but it got me jumpy again.

I looked in my rear-view all the way home. In fact I was so busy looking behind me that I didn't notice the police car in JoBob's driveway until I'd almost run into it. I got out clutching my shopping bag, my heart thumping, wondering if Wal had woken up and tried to assault Enid and Harvey. What now?

To my relief, Fiona Bligh and Bill Barnes were loitering near the galahs. At least it wasn't Cravich and Blake.

'Howdee do,' I called as I ambled down the driveway towards them. ''Sup?'

Bligh continued looking intently in the cage but Bill gave me a big wave. 'Hi Tara,' he said. 'We've brought Brains her treat like we promised. No one home at the front, so we found our own way in.'

'OK.' I smiled brightly at him, but a little alarm bell went off in my head. Were these two scoping me out? 'That's nice of you.'

'Do they both like treats?' asked Bligh. She had her finger in between the wires trying to entice Brains with a fruit stick.

'Sure,' I said, 'but be careful of Brains because she likes to—'

'Aaagh!'

'—bite,' I finished, lamely.

Bill burst out laughing.

Fiona tucked her hand under her armpit and glared at me. 'We wanted to talk to you too. Got somewhere we could go?'

I nodded nervously. Surely Enid, Harvey and Wal had gone? 'OK This way.'

They followed me out the end of the driveway and across to my flat. I hesitated at the door. 'Just let me make sure all my undies are put away,' I said, then rolled my eyes at Bill. 'Girl on her own, you know.'

Bill grinned but Fiona Bligh wasn't buying it. 'You're not thinking of hiding drugs are you, Tara?'

'I've already told you, that's not my thing. Just give me a moment to make my bed.'

I slid the door open, stepped in, and slid it shut behind me. To my amazement the place was immaculate. Not immaculate the-way-it-was-before-Enid-rocked-Harvey's-world, but immaculate like an army of cleaners had been through: not an item of clothing or a cushion out of place. I inhaled a lung full of air-freshener and noted the empty rubbish bin. *WTF?* Dazed, I opened the door for the cops.

Bligh stepped in first, sniffing the air, followed by Bill, whose quick scan of the room lingered on my bed and lacy pillow slip.

I pointed to the couch. 'Take a seat if you want. Now, what did you want to talk about?'

Bill dropped his butt down but Bligh stayed standing. I liked Fiona, but she had a bit of a stiff attitude. Her turquoise aura got grey streaks through it when she was like this. Bill's, on the other hand, was permanently fuzzy and soft, like a halo of green fur. I'm not sure he'd picked the right profession.

'Where do you buy your petrol?'

'Huh?' I said. 'Wherever's cheap. Why?'

'What about the servo on Forest and Gugeri?'

'Sometimes. Not often.'

'When did you last buy it there?'

'I'm not sure,' I said, confused. 'Why do you care?'

'Sam Barbaro pumps petrol there.' She said flatly, studying my reaction.

'Good for him. But what's that got to do with me?'

'Had you ever met Sam Barbaro before the night of the

attempted burglary?'

I stared at her. 'I've already told you I'd never seen him before in my life. I don't make a habit of hanging out with burglars.'

'No need to get smart, Sharp, just answer the question.'

'No, never before,' I said solemnly. 'Why?'

'He's been bailed. We don't know who really put up the money but Peter Delgado is fronting it. He represents Johnny Viaspa, in case you didn't know. There's been some talk at the station that you might have been an accomplice, not a hero,' Bill blurted out.

'Bill,' admonished Fiona. 'Zip it.'

'You don't believe that, do you?' I gasped at Fiona. 'Cripes, why would I want to be robbing Euccy Grove grannies? And where would I get bail money?'

'Not just any granny,' said Bligh. 'Eireen Tozzi.'

'*What?*'

'You didn't know who it was?'

I shook my head, dumbfounded, not enjoying the curdling feeling in my stomach. 'No idea. I only saw the picture of me and Whitey. That was enough. Didn't bother to read the article.'

After a moment though, I grinned. 'No wonder he ran for it. She's got a reputation for being a tough old goat.'

'You chose the wrong time to go to a party at Coke Road and be seen in the company of people like Peter Delgado, Sharp. You need to be careful. I believe you've registered a new business recently.'

'So?' I should have been less bolshy but this friendly 'chat' was starting to get on my nerves.

'Would you care to describe it?'

I shrugged. 'Communication analysis.'

Bill snorted with laughter but Fiona remained deadly serious. 'Garth Wilmot says you're inclined to be impulsive.'

'Why have you been talking to Garth?'

'Just a bit of background checking.'

'You're doing background checks *on me*?'

'On everyone at the Coke Road party,' groaned Bill.

'Barnes!' snapped Bligh.

'What would an accountant know,' I said. 'His idea of impulsive is to take his shoes off after work.' *Remember to kill him.*

Fiona walked around the couch and made a show of looking into every nook and cranny my tiny garage apartment had to offer. 'Tell me, Sharp. What would a known petty criminal by the name of Wallace Grominsky, and Harvey Tsao, an ASIO recruit, be doing at your place at the same time?'

Tsao. Was that his name? And ASIO? WTF? 'Having Social Skills Coaching. You know, how to get along with people,' I said sweetly. 'There's room in the class if you want to sign up.'

Bill looked like he might explode from trying not to laugh. But Bligh remained sombre. 'Listen, Cravich and Blake wanted to make this call. So don't tick me off or next time I won't insist on doing it.'

Bill's expression sobered. 'She's right, Tara. She had to take some crap to keep them off your derrière.'

Bligh grunted and turned to leave.

'Thanks, Bligh.' I sighed. 'I appreciate it. And Wal and Harvey both answered my advert in the local paper. Simple as that. I guess there are a lot of lonely people out there.' I ventured another smile. 'So I suppose the blue car that was following me today was you guys then?'

Fiona spun on her heel and pinned me with a look. 'What blue car?'

'A BMW. Five or six years old?'

'Did you get the licence plate?'

'No. I-I wasn't sure whether it was really following me or if I was imagining it. Why? Isn't it one of yours?'

She shook her head. 'No. We're not tailing you, Tara. But if you think someone is, you'd better be extra careful. Don't go anywhere alone if you can help it and stick to areas of the city that you know.'

'You're kidding me?'

She looked insulted. 'If you get a number plate, let us know.' She fished in her pocket and pulled out a fridge magnet in the shape of policeman's cap. 'Here's the station number. Ask for me or Bill.'

They left then, Bill dutifully following a step behind dour Fiona. He gave me a wave from behind his back and the 'thumbs-up'.

I liked Bill.

Chapter 19

My chat with the local constabulary left me with a severe case of anxiety hunger. So I went up to JoBob's to raid the fridge. My one stroke of good luck for the day was that they were out at golf—the beauty of Dad being a semi-retired trader—so I wouldn't have to field difficult questions.

Armed with nuts, brie, water biscuits, a bag of cherries and some microwave popcorn, I headed back to my garage flat, locked the door and shut the curtain. Today was officially over for me until Bok picked me up to go to Club Eighteen.

I popped the corn then scoffed all my borrowed goodies. Feeling a little better, I tried on my new dress, swapping shoes until I got the right pair. Satisfied, I hung it up on a picture hook and lay down on my bed, pondering the mystery of who had cleaned up my room, until sheer puzzlement put me to sleep.

I woke up an hour later, really thirsty from the popcorn.

My watch told me I only had an hour until Bok arrived, so I guzzled a couple of glasses of water and scurried across to the shower, donning a black slim-line skirt and dressy shirttop. I pushed my hair into combs and daubed eyeliner and blusher in the appropriate spots. A pair of flats (I was working!) and my beloved quilted fake Marc Jacobs handbag completed the outfit.

I sat on the couch, sent a couple of texts then read my email. One was a rather jerky message to Mr Hara saying that I wouldn't be working for Peter Delgado anymore and that I hoped Mrs Hara was enjoying snow skiing; another to Smitty saying thanks for cake and for diverting mad female stalkers. I composed a last one to Garth, telling him he was a jerk for blabbing to the cops, and then thought better about sending it. Knowing my current luck, it would be used in evidence against me.

Trying to ignore the faint smell of Wal Grominsky's body odour on the cushion covers—ugh—I then deleted some porn spam from my inbox and took time to study the photo Mr Honey had sent me of his girlfriend. She was a handsome brunette with a fierce set of abs showing beneath her midriff top. I couldn't see auras in photos but I was betting hers was as streamlined and determined as her gym-junkie figure.

That was the thing with auras. It wasn't just their colour that told you things about the person. They had texture too. Some were fuzzy, or stripy, or ragged at the edges. Some were graded, fading out of their colour, while others had a definite edge. According to Mr Hara, the thin, well-defined auras tended to surround people who liked to be in control and who calculated their life within an inch of itself. I mean to say, abs like hers took grit.

When Bok rang to say he was waiting outside, I squirted myself with Very Valentino and locked the door tight.

As I walked down the driveway I could see Dad in the kitchen window. 'Do you want me to cover the birds?' I called out.

Dad waved to me and nodded. He looked tired and a little drained. Living with a vampire lady can do that to you.

I tipped some seed into the birds' three feed containers and yanked the cover down. It wasn't dark yet but they were already hunkered down for the evening, heads tucked under their wings. *Cu-ute*. And hard to believe one of them was a crime fighter who'd nearly bitten the top off a policewoman's finger.

Bok and I took the beach road to enjoy the sun swimming its way down below the horizon. He was dressed in black shirt and pants and his hair was as glossy and smooth as a Pantene commercial.

As I told him about my date with Nick Tozzi, Fiona Bligh's visit and the blue BMW, his serene expression gradually changed into pursed lips and a frown.

'I don't like this, T. This is not like any stupid thing

131

you've done before.'

For once I didn't argue with him. He was right and I was sitting on a belly full of jitters. 'I've told Mr Hara I'm quitting on Peter Delgado.'

'Might be too late for that. Without being too dramatic, these guys don't like anyone knowing their *business*.'

My phone rang: a private number. I answered it and listened.

'I can hear you breathing, Ms Sharp. This is Peter Delgado.'

'Hello,' I croaked.

'I believe the police have just paid you a visit? I want you to come into my office first thing on Monday morning 9AM to further discuss your contract. In the meantime, think carefully about who you talk to.'

I shut my phone and stared out the window: one lone windsurfer on the roughening water in the fading light. He was game.

'T?'

'Delgado wants me to come in first thing on Monday morning. He warned me not to talk to anyone.'

Bok slapped the steering wheel. 'You'd better cancel on Tozzi.'

'I *can't*, Marty.'

That was low. I only used *Marty* when I really needed something. And I needed to see Nick Tozzi, not just because he was delicious and my blood got hot every time I thought about him, but because he was a decent bloke and he deserved to know that Johnny Vogue had it in for him.

Bok snagged a park right opposite Club Eighteen and we sat in silence while he negotiated the reverse parking. As I went to unclip my seatbelt though, he grabbed my hand. 'I'll help you, T, whatever you want. But you've got to promise me you'll consider things before you act. You overheard Viaspa threatening to plant drugs on Nick Tozzi. This is too heavyweight for you to be impulsive.'

'I promise.' I gave him a quick smile and a kiss on the cheek.

Chapter 20

It took me a moment or so to mentally gear up to meet Lloyd Honey's intended. I hadn't been inside Club Eighteen for a couple of years. The bar, which doubled as a nightclub after 11PM, had always been a hangout for school leavers and made me feel like old meat these days. In the early hours of the evening, though, you could grab a meal and a drink there without having to queue up for the loo or the bar. Around dinner time, the clientele tended to be older. Bok gave me a little nod—his silent seal of approval—for my wardrobe choice.

The interior of Club Eighteen was pretty standard club fare: bar, dance floor and booths—the latter all in black with polished chrome trim. The aircon struggled to suck smoke and whatever out of the air, and the industrial-grade red carpet looked like it had been through a holocaust. Clubs always smelled stale before midnight, until the aftershaves and perfumes and drink spills filled them up.

Club Eighteen sat right above the Fresh Flesh Gym,

which explained why Lloyd Honey's girlfriend liked to duck in there with her friends after a late Saturday afternoon workout. She was easy enough to pick out among a bunch of six women still in their gym gear, drinking shooters and flirting with the hunky waiters.

Club Eighteen had always been good for hot waiters. I'd forgotten how good! Bok and I took a booth right next to the girls and I tried not to gawk at the guy who arrived to serve us. Six feet tall with curly black hair, a dead straight nose and perfect white teeth, he could have been a model, and probably was.

'My name is Edouardo. What can I get for you this evening?'

I resisted saying 'two of you' because it wouldn't have been original. Edouardo was the kind of guy who got hit on by everyone—even Bok was giving him a detailed appraisal.

'Dark and Stormy.' I came over all husky. I swear I couldn't help it, my voice does that sometimes. 'But my friend is driving so he'll have an OJ.'

'He must be a good friend,' said Edouardo, smiling. His aura was ultramarine blue, like the water around Rottnest Island; glorious.

Bok scowled.

'Yeah,' I laughed. 'Can't you tell?'

After Edouardo took his muscled butt off to get our drinks, Bok and I got to chatting.

'How's the mag going?' I asked.

It was a tough job convincing advertisers that a Perth-based magazine might have national appeal. Bok was spending too much time wooing advertisers and not enough finding content. The deadline for the first issue was just weeks away.

'Torrid,' he said.

The gym girls were already eyeing Bok off, between grabs at the passing Edouardo. I suppressed a sigh. It was often like that when I went out with Bok—he got way more attention than me.

'Can I help?' I offered.

'Yes, by staying out of trouble. I can't afford the time to babysit you.'

I poked out my tongue. 'I didn't ask you to.'

'Who's paying for the drinks?' he asked.

My phone beeped a message arrival, which saved me from answering him. My heart fluttered when I saw it was Nick Tozzi's PA sending through the breakfast details. A Place on the River at 7AM.

'Who is it?' asked Bok.

'Tozzi's PA,' I said as I sent back a confirmation. 'He's taking me to A Place on the River for breakfast.'

'It's not open for breakfast on Sunday,' said Bok, who knew every posh restaurant in Perth by virtue of having to entertain mag people. If he said it wasn't open for breakfast, then it wasn't.

'Dunno,' I said. 'Guess I'll see.'

'*We'll* see.'

'You don't have to come, hon. Honest, I'll be fine.'

Bok gave me a superior, knowing look. 'Let's see how we get through this evening first.'

On cue, a shriek went up from the gym girls. Lloyd Honey's fiancée had pulled Edouardo onto her lap and was running probing hands up and down his thighs. Edouardo was politely trying to disengage himself.

Catching my eye, he cast me a desperate look.

'Back in a tick,' I told Bok.

I jumped up and marched over to Edouardo.

'What sort of a boyfriend are you?' I shouted. 'You ask me to bring my brother down for a drink, and here you are lap dancing with another woman.' I slapped a hand on the table, causing the accumulated shooter glasses to jump, then I drew myself up to my full, bicep-worthy height. 'Explain yourself, Edouardo, before I tear your manhood from you.'

Mrs Honey-to-be dropped Edouardo off her lap like a hot potato.

He collected himself from the floor and gave me an apologetic peck on the cheek. 'Bella, it's not what you...'

'A little mish-undershtanding,' interrupted the three-quarters-pissed Mrs Honey-to-be.

I propped my hands on my hips, ignoring Bok's despairing body language in my corner sight. '*How* is it?'

'Lishen,' she said. 'Bring your brother over here and I'll buy you both a drink and s'plain.'

I pretended to consider it for a few moments before

grabbing my opportunity to check her out. 'Very well. But hands off my man!'

The girls raised their hands in the air and giggled, and Edouardo scuttled off.

'Now, what's your brother's name?' Mrs Honey-to-be asked.

I dragged Bok from our booth. 'You're nuts,' he hissed at me. 'What's with the fake accent?'

'My disguise. Don't knock opportunity,' I growled back.

We squeezed in on either side of Honey-to-be, and I introduced us simply as Martin and Tara.

Edouardo brought a fresh round of shooters, and Mrs Honey-to-be threw her credit card at him. He caught it with a deft hand and gave me a heart-melting smile of gratitude.

'Are you all celebrating?' I asked them innocently.

The girls raised their shooters at my enquiry and in one accord, downed them.

'Yes! Yes! Yes!' squealed Mrs Honey-to-be. She nuzzled up to me and I got the distinct impression that she didn't mind which side of her meat she got gravy.

It's hard to see a person's aura when you're too close to them but sometimes I get a little charge from it, like static electricity. Mrs Honey-to-be's aura was an annoying prickle, neither pleasurable nor strong enough to be really awful.

Bok slid his shooter along the table in my direction.

'I'm driving, *remember*?' The girl on the other side of him was already playing with his hair.

I drank the two small glasses of murky liquid in two gulps. 'What's the occasion then?'

'We-ell,' she drawled, confidingly. 'I've snagged a rich geeko and I'm getting married.'

'But do you love him?' I asked lightly.

She brushed her arm against my breast and gave a little flutter of her eyelashes. 'As much as I can, as much as I can.'

I mumbled something about the loo and squeezed up onto the back of the seat, climbing over it rather than dislodging the gym girls from their fawning over Bok.

I took my time having a breather in the loo, and then stopped for a glass of water at the bar on the way back. Edouardo was only too happy to get it for me. 'Let me buy you a drink—to say thank you for rescuing me,' he said.

I shook my head. 'Don't worry about it. I expect you get it all the time. Serve's you right for being so good-looking. You need a bodyguard or a minder.'

He looked a bit embarrassed. 'I never know what to say when a woman grabs me. It seems rude to shake her off but I hate being...'

'Pawed,' I offered.

He nodded. 'Thanks again. Maybe ... can I buy you dinner later instead of a drink?'

I stared at him, surprised. He had to be five years

younger than me at least. 'No need to take gratitude too far,' I said, trying to let him off the hook.

'No, really, I'd like to. I've only been in Perth a few weeks—I'm from down south. Haven't met many people yet.'

He suddenly looked really young; fresh from his mother's nest.

'Sure.' I fished in my bag for a business card. Bok had printed them up for me on his colour photocopier at work. 'Here's my number.'

He gave me a huge, gorgeous grin. 'Great. I'll be in touch.' He squinted at the crumpled card. 'Tara Sharp.'

'Bye, Edouardo.'

On the way back to the table my phone rang. 'Ms Sharp, are you in place?'

'Lloyd?' I whispered.

'Yes. She's just phoned and I'm coming to pick her up.'

'I'm all set,' I said. 'See you soon.'

I climbed over the back of the seat again and plonked down next to Lloyd's intended.

What had I learned about her? She had a prickly but not dangerous aura; she was probably bisexual and damn happy to spend his money. Did she love him? *As much as she could.*

All those little pieces of information would mean something in a few moments when I saw them together. Building evidence, like Mr Hara had suggested, was helpful, but until you saw the energy flow between people you couldn't really know.

I talked weights with the gym girls while I waited for Lloyd to arrive, cogitating all the while on how opportunity could be so double-edged. I'd grasped it with Peter Delgado and it had landed me in a 'situation', whereas tonight it had landed me an invitation to have dinner with Edouardo. Go figure.

'Darling? Are you ready?' said a honeyed voice.

I turned around and saw Lloyd, Porsche key ring in hand, brow furrowed.

What interested me more, though, was the expression on his intended's face; beneath her solarium tan her skin was aglow. Her aura ceased prickling me and smoothed out.

I felt a huge relief. She actually liked him. He soothed her.

She climbed over Bok to get out of the booth, taking a second to whisper something in my ear before she did.

'If you, and that delicious man of yours, ever want a threesome, you can find me here on Saturday nights,' she said.

I nodded, unable to think of a suitable reply.

As the two of them left, Lloyd stopped just short of having to use a fireman's lift. I could picture them in twenty years. She'd still be getting pissed and picking up strangers, and he'd be … well … maybe that would depend on what I said to him when he rang me on Monday morning for my assessment.

And what would I say? Whatever it was, it might affect the rest of Lloyd's life. I used to malign clairvoyants and palm readers for the same thing: the power of their suggestions influencing a person's life decisions. And here I was, running the same agenda.

'Can we please go?' said Bok. His hair was now in three braids, one of which had been curled up and pinned into a bun.

I giggled and slung my arm around his neck. The D&S and the shooters had started to make me feel a little woozy. 'Home, Martin!'

Chapter 21

I set the alarm for 5.30AM, slept through it, and woke up at 6.30. That left me fifteen minutes to get dressed and fifteen minutes to drive to A Place on the River.

I cribbed five minutes to throw on some makeup, telling myself the roads would be quiet at that time.

Dress. Check.

Sandals. Check.

Handbag. Check.

I ran out the door at 6.55, stopped for thirty seconds to rip the cover off the birds, and then belted up the driveway to Mona. And read Bok's text saying that he couldn't make it (YAY!).

Down the highway—through three suburbs in seven minutes—only to get caught in a road detour at the last set of traffic lights before the river.

I finally arrived breathless and sweating (having run the whole length of the pier to the restaurant) at 7.15.

Bok had been right, the place was closed on Sunday

mornings.

I leaned on the railing to catch my breath and stared into the water, feeling kinda stupid and deflated. Was Nick Tozzi having some kind of weird joke with me? Or had his PA made a mistake?

As I turned away to head back to my car, a voice called out. 'Tara!'

Nick Tozzi was standing on a low jetty along the side of the restaurant that faced out towards the centre of the river.

I should say now that the Swan isn't a meandering little snippet of a thing, but a deep blue, immensely dignified river of sweeping proportions: ideal for yachting and water-skiing and board-sailing. A Place on the River kinda dangled on the edge of a long pier that floated out on the Swan like a piece of bait on a hook, daring a high tide to come in and swamp its expensive jarrah floors.

With relief I waved and made my way towards him down a set of bleached-wood steps and through an unlocked barbed-wire gate.

His caramel aura burned golden bright against the sparkling water, making it almost impossible to look straight at him. I fumbled for my sunglasses and, fortunately, got them on before I reached him.

He smiled and shook my hand formally. On the little table behind him was a thermos, two mugs and a paper bag. 'Thanks for coming. I hope you like croissants?'

I noticed then he was wearing tracksuit pants and an old

windcheater. 'I hope you don't mind me being overdressed.'

'Sorry, I should have explained. I hate overeating at breakfast. I know the owner of this restaurant well and he lets me use this place out of hours, as long as I feed the cat.' He pointed at the fat moggy watching us from the top of a wide spit post. 'If I don't bring my phone, I get to eat in perfect quiet. Sometimes I even bring a fishing rod.'

But do you bring your wife? The question burned on the tip of my tongue. 'Sounds like a good arrangement.'

He waved his hand in a gentlemanly gesture. 'Please have a seat. Do you take sugar in your tea? I forgot to bring some.'

'Is there honey for the croissants?' I asked.

He reached for the paper bag and fished out four little sachets.

'Phew!' I gasped in mock relief. 'I think I'll survive.'

He laughed, and suddenly it was like we were old friends. We sat and chatted about our favourite bakeries, the best tackle to use for bream, and the NBA finals. As we did, his face relaxed and his aura subsided into something less fluorescent.

We ate the croissants over the paper bag and swept the crumbs between the planks to the fish.

When our chitchat eventually ran out we sat in companionable silence and stared at the scant morning river traffic: a rowing eight going home and the South Perth ferry in the distance.

He was right. It was peaceful. I hadn't had breakfast

outdoors in ages.

I'd almost forgotten I was there for a reason, when he finally cleared his throat. 'Tara, what were you doing at one of Johnny Vogue's parties? It's presumptuous of me to ask, I know, but he's not good company.'

I dragged my gaze from the pearly morning blue of the river and risked removing my sunglasses. He was leaning forward, his forearms resting on the table—not trying to intimidate—but signalling how serious he was. It was important he could see the earnestness in my eyes too.

'Before I answer that, you have to tell me something. At that party when I told you I used to play basketball, you said "I know". What did you mean?'

'You don't remember, do you?'

'Uuh?' I shook my head. 'Remember what?'

'Do you remember your under-sixteen state championships?'

I sat up straighter. 'Yep, I'll never forget them. We played the Fremantle Cougars in the grand final. We beat them by two points on the buzzer.'

'*You* beat them by two points on the buzzer.'

I blushed. 'Lucky shot. Can't pin a whole game on the last two points scored.'

'Yeah. But not everyone can step up under pressure. You like to win.'

I stared at his face. There was a whole bunch of things going on there. I tried to blank out his words and concentrate on his micro-expressions—the tiny fleeting facial movements that everyone made. What I saw was conflict. And his aura was giving faint flickers.

'Tara?'

'Uh, sorry. Just remembering. So what does that have to do with you knowing me?'

'Do you remember the Cougar's assistant coach?'

I screwed up my face as I tried to recall the game. The coach of the other team I knew well, but the assistant … I had a vague picture of a tall, incredibly skinny guy with acne and dark hair.

My eyes nearly popped out of their sockets. 'Hookman! *You're* Hookman?' I stared at the width of his shoulders and couldn't equate them with that skinny guy of twelve years ago. 'What did you do, swallow the entire North American supply of steroids?'

He looked slightly affronted then laughed. 'Are you always so straightforward?'

'Only when I'm shocked.'

'Well, in answer to your question, no, I was clean. But I did a tonne of weights. I had to—to survive.'

'Wow.' I sat back in my seat as I processed what he'd just told me.

'Now it's your turn. How did you come to be hanging out with the likes of Peter Delgado?'

I sucked in a large breath and expelled it. Then I gulped down my last mouthful of tea. It was a good brew, with tea leaves in the bottom. Russian, I thought.

After Peter Delgado's warning phone call the night

before I'd decided not to tell Nick Tozzi too much. But knowing he was Hookman changed things. Silly isn't it? I didn't know Nick at all, but now it felt like I did.

It was the same as the old school tie, or the kid next door to you as you grew up, or vacation friends. Some associations—however brief—give you belief in a person. Or maybe it's a case of context. Whatever the case, I found myself spilling most of the truth.

'My work is kinda unusual.'

He smiled. 'Why am I not surprised?'

'Well ... I specialise in non-verbal communications,' I explained. 'I have my own business. Peter Delgado approached a ... company I ... sub-contract to, and I ended up with the job.' Well that was pretty much true, leaving out Hara's warnings and the bonus enticement. 'Delgado wants me to get close to you.'

'Me. Why would he want you to do that?'

I broke out in a light sweat. I liked Nick, and for some ridiculous reason I trusted him, but he was a powerful business man. You didn't get to be that by being sweet and fluffy. I had to be careful here. 'You're the best one to answer that.'

'Is he working for Johnny Viaspa?'

'I don't know,' I said, honestly. 'It seems that way.'

'Viaspa's a criminal, Tara, and you're not. You're straight up and honest.'

For some reason I felt he'd given me a huge compliment of which I wasn't worthy. Not while I was holding back on him. Or maybe that's what he wanted me to think. I glanced at his aura. It was stable enough. 'I overheard Johnny Vogue talking about you and your wife.'

'Antonia?' Nick's aura flared so strongly I had to shut my eyes for a second and wait for the after-image to fade.

When I opened them again he was staring at me with such intensity that my heart began to pound. Nick Tozzi was a hard man to deny.

'He was on the phone to someone after you left the party, just before the police bust.'

His frown deepened. 'I heard about the raid. Wondered how you fared.'

'I knew one of the cops, so after they asked me a few questions, they let me go.'

'What did Viaspa say?'

'I think he wants to ruin you financially,' I said.

'What about Antonia?'

I shrugged and looked back at the river. 'He said something like "she'd come crawling".'

Nick leaned across the table and grabbed my arm. 'You're not inventing this are you, Tara? To wind me up?'

I pulled my arm from his grip, got up and stuck my hands on my hips. I could feel my chin jutting out a mile. 'Excuse me? You're the one who was just telling me how honest I was. I didn't have to come here today. I sure as hell didn't have to tell you anything. In fact, I wish I hadn't. It's just going to cause me aggravation. Thanks for breakfast.'

I grabbed my handbag, marched off through the gate and up the steps before he could reply. By the time I was at the end of the pier, I'd cooled off a little. I guess it'd been a shock for Nick to hear that Perth's crime lord had marked him.

Still, I felt tingly, and upset.

As I left the pier and started to walk across the empty restaurant car park towards Mona, a blue BMW came from nowhere, straight at me.

Chapter 22

I froze, not knowing which way to jump.

A shout from behind me urged me to run. It snapped my paralysis and I leaped back onto the pavement. I saw some things really clearly: scratches on the duco, a plastic spider swinging from the car's rear-vision mirror, the mask and hoodie that hid the driver's identity.

A split second before the car smashed up over the kerb, I threw myself backwards off the retaining wall and into the river.

There was a loud thunk, followed by a roar of acceleration, and the car drove off, leaving me a quivering mess in the water.

I dragged myself out of the water and the next thing I knew, Nick Tozzi had his arms around me and was talking quickly. 'Are-you-alright? What the hell was that? Tara, *are you alright?*'

I couldn't stop shaking. My back hurt and my calves and elbows were bleeding.

'Shit!' he said. 'Here.' He yanked off his windcheater, leaving himself bare-chested, and slipped it around me.

At any other time I would have drooled at the sight of such a mountain of muscular flesh, but right now I barely registered.

'Is the Monaro your car?'

I nodded.

He picked me up and carried me over to it. I leaned against the bonnet while he fumbled in my bag for the keys. When he got it open he levered me down into the passenger seat.

I continued to shiver.

'I dropped the thermos on the pier. I'll just grab it.'

I grabbed his arm in alarm. 'P-please d-don't l-leave m-me,' I stammered.

He hesitated and nodded. 'Move over,' he said, then got in and put his arms around me.

I burrowed into his shoulder like a little kid and we sat like that until the worst of my shaking abated.

I raised my head eventually. 'S-sorry, Nick. S-scared the crap out of me.'

His face was a mixture of emotions which I wasn't in a clear enough mind to decipher. 'Any idea who that was?'

'Not exactly … Peter Delgado warned me off talking to anyone. But I didn't think he meant it this seriously.'

This time Nick gave me the exact same look Bok had the day before. 'Tara, I don't know at what level you're involved with these guys, but I'd say you're out of your depth.'

'I can see that. Just not sure how to swim back to the shallows.'

'You said you worked for someone else. Can he help you?'

'He's away,' I said flatly, feeling kinda strange now, like I might be sick.

'I think you should contact him and let him know. I also think you should go to the police.'

I thought of Cravich and Blake. It'd just be my luck if they got the case. 'Not yet.'

'When then? On the way to the mortuary?'

I could see he wasn't joking.

'OK. I know someone at the local station. I'll talk to them.'

'You live alone?'

'No. Out the back of my parents' house in a granny flat.'

'I assume you don't want to tell them about this. Have you got a friend who could come and sit with you for a while?'

I thought about it. Smitty would be having her one sleep-in for the week, but Bok might spare me an hour. 'Sure.'

'Right,' he said, reaching into my handbag to find my phone. 'I'll drive you home. You call them on the way and get them to meet you there.'

'What about your car?' I glanced around the empty car park. I didn't want him to drive me home because I had a strong suspicion I was about to cry and not stop.

'No problem. I jogged here.'

He stuck the keys in the ignition and Mona growled into life. He caressed the steering wheel. 'Haven't driven one of these since I was a teenager.'

'Yeah, well treat her with respect.'

'Nothing less,' he said and reversed out.

Chapter 23

I rang Bok on the way home. I didn't have to explain, he could tell by the tone of my voice.

'I'll be there in ten minutes, T.'

'Thanks, hon.' I glanced down at my wet, sandy dress. 'Bring a coat for me. Love you.'

I only ever told Bok I loved him when something terrible happened or I was really drunk. I think this morning's episode qualified as the former.

I glanced across at Nick Tozzi. His face was in a grim set, and from what I could see his aura had hardened. His hands moved restlessly on the wheel like he wanted to punch something. I detected micro-expressions that signalled controlled emotions.

'That your boyfriend?' he asked.

'No. My best friend,' I said. 'Turn left off the highway at the next lights, third on the right. Number 25 Lilac Street.'

His hands relaxed a little then and we continued in

silence while he followed my instructions.

'Park on the road. The driveway is for my parents and their birds.'

He raised an eyebrow but didn't ask.

It made me remember something though. 'There's another thing I should tell you.'

He groaned as he turned off the key and snapped the hand brake on. '*More?*'

'I caught a burglar the other night.'

His eyes widened. 'What do you mean by "caught"?'

'Well, I just collided with him, the police caught him. Here's the thing,' I finished. 'The woman he tried to rob was your mother.'

'That was you?' He gave me a strange look.

A car pulled up behind us. I glanced in the rear view and waved at Bok. 'Thank you for everything. Do you want to borrow my car to drive home?'

'No. Keep your head down. I'll be in touch.' He got out of the car and jogged off down the street.

I'll be in touch. What did that mean?

A moment later Bok tapped on my window. He held a coat in one hand and a white paper bag in the other: vanilla slices, bless him.

I wound down the window and took the coat. Then I shimmied into it, got out, and locked the car.

Without a word, he slung his arm around my shoulders and we walked down to my garage together. Even if JoBob happened to be looking out the window they wouldn't stop me for question time if Bok was there.

After showering, I got changed and lay down on the bed. While Bok made us both some tea and found two saucers for the slices, I told him what had happened. He brought a tray over and sprawled across the end of the bed.

'You should call the cops, T,' he said between mouthfuls. He liked to eat vanilla slices the proper way, in sharp, precise bites.

I glanced over to the fridge where I'd stuck Bligh's magnet. 'If I do that I'm going to have to tell her that I think Sam Barbaro tried to run me over.'

'Why do you think it's Barbaro?'

'He told me he'd get me.'

'Might have just been talk.'

'Might have. Might not. Delgado posted bail for him, Bligh said so. Seems coincidental that Delgado then warned me not to talk to anyone.'

'True.'

'If I go and see Delgado tomorrow, maybe I can make this all go away.'

'But what are you going to tell him? That you've told Nick Tozzi you're supposed to be spying on him?'

I sniffed, and before I knew it, was bawling, tears dripping off my chin onto the vanilla icing.

Bok took the tea and the slice away from me and put them on my bedside table. Then he grabbed my shoulders and made me look him in the eye. 'You've had a shock, T.

But you've got to get a grip and think things through.'

I shrugged him off and buried my face in my pillow.

'I mean,' he continued. 'I suppose it's possible that it *wasn't* Barbaro who tried to run you down. You didn't really see who it was. The whole connection with Nick Tozzi could be accidental. I mean you've only got a very little piece of the picture.'

He was trying to calm me down. And it worked. My survival instinct righted itself. I let go of the pillow and sat bolt upright. 'You're right.' *I need to know more.*

'Good girl,' said Bok, relieved I'd stopped blubbering.

I kissed him on the cheek. 'What would I do without you?'

His relief turned to suspicion and he tapped my head. 'What's going on in there?'

I gave him a determined smile. 'Nothing. Now you go home and I'll call you later. I'll be fine. I won't go out.'

It took a few minutes and a promise, but I managed to convince him.

'You *will* call the cops if things don't pan out well with Delgado tomorrow, won't you?' he begged. 'I don't want to be the one identifying you when they pull you out of the river.'

'Cross my heart and hope to—'

He kissed me back. 'Don't say that, T. Never say that.'

I locked the door behind him and counted to a hundred to make sure he'd gone. Then I made a couple of calls.

The first was to Nick. He didn't pick up so I left him

160

a message, thanking him again and asking him to ring me ASAP.

Next I turned on my laptop and opened up my class files, looking for a contact number for Wallace Grominsky.

Wal answered quickly. 'Yeah?'

'It's Tara Sharp.'

'Who?'

'From your Saturday class.'

Silence. 'You mean Teacher Tara.'

'Err, yes.'

''Sup, Teach.'

'Did any of you tidy up my flat before you left the other day?'

'Uuh?'

'You, Harvey or Enid?'

'Nah. Least there was no one around when I woke up. I jus' left. Didn't notice no tidying.'

'Oh. OK. Anyway, I'm ringing because I might need a part-time bodyguard. Would you be interested?'

'True?' His voice brightened. 'Can do. Any night but Friday this week. I'm gigging for the Scorched Torches.'

'I'm a bit strapped for cash, Wal, but I can offer you free classes. How does that sound?' What was I saying?

There was more silence while he considered it. 'Guns or knives?' he asked.

'Just you,' I said, my heart fluttering. 'You know, just a presence.'

'Oh.' That disappointed him. 'Well, I guess so. As long

as I don't get bored.'

'Thanks. I'll call you when I need you.'

He hung up before I did.

Chapter 24

Before I could dwell too much on hiring someone who was mentally unbalanced as a bodyguard, I bundled my dirty washing into a towel and headed up to JoBob's.

Dad was sitting in his chair reading the Sunday papers and the Vampire was poking around her Doulton china collection with a miniature feather duster.

'Morning all, is the washing machine free?' I asked, detouring via the fridge. Hmmmm… Leftover homemade peach kuchen and some caviar on slightly soggy biscuits; JoBob had been entertaining. If only I hadn't just eaten a vanilla slice…

'Hello, love.' The newspaper didn't move.

'Tara, what was that fellow doing here so early in the morning?' asked the Vampire.

'His name is Martin, Joanna, and you've known him for fifteen years. And we … err … went out to breakfast.' It seemed ridiculous having to answer questions like that at my age—but *you* try living at home when you're an adult.

'And who was that pleasant well-mannered man that rang for your number the other day … Nick someone or other?'

'Tozzi,' I said, and then immediately wished I could take it back.

The duster froze. 'Tozzi? You mean *The* Tozzis?'

I sighed. It was always *The* Tozzis or *The* someone or other.

'I guess so.'

'Then he's one of Eireen's boys? They're the only Tozzis in our area.'

'How do you know he's from *our* area?'

'Tara!' said Dad, in a warning tone.

I popped my head out of the fridge. 'You know Eireen Tozzi?'

Joanna looked surprised. 'Of course I do. She was friends with my Aunty Bel. She sponsored your father and me into the golf club.'

I grabbed a celery stick to keep my hands away from the kuchen. This might be the opportunity I needed to join some dots on the Johnny Vogue and Nick Tozzi picture puzzle. 'Actually I've been thinking of visiting her. You know, to see if she's alright after the burglary the other night.'

'You have?' Joanna carefully put down the cream jug she was holding and gave me a full motherly scrutiny.

I crunched the celery noisily and grinned. 'I just thought it would be good manners to introduce myself, and, of course, I'm very well brought up.' I hadn't pulled the 'Good Manners' card in a long time.

In the long, loaded pause that followed I noticed the newspaper twitching. Dad knew I was up to something.

'Well ... I suppose I could call her and see, if you promise to dress appropriately,' said Joanna. She eyed my trackies and ribbed singlet.

'I'm free this afternoon,' I said. 'And I have a nice white Laura Ashley dress that I just bought.' *If I wash and dry it quick smart.*

'Laura Ashley,' mused Joanna, as she walked to the telephone. 'How nice. Then I'll wear my Perri Cutten suit.'

Damn.

Eireen Tozzi lived in an old Euccy Grove mansion that posed arrogantly in the middle of its eighteen hundred squares. The long paved driveway was lined with white gums and paperbark trees, and curved like a gracious sweep of a hand to the front door.

I half expected a butler to let us in but it was Eireen herself, wearing a jinky little hound's-tooth suit and smart black pumps. She was small but solid for a lady of seventy, with thick shoulders that would have once rivalled my own. They were a little hunched now though, and she leaned on a tortoiseshell-coloured stick. Her hair was defiantly black, dyed within an inch of its life and stiff with hairspray. Her nails were pale pink and beautifully manicured. Most interesting though was her electric blue aura, which was strong and bright and flowed around her like a river. On Mr Hara's colour chart, electric blue meant powerful and domineering. Well, I was guessing he got that right!

'Hurry up, Joanna, the dust will get in,' she scolded, ushering us past. 'Who have you got there?'

'Good afternoon, Eireen. This is my daughter, Tara.'

The sharp eyes looked up at me through the gloom of the topaz-marbled entry hall. 'Nice big girl.' She pointed her stick. 'This way. Jessica's put out some cake and sherry for us.'

Joanna and I perched on an enormous peony-patterned couch while Madame Tozzi settled into a matching armchair and popped her legs up on a footstool. 'Joanna, get that girl of yours to serve.'

Clearly, Eireen was used to giving orders. I found myself wanting to curtsy, and say 'yes ma'am'. Instead I went over to the sherry decanter and poured three stiff ones. It was only three o'clock in the afternoon, but I, for one, had had a bad start to the day. I popped a glass and a slab of Madeira cake on Eireen's occasional table and then passed Joanna hers. As I took my first gulp of plonk, Eireen cut to the chase.

'So what is it you want, young Sharp. Girls like you don't visit old women like me on Sunday afternoons, especially with their mother. Are you in love with my Lui maybe? I do wish he'd settle down. No, I think you'd better suit my little Nicky, if he wasn't already wed to one of those skinny inbred Falks. All the girls love my Nicky. I can tell you right now I won't hear a word against my boys.'

The sherry climbed into my airways, bringing tears to my eyes. 'I've come to see how you are after the burglary, Mrs Tozzi. I'm the one who knocked the burglar down.'

Eireen swallowed the entire glass without wetting her lips. Her bright eyes bored into me. 'Yes, the police spoke to me. What on earth were you doing in my laneway without your pants on?'

Joanna looked as if she might faint. Instead, to my dismay, she hastily copied Eireen, downing the contents of her glass in one go. Mum didn't—couldn't—hold her liquor. This did not bode well.

'I *was* dressed, Mrs Tozzi, it's just that one of our pet birds escaped and I was chasing it. It flew into a tree. My pants were too tight to climb the fence in … it was dark … I didn't think anyone would see me.'

'Hmmm … expected you would have brought your child up better than that, Joanna,' said Eireen with disapproval.

Mum thrust her glass at me for a refill and gave a nervous laugh. 'Oh you know the young, Eireen. They have different notions about modesty than we did. And of course she did help catch your burglar for you.'

Joanna was sticking up for me? Jeez!

'Yes, yes. I suppose.' Eireen waved her glass. 'While

you're there, girl, top-ups all round.'

Girl? I checked my Laura Ashley dress to see if it'd suddenly sprouted a maid's apron? Nope.

This time I filled their glasses to the brim, and returned to my allotted spot on the couch on top of a purple peony.

'Did the burglar take anything, Mrs Tozzi?' I asked.

The old girl gave me a sharp look, which I countered with something meek and innocent. 'What I mean is … we only live a few streets away from you, I worry about my parents,' I said.

Mum's icy stare of disbelief snap-froze the hair on my arms.

'He was just trying to scare an old woman, I'm sure. Took nothing. Just made a mess. Tipped things out all over the place. My Nicky's things from college. Everywhere.' She covered her face with trembling fingers. 'How will I *ever* clean it all up? Nicky says he'll help but he's so busy with his work. He's very important, you know. And Antonia … *she* wouldn't even help a person into their grave.'

It struck me that Eireen was foxing, playing helpless. I wondered why.

'What about your housekeeper?' ventured Joanna, downing the second glass almost as quickly, her cheeks flushed.

Eireen put her hand to one side of her face and whispered aloud. 'Never trust the staff with personal things.' Her aura faded to a pale eggshell blue and suddenly she looked like a lonely old woman.

'I'll help you tidy things, if you'd like?' I offered.

Mum's eyes bulged.

'Would you?' said Eireen, fluttering her stubs of eyelashes. She reached over and patted Mum's hand. 'Joanna, what a good girl you have here. Come on Tuesday at three.'

After a bit more chitchat, the housekeeper, Jessica, arrived to take away the sherry and let us out.

Joanna wobbled down the driveway without speaking a word to me.

In fact, the walk home was conducted in the worst of mother–daughter silences. When we arrived at the front door she turned on me. 'I will only say this once, Tara. Never, EVER take your pants off in public again.'

Chapter 25

I woke on Monday morning feeling heavy with dread about my meeting with Peter Delgado. How could I face the man who'd probably tried to have me run over yesterday?

And what would I say when I called Mr Honey? *Your fiancée likes you well enough but she'll never be faithful.*

I lay in bed suffering a huge reality check about what I'd got myself into. Maybe trying to turn my 'talent' into a business opportunity had been yet another bad choice in a long series of bad choices. Not that my previous bad choices had got me in trouble with the local bad guys. They'd all been silly things: falling in love with a Mauritian con man, skinny-dipping in the fountains of the old Parliament Place, growing pot in the uni hydroponics lab.

Now it seemed that my choices were getting worse not better. Even Mr Hara's lessons hadn't been enough to save me from myself.

Mr Hara.

I fumbled for my phone and sent him a text. 'Wen r u back? Need urgent advice. Tara.'

That done, I rolled out of bed and into gym shorts.

My first mouthful of cereal got stuck in my nervous throat and I abandoned the idea of breakfast. I started worrying again over who had tidied my room while I was out. What if Peter Delgado and Johnny Vogue had sent someone in after Los Trios left, and planted a bug?

I rang Garth. He sounded early morning grumpy. 'Wilmot.'

'Garth, it's Tara. What does a bug look like?'

He paused. 'Six legs, exoskeleton—'

'No, I mean a surveillance bug.'

'Why are you ringing me at 7AM to ask that?'

'You read spy novels. I just thought you might know.'

'Well, I don't.'

'Oh.'

'Tara? What's going on?'

'Nothing. But I'd appreciate it if you didn't discuss my recent past with anyone.'

'You mean Constable Bligh?'

'If the name fits…'

'So you want me to lie to the police? You can be so annoying, Tara. I mean, it's your fault they were asking questions in the first place.'

I'd give him annoying! 'And you're such a pompous prat sometimes, Garth,' I said and hung up.

Bok rang almost immediately. 'Everything OK?'

'Dandy.'

'I want you to cancel your appointment with Delgado.'

'Why?'

'I can't come with you. The national head of marketing is flying in from Sydney unexpectedly. I have to pick him up from the airport.'

'No probs,' I said calmly. 'I've got a contingency plan.'

'T?'

'I've hired a bodyguard. Nothing major, just someone to watch my back.'

'You've whaaat!' shrieked Bok, his voice rising to that kinda strangled, can't-get-enough-air-in-my-lungs pitch.

'Take a deep breath,' I said. 'It's under control. Delgado's not going to do anything to me in broad daylight at his office. I'll call you straight after. Bye.'

I sent a quick text to Wal telling him where and when to meet me, then switched my phone off so Bok couldn't call me back. Chucking the phone in my backpack, I headed out the door to the gym.

Like lots of people, I have a love–hate relationship with exercise. I love being fit but I hate doing the work to get there. On top of that, many years of competitive sport has given me an overdeveloped conscience: too long without a workout of some sort and I begin to feel guilty.

Plus, the way things were going in my life I might need to be able to run fast.

This morning's class was boxercise, which I'd found I had a reasonable talent for. In my very first class, I'd accidentally punched Craigo in the jaw, knocking him down on his tight arse. Since then, he'd always stood behind me to correct my movements.

I let all my worry and frustration work its way out during class until I'd raised a huge sweat and cleared the space on the floor with my flailing limbs.

Craigo came over to me as I was stuffing my towel back in my gym bag. 'Everything alright, Tara?'

His accent was slightly European and his aura was a tasty green, like mint jelly.

'Sure,' I replied. 'Why?'

He shrugged in his way. 'No reason. Listen, I've entered a team in a triathlon next weekend and the girl doing the running section has pulled out with an Achilles injury. Is there any chance you could fill in? I've heard you used to be a runner.'

'Triathlon? How far?'

'Just a standard ten-k run. Three thousand dollars prize money split three ways.'

I hadn't run ten kilometres in over ten years—but the thing about ex-athletes is this: we hate letting anyone know that we're not fit. And what the hell, we might win, and I needed the money. I'd made some crap decisions lately, this one couldn't be worse than the others. 'Sure,' I said.

'Fabuloso!' He pulled a flyer out of his bumbag. 'Here are all the details. I've also written my phone number on the back. See you at the course an hour before the start.'

I tucked it in my bag on top of my sweaty towel. 'No problemo.'

I sauntered nonchalantly over to the noticeboard, as if I accepted invitations to do team triathlons all the time. Nothing new had been posted, but I spared a moment to smirk at the over-fifties photo again.

By the time I climbed into Mona, though, I was cursing my stupid ego for accepting, and trying to think of which illness I could suddenly develop. The whole dilemma kept me distracted while I drove home, showered, got into jeans, heels and a t-shirt, and headed for Klintoff House.

Amazingly, Wal was early, loitering outside the front door like a criminal, in black, skin-tight jeans, a black singlet that showed off his maze of tattoos and brawny roadie's shoulders, and black Doc Martens boots. His hair was in a plait secured by an elastic band that sported a dangling skull's head. To top it off he was smoking a black Sobranie.

Bogan City channelling Russian Mafia.

'Nice ciggies,' I said.

He nodded and blew a smoke ring. 'Keep them for special occasions.'

I didn't dare ask why this was a special occasion. 'OK. I don't need you to say anything or do anything. Just sit in the waiting room and look like you might tear the place apart if I don't come out of my meeting.'

'Right on.'

Right on? Who said 'right on' anymore?

I started to walk in the front door but Wal jumped in front of me, maintaining a head-swivelling surveillance as we crossed the lobby and headed up in the lift.

'We're in the lift, Wal,' I said. 'And it's just you and me.'

'Vigilance is next to godliness,' he replied.

He kept up the same behaviour out of the lift and into the offices of Positoni & Kizzick.

Giggler Francine was at the desk, listening to her dictaphone and clacking on the keyboard with her acrylic nails. When she saw Wal, her eyes bugged and I noticed her right hand reach under the desk. Then she saw me and her hand relaxed.

So Peter Delgado had one of *those* buttons. I wonder who it was hooked up to. I bet it wasn't the local police.

'Take a seat, please, Ms Sharp and Mr...?'

'Grominsky,' said Wal with just enough surliness to be scary.

While we dropped our bums on the appointed chairs, Giggler removed her dictaphone, got up and walked over to the filing cabinet. Her red skirt was so tight, and short, she reminded me of a frankfurter sausage that had been dropped into hot water.

Obviously it didn't conjure the same image for Wal. He sat bolt upright like someone had shoved a packet of frozen peas down his pants.

'You didn't tell me to wear white to the party,' I said to her in a conversational tone.

'Excuse me?'

'You were supposed to tell me to wear white.'

We locked eyes for a second. Hers were wide and feigned confusion. Mine were glowering and full of 'I won't forget it.'

'Oh, I'm sure I sent you a message. You must have forgotten.'

'No,' I said steadily.

She looked away first, a flush rising up her bare neck.

I settled back in my chair with folded arms, and continued to give her my stare. I was psyching myself into controlled anger mode. Best antidote I knew for being scared witless.

Delgado walked through the door a moment later. His dark brown aura was pulsing a little but it rippled when he saw Wal.

Wal, thank whoever, had stopped ogling Giggler and assumed his most menacing look: faint sneer beneath the cheap sunglasses, legs wide apart, muscular forearms crossed in front of a barrel chest.

I stood up.

'Morning, Ms Sharp and...'

'This is my associate, Mr Grominsky. He works with me from time to time,' I said.

Wal liked the 'Mr' tag, I could tell from the slight lift of his stubbly jaw.

'This is a private meeting, Ms Sharp,' said Delgado. 'Between you and me.'

'Of course,' I nodded. 'Mr Grominsky is accompanying me on to my next appointment. He'll wait *right here.*'

Delgado looked annoyed. 'Very well.' He held the door open for me.

'Back shortly,' I said to Wal, and walked in.

This time I was too nervous to enjoy the luxury of the Chesterfield.

Delgado shut the door and sat down behind his desk. 'Last Saturday night has had some unfortunate ramifications for you,' he began.

'It sure has,' I agreed. 'I don't remember you mentioning anything about the likelihood of a drug raid at the party.'

'I was referring to the fact that you eavesdropped on my client. Mr Viaspa is not happy. However, I've convinced him to overlook your faux pas, if you provide useful feedback to us.'

'My ... *faux pas?*'

'Yes.' He stared at me. 'Now, Nick Tozzi...'

Crunch time! Did I outright refuse and leave? Did I tell him maybe, and then do no such thing? Or did I do as he and Johnny Viaspa wanted me to—spy on Tozzi?

I discounted the last one immediately. Nick Tozzi had bought me croissants and picked me up, soaking wet, out of the river. My alliances were cast. Besides, in some ways Eireen Tozzi scared me more than Johnny Vogue.

The first option didn't thrill me much either. I liked to think I had reasonable integrity, but I didn't want to end up wearing concrete boots because of it.

'Getting close to someone takes time. And our first meeting got interrupted, so I think you're going to have to be a lot more specific if you want information quickly. What exactly did you want me to find out?'

'We believe that Mr Tozzi is in some financial difficulty. We want you to ascertain how much.'

'Why?'

'You already know more than is healthy for you, Ms Sharp. Keep your curiosity for Tozzi. And then bring the answers back to me. You have a few days.'

'Or?'

Delgado got up and walked around the desk. I didn't like the way his aura was vibrating, or the tense, coiled look of his body, so I jumped up off the Chesterfield and backed towards the door.

He followed me until I was pressed against the handle.

'Your faux pas may be considered irredeemable.'

'That sounds like a threat, Mr Delgado.' The undercurrent of his psychic energy was drowning me. 'What will you do? Try to run me over on the street?'

To any normal observer Delgado didn't appear to react. But I saw a number of signs suggesting he didn't take my bait. For one, his aura didn't change. Second, his eyes widened the tiniest amount and his eyebrows rose. Third, the psychic undertow stopped sucking me down.

He was surprised.

Crap. Maybe it hadn't been Sam Barbaro. Or, at least, not on Delgado's bidding.

'You wouldn't want to put ideas in my head,' he replied. 'Saturday then, Ms Sharp.'

I fumbled behind for the handle and almost stumbled out of the door when it opened suddenly. Wal must have been standing at the door because he caught me.

He looked at Delgado and then me. 'I was just coming to get you,' he said, meaningfully. 'We're late for our next appointment.'

I nodded, relieved.

Chapter 26

I offered to buy Wal a coffee and cake. He'd surprised me by acting pretty much the way I'd wanted him to: threatening but passive.

If that was the silver lining on my day then maybe I needed to reconsider the direction my life was going in.

I mulled over that, and other things, while I waited in the queue at the OBH café, one of the most popular hotels on the beachfront. On summer weekends the foot traffic completely outnumbered the cars as the stylish young ones migrated up and down to the different pubs, like gorgeous butterflies sampling pollen. I'd done it myself a few years ago, but now I preferred to avoid that area on Sunday afternoons.

I picked the OBH café because Wal wasn't a Latte Ole kind of guy. And call me shallow, but I didn't really want anyone I knew to see us and think we were *together*.

My message bank carolled when I switched my phone on. I'd missed calls from Mr Honey and Nick Tozzi.

My heart did a little bit of a hoola. I called him right back.

'Tozzi,' he answered.

'Sharp,' I snapped back.

He paused and I wished I could see what that warm aura of his was doing.

'Are you alright?' he asked.

'Are you?'

He expelled a breath into the phone. 'Hold on a moment.' A few rattling, crunching moments later he came back on. 'I'm not the one somebody tried to run over.' It sounded like he was out in the wind with his hand cupped over the phone.

'Oh that,' I said airily. 'No problem.'

'I hear you made a social call on my mother?'

'Umm…' The conversation wasn't going the way I'd hoped.

'Whatcha want?' interrupted the waitress in a timely manner.

'One English Breakfast tea, one short black and two custard tarts,' I replied. 'I gotta go, Nick.'

'Hang on a—'

I stuffed my phone in my pocket. A light sweat had broken out over my body. I hadn't expected that Eireen would tell Nick about her Sunday visitors—but in a way, it was kind of endearing that she had. And Joanna would approve—a son who talked to his mother.

Speaking of which, I didn't think mine was talking to

me. I sighed and returned to Wal, who was jiggling his leg and darting looks around.

'Everything alright?' I asked, plonking our number 23 table weight down.

He fixed on me for about a second before resuming his routine. 'No offence or nothing, Teach, but don't really wanna be seen with you.'

I nearly laughed. 'No offence taken.'

'It's just … you're OK and everything … but if any of me mates see me in a caff like this, with a chick like you—'

Chick? 80s PTSD threatened. The tea and tart arrived, delivered by a young guy who looked half asleep. After he'd shuffled away, Wal continued. 'That stiff you just met works for Johnny Vogue, doesn't he?'

I nodded unhappily.

'I'm thinking that you'll be needing my services again then.' He picked up the custard tart in one hand and sort of siphoned it into his mouth like it was a line of jelly, then he swallowed the short black in a gulp. 'Next time you might want to think about guns or knives. Later.' He got up and slouched off.

My nerves, which had been starting to settle, took up with their own version of the salsa. 'Later,' I managed to whisper in his wake.

I ate my tart with a spoon, in ladylike bites that would have made Joanna proud. Each mouthful of custard seemed to soothe all that was wrong in my world.

By the time I'd squeezed three cups from the little

Bodum teapot I felt calmer; enough to walk across the road and find a seat on one of the grassy terraces above North Cottesloe Beach.

I needed some time to think.

How was I going to get Delgado and Johnny Vogue off my case? Delgado was smart enough not to threaten me with anything specific. I could go to the police but then things would get out of my control—which meant I had to find out about Nick Tozzi. Why did Johnny Vogue want to ruin him? If I knew more, I might be able to figure something out.

My phone vibrated in my pocket. It was a text from Mr Hara. 'Back Friday. Freeze.'

What in the sugar-daddies did that mean? He was freezing? Or he wanted me to freeze? When your boss writes less comprehensible English than he speaks, text can be a tricky way to communicate.

'Pardon?' I sent back.

'Yes. OK,' he replied.

Aaaagh!

Chapter 27

I took some deep breaths. The sea was sparkling today, slapping into the large man-made rock wall (referred to by locals as *the Groyne)* like they were old friends. Inside the protective arc of the Groyne, foam curled around a concrete pylon, the one remaining evidence of a long-decayed shark net. The seagulls were on-song, squawking in annoying unison. They seemed to be telling me that the time had come to ring Mr Honey.

Somehow the morning's interlude with Peter Delgado had given me back some perspective. I knew what I was going to say.

I found Mr Honey's number in my directory and hit the call button.

He answered it on the second ring.

'Hello, Lloyd?'

'Ms Sharp, is that you?' he sounded so anxious, poor fellow, that I wanted to reach through the phone and pat his shoulder.

'Yes it is. Would you prefer to talk on the phone or in person?'

'Where are you now, Ms Sharp?'

'Err … North Cott on the high wall.'

'I could be there in ten minutes.'

'Fine,' I said. 'Make it fifteen and bring some hot chips for the seagulls.'

I settled into people watching while I waited, but not much was happening midmorning on a weekday. Just some kids wagging school and a few retirees working on their baked-potato suntans.

'Ms Sharp?' Lloyd was standing behind me holding a greasy paper bag.

I patted the seat. 'Well done, Lloyd.'

He sat down and passed me the bag. I reached into it and threw some chips down the embankment. Gulls came from everywhere—the roof of the tea rooms, the tip of the pylon, from underneath parked cars. The squabbling was cacophonous but gratifying. We waited for them to quieten before either of us spoke.

I went first. 'So, what would you like to know? I'll give you a written appraisal but I do like to talk face to face with my clients as well.'

'No. Nothing written,' he said hurriedly.

'Then fire away. And please call me Tara.'

Silence returned for a bit. It was hard for anyone— especially a guy—to discuss personal things with a near-stranger. I sat staring at the sea, giving him time to work up to it.

'Do you think she really likes me, Tara?'

I turned and gave him a square-on look. 'Absolutely and without a doubt.'

Happiness transformed his face. 'Really?'

I nodded. 'Really. All her non-verbal cues indicate so. And I was able to discreetly question her as well. She thinks you're—'

'Thank you so much.' He reached into his wallet and peeled out three hundred-dollar notes.

'Woah!' I held up my hand. 'Yes, I did work two hours, expenses included. But don't you want to know anything more?'

He peered at me through his many layers of optical glass. I think his eyes were blue, but it was hard to tell. The colour was washed out by the glare. 'Well I already know a lot of things about Jenny. For instance, she's a woman of appetites that I could never hope to satisfy. If I wanted to uncover *all* her secrets I'd hire a private investigator. The truth is I don't really care about them. What I didn't know was if her feelings for me were genuine. That's why I came to you, Tara. A private investigator couldn't tell me that. Nor could a clairvoyant.'

'Oh. Right.'

'If she likes me then we've got a chance of making a real go of our marriage. Do you see?'

'Likes you or loves you?'

'I personally think "like" is what gets you through

the long term.'

I let all that sink in for a moment. 'So you're happy with my services?'

He held out the cash again. 'It might seem silly to you, Ms Sharp,' he said, reverting to formality again. 'But you're an independent viewpoint with nothing to gain. You would have gotten paid no matter what you'd told me. Therefore I'm calculating that you're telling the truth—at least from your perspective. I can't get that non-bias from friends or family.' He stood up. 'Thank you again. I'll make sure I recommend you. And if I can ever do anything to help you, I'm more than willing. I run a genealogical databank as one of my internet businesses. It can be quite useful for background information.'

Handy! 'Bye Lloyd.'

I watched him go, not quite knowing how I felt about what had just transpired. On the one hand, I felt a bit flat. He hadn't really believed in my expertise, just my lack of bias. I had a long way to go before my talent had credentials. On the other hand, I had three hundred dollars cash, which meant I could buy phone credit and some petrol and still have some leftover. YAY!

I decided to stick with the latter feeling, and bounded across the road and around the corner into the Cott car park.

My good mood deserted in an instant.

Mona had been covered in graffiti. Eloquent words like 'bitch' and 'whore' written all over in fluorescent paint.

There was no one else in sight, other than the bottle shop attendant, who peeked out of the doorway from behind his till.

I stormed over to him. 'Did you see who did that?'

He shook his head. 'I just started. Came in through the hotel. Looks like you've pissed off someone,' he said unhelpfully. 'Cost a bit to get that re-sprayed.'

I felt like punching him. I wanted to find the vandal even more, and strangle them. My car was holy ground.

Fighting back tears of rage, I rang Wal. I couldn't go home with Mona in this state. Not to Euccy Grove. Not to JoBob. 'It's me again.'

He didn't seem surprised. 'Yeah, Teach?'

'Do you know any cheap spray painters?'

'I know a guy over Bunka way.'

Bunka was a light industrial area adjacent to Perth's more dubious suburbs. Lots of business got done in the Bunka, most of it involving cash. It was also the place Johnny Vogue had mentioned on the phone. Monday, he'd said. Well, today was Monday. Maybe I'd get lucky and find the warehouse. It couldn't hurt to look. 'How much for a re-spray?'

'Your car?'

'Yes.' I told him what had happened.

'Wait and I'll call you back.'

I examined Mona while I waited. I wasn't a person to bear grudges—life was too short—but if I ever found out who'd done this...

My phone rang. 'Wal?'

'This guy owes me a favour. Throw in a hundred bucks cash for beer money if you don't mind what the colour is. Will take a couple of days though.'

'Awesome. Thanks.'

He gave me the address. 'His name is Bog.'

'B-o-g?'

'Yeah. Spray painter's joke.'

'Fair enough.'

I put on my sunnies and dug around under the back seat until I found a cap. Jamming it down over my head, I headed for Bunka territory.

Chapter 28

Every traffic light on the way to Bunka seemed to be red, every road congested. It seemed that The Almighty wanted the entire population of the western suburbs to see my graffitied car, slowly and in graphic detail.

A police car passed me going in the other direction—Cravich and Blake. They clocked me, their heads turning simultaneously to gape at Mona. I half expected them to turn around and follow me but they continued on.

I drove east, across the causeway, along the Eastern Highway towards the hills. Veering north, I followed the street directory and found Wal's spray painter in a tin shed on a back block in Bunka. The yard reeked of thinners and was cluttered by dead car bodies. Razor wire ran along the top of the fence. I parked between a nineties Landcruiser and an even older Datsun.

Bog was inside the shed prepping a metallic blue and rust Holden. A mask hung from his neck and his long black ponytail was speckled with a rainbow of paint, unlike his aura which was thick custard yellow.

'Hi,' I said. 'Wal sent me.'

Bog looked me up and down. 'Grominsky's taste's gone upmarket.'

I swallowed hard, not knowing who should be more upset by that notion—Wal or me? 'We're just … friends.'

'Sure,' he said.

We walked out into the yard to look at my car. He gave a low whistle. 'Nice wheels. Used to own one like it. Heavy on the corners but craps it down the straight.'

'Yeah. I used to dream about racing it.'

'True?' His eyebrows shot up. 'Let me know if you ever do. I got a hankerin' that way meself. Meantime, looks like you got yourself some trouble.'

'Shit happens,' I said in my plumiest voice.

He started laughing at that, grabbing his belly and rocking back and forward on his feet. When he finally stopped, he wiped his eyes. 'Can do a freebie but only got this colour,' he said, grabbing hold of his ponytail. He isolated a section of it and waved it at me.

The section of hair was tinted with burnt-orange paint reminiscent of a far north sunset. A great colour in the right context. Western suburbs was not the right context, being more black, powder blue or white. 'Uuuh, that all you got?' I asked.

He frowned. 'What d'ya want for free? Gold plate? Diamond studs?'

I sighed. Having no money stunk. Still, Mona wasn't

really a western suburbs kind of car anyway. 'Sorry. That'll be fine.'

'Fine,' he said, mimicking my accent.

I pulled a face.

'Gimme two days.' He reverted to his normal accent and held out his hand.

I rotated the key off my key chain and passed it to him.

His hand stayed outstretched.

It took me a second and then I clicked, extracting a hundred dollars cash from my jeans pocket. 'Enjoy.' My teeth weren't quite gritted. Almost. Now I only had two hundred left from my first job. 'Say Bog, you don't happen to know if Johnny Vogue keeps a warehouse around here?'

His expression got shifty and his aura contracted a little. 'He ain't good company, that one.'

'Sure,' I said, and waited.

His gaze drifted to my purse and stayed there.

I caught his drift quicker this time. 'How much?'

He didn't answer but lifted his chin and rolled his eyes.

Reluctantly, I pulled another fifty from my pay and waved it at him. 'Don't be shy.'

He snaffled it faster than Brains swiping an almond. 'I heard he's got somethin' a coupla blocks over, jus' before you hit residential. Machinery out the front. Can't miss it. But you don't want to be walkin' round there without some muscle.'

'Where's the train station?'

'A few blocks past that again.' He frowned. 'You're

not dressed right either.'

I looked down at my black flats and designer jeans. 'What do you mean?'

He scratched his head. 'You got someone who can pick you up?'

'I'll be fine,' I said, lifting my chin. And really, I could only afford the train.

He shrugged and turned back to his car. 'If you're still alive, come back on Thursd'y mornin'.'

I marched off up the long driveway and turned right in the direction he'd pointed me. This part of Bunka was all light industrial, and busy with tray-backs and vans ducking in and out of lots. The sun was shining and everything looked harmless enough. The smell of thinners was gradually overrun by the flavour of cooking wheat from the Sanitarium Factory. Weetbix. Yum.

After two blocks I wished I'd worn sneakers, even though I was wearing flats. My narrow shoes were squashing my toes together and the sharp little heels sunk into the blue metal-covered dirt. No bitumen here.

Feeling blisters coming on, I took a shortcut through a laneway bordered by tall tufts of spear grass. On one side was a chained yard with a large warehouse in the centre of it and several mechanical diggers parked outside. On the other side there was a refrigerated storage compound. The airconditioner ducts in the compound roared like jet engines and the hot blast of exhaust fanned up a willy-willy of dust. I danced sideways to avoid it but my heel got caught in a stormwater grate, and sent me toppling as it snapped off. I slammed against the compound fence then slid ignominiously into a clump of spear grass.

I sat there for a while, feeling stupid, until a sleek, black HSV near the warehouse door caught my attention. It wasn't a Bunka kind of car.

Maybe I'd just sit a while longer.

My patience was rewarded within a short time. A round-faced, bulky guy in a suit left the warehouse and ran to the car, hastily opening the back door to climb in. He looked nervous. My memory for faces stirred but couldn't place him.

I pushed aside the grass for a better look, doing my best to ignore the smell of dog urine and the telltale signs of scalded yellow blades.

A few moments later, Johnny Vogue joined him, and the HSV drove out of the compound in a hurry.

Suddenly spooked, I got up and hobbled out of the lane onto the road.

The landscape on this side of the block was completely different. No more little factories or car yards; only a carpet of red-tiled, fibro houses with half-starved dogs roaming many of the gardens. At the sight of me the entire dog population of the street seemed to begin barking.

As I stood on one foot trying to decide whether to go back the way I'd come, a battered station wagon drove past me slowly. The guy driving it was bald. His passenger hung a heavily tattooed arm out the window and stared.

The back of the car was jammed with enough speakers and amps for a Kiss concert, though it was pinging out hip hop. They cruised to the end of the street and turned around for another drive-by.

I didn't need to be able to read their auras to know their intentions weren't in my best interests. Bravado deserted me. I started walking briskly away from them while I grabbed my phone from my bag and rang Bok.

Message bank.

Smitty.

No answer.

Garth.

Message bank.

Aunt Liv.

Number disconnected. (She must've forgotten to pay her bill again!)

The music grew louder again as the car did another drive-by.

I fumbled through my phone directory. Maybe I should ring the Euccy Grove cops and ask for Bligh. But a little streak of stubbornness stopped me. Being laughed about over car graffiti was one thing. Being dubbed stupid for getting myself in trouble in Bunka was quite another.

And I had been stupid. Stupid, stupid, stupid. Who did I think I was? Jackie Chan?

I bent down and slipped my shoes off. Should I run into one of those houses and ask for help?

Not if I didn't want to be savaged by a dog.

The car was level with me again. Then it accelerated and crashed across the footpath, blocking my way.

'Looking for someone?' shouted the bald guy over the music.

Something warned me not to talk at all. Instead, I stepped right around the back of the car onto the road. My stomach felt like a bag of hot liquid.

The car reversed roughly. 'Hey, bitch!'

My jaw set at that. I walked across the road to the other side. The train clacked along in the distance. I couldn't be too far from the station.

Tattoo guy opened his door and tried the smoother approach. 'Hey, baby. Wanna fuck a real man?'

My phone rang and I put it to my ear automatically.

'Tara?'

'Yes Dad?'

Tattoo got out of the car and started to walk after me. I quickened my pace.

'You're puffing, dear—are you alright?'

'I'm out for aaah … mmm … power walk. Said yes … to a … triathlon next weekend.'

'Oh. Well. Good for you. Can you feed the birds tonight? Your mother and I are going out for an early dinner and then on to the opera.'

Tattoo sprinted past me, laughing and flapping his arms. He dropped into a tackling crouch.

'Sure. Gotta go. Call you later.'

Later? I was about to be abducted and raped.

I hooked my bag over my head and shoulder so it wouldn't slip off and bolted across the road.

My quick move took Tattoo by surprise; and my speed.

By the time I heard his pounding footsteps chasing me, I was almost at the end of the street.

Baldy didn't stop to pick up Tattoo like I'd banked on, and the car roared after me, door still open and swinging.

Just as I hit the intersection, a white Commodore cornered wildly into our street on two wheels and spat out a short spray of gunfire.

Baldy hit the brakes and squealed past me. The wagon's tail swung around in an untidy 180-degree spin and fishtailed after the Commodore, which was driving straight at Tattoo.

I didn't wait to see the outcome, but kept on running in the direction I'd heard the train. Three streets over, the station appeared, perched high on a litter-strewn embankment. I ran up the steps to the platform, then straight past the group of skanky teens throwing bottles onto the track.

The station had one heavily barred ticket office— now closed—and two toilets. The ladies seemed the safest option, so I locked myself in the first toilet and pressed phone numbers wildly until someone—*anyone*— answered.

'Tozzi.'

'Thank God! Nick—it's—Tara,' I gasped. 'Need—*huge* favour.'

'What's wrong?' he said sharply.

'Everything!' I took a couple of deep breaths and told him what had just happened.

'Which station are you at?'

I tried to remember the sign I'd run past. 'Burnside, I think. I've locked myself in the loo.'

'Sit tight.'

'Won't move a sphincter,' I assured him.

I put the seat cover down and perched on the top of the toilet. I'd dropped my good shoe somewhere and only had the one with the broken heel. My feet were grazed and filthy and didn't bear looking at. Now that my breathing had evened out, I began to shake all over, like I'd been in a freezer for a couple of hours.

I tried occupying my thoughts with the graffiti on the walls and door. Especially the list of gang names scratched into the wooden door. I was guessing that a gang altercation was what had just saved me from being dumped, raped or dead, in some vacant lot.

'Hey lady, you got any fags?' said one of the young girls from outside, banging on the toilet door.

'Don't smoke,' I said, wiping any trace of 'posh' from my voice.

'Got any money?'

I closed my eyes and pressed my fingers to my temples. I didn't get headaches much but I had a doozy coming on. This was clearly not my day and right now I didn't feel like taking on a bunch of bored teens. 'How much?'

'Just wanna buy some smokes for me and me boyfriend.'

I passed a twenty-dollar note under the door. 'Do me a favour. When a big guy turns up in a flash car—I'm talking *real* big—let me know.' I followed it with another twenty.

'Watcha doin' in there?'

'Thinkin',' I said. 'We had a fight. But he's comin' to get me so we can make up. Just let me know, OK?'

She giggled. 'OK. What's ya name?'

'Tara.'

'What's his name?'

'Nick.'

'I'm Cass.'

'Thanks, Cass.'

'No prob.'

Silence. She'd gone outside. I could hear her recounting our conversation to her friends. A guy—probably her boyfriend—urged her to come and hassle me for more.

'Nah. Leave her alone. She's got man problems,' said Cass.

The other girls in the group tittered. Then I heard them banging at the cigarette machine.

Vive la sisterhood!

While I waited for Nick, I thought about the things that had happened to me in the last few days. Had Johnny Vogue and Delgado tried to have me run over and then trashed my car? The words 'whore' and 'slag' didn't seem to be their style. I mean, why would Johnny Vogue bother to taunt me when he could straight out 'disappear' me? I was so deep in gloomy rumination that it took me a while to register that Cass was back.

'Tara?'

'Yeah,' I croaked.

'I think your Nick's here. He drive an SUV?'

'Err—what's he look like?'

'Frickin' huge. Like a bear. And hot.'

'That's him.' I opened the door and peered around. My messenger was a small, plump young girl in torn tights and a wrap-around skirt. She wore thick purple eye shadow and a spray of piercings on one side of her face: ear, nose, half-lip and eyebrow. Smoke curled out from the cigarette pinched between her thumb and forefinger. She lifted it to her lips and sucked on it like a bloke.

I suddenly felt cowardly, hiding in the toilet from a bunch of young kids.

'He rich or somethin'?' she asked.

I limped past her to the mirror, feeling the need to comb my hair and splash my face before I went outside. 'He used to play in the NBA,' I said.

'Wassat? Footy or somethin'?'

'Basketball.'

'He famous?'

'In a way,' I said, and tucked the comb away in my Marc Jacobs.

'My cousin's got a bag like that. Got it in Bali. Real nice. I wanna go there one day,' she said, following me outside into the glare.

Nick was standing in the car park adjoining the platform, leaning against his four-wheel drive and fielding commentary from Cass's friends.

Cass paraded ahead of me like she was my chaperone. 'Got your missus here, Mr Big 'n' Famous,' she announced when we got close.

Some of the boys catcalled at that. Like Cass, most of them were heavily pierced. But they wore ragged Metal t-shirts over their torn baggy shorts.

Nick didn't even raise an eyebrow. He just walked around to the passenger side and opened the door for me.

I hopped straight in and waited for him to shut the door and return to the driver's seat.

Cass came close to the window and gave me a slow wink.

I winked back. Then I emptied my handbag out on the floor and pressed the window button so that it opened.

'Here,' I said, passing out the bag. 'It's yours.'

She grabbed it with both hands. 'Truth?'

'Yeah. Truth.'

'Thanks, Tara.'

'Take care, Cass.'

Then Nick was reversing purposefully out of the car park.

I looked in the rear view. One of the boys threw a bottle at the back of the car as we accelerated forward. Cass hit him on the head with her new bag.

'Are you *insane*?' asked Nick.

I looked over at him.

'I mean—first you come out to Bunka alone, then you wander *by yourself* through Burnside and apparently nearly get shot in a gang fight. You ring me up to be rescued, and while I'm obliging your stupidity, you give your handbag away to a delinquent kid.'

'How do you know she was a delinquent?' I said defensively.

'They threw a beer bottle at my car. What would you call it?'

'Bored.'

'I get bored too. I don't do that.'

'But you come from a privileged background—'

He slapped his hands against the wheel in anger. Heat poured from his aura. 'There was nothing privileged about my parents' lifestyle when they came to Australia. They were hardworking migrants who deserved what they got. I wasn't born into status. *My* great-grandfather wasn't lord mayor of Perth.'

I stared at him open-mouthed. 'How do you know that?'

He fell silent then, concentrating on the road.

It took a little while for it to sink in that he'd been checking me out—the same way I'd been checking him out. Maybe it was stress release, but I burst out laughing.

He gave me a sideways glance and shook his head. 'See. Mad!'

His aura cooled to something less scalding. Mostly

auras were a visual thing for me, especially with strangers. In intimate or tense situations I could feel energy. But there were very few people whose aura I was temperature-sensitive to. I hoped my receptivity was because I found him so damn appealing, not because my weird talent was getting stronger. I'd have to check with Mr Hara.

'I saw Peter Delgado this morning.'

He didn't say anything.

'They want me to continue to spy on you. Find out if you're in financial difficulty.'

'And what did you say?'

'I stalled. Figured that might give you and me time to find out what's going on.'

'I appreciate you being candid with me, Tara. But *I'll* be the one finding out what is going on. *You'll* be the one staying in with the blinds down and the phone off the hook.'

I chewed my finger for a bit as Bunka disappeared. I didn't much like the sound of that. I'd been going to tell him about seeing Johnny Vogue at the warehouse, but decided to keep it to myself.

Our conversation dried up as we headed along the Eastern Highway. A few minutes later, Nick took the city lane instead of the bypass.

'I'm going to stop at my office. You can wash your feet and tidy up there before I drop you home,' he said.

'Umm … thanks. Sorry to interrupt your working day,' I said.

We drove in silence the rest of the way.

Chapter 29

Nick Tozzi's office was in a sleek, discreet building in East Perth, not far from the famous sports ground known to cricket fanatics around the world as the WACA. Royal Perth Hospital was within spitting distance, as was a small inner-city park that boasted a desultory rose garden and some paint-flaked benches. Right now a couple huddled on one of the benches, sharing sips from a flagon of port.

Nick slid his four-wheel drive down the alleyway behind the building, and into a bay stencilled *Tozzi*.

'My great-granddad might have been lord mayor but I don't have my own parking spot near the centre of the city,' I observed dryly.

He got out of the car and came around to open my door again. Another gentlemanly gesture—if he hadn't been frowning. 'Are you always so acerbic with your rescuers?'

'I prefer to think of this as a friend doing a favour for a friend. I didn't need rescuing.'

'Yeah, right,' he said with sarcasm.

We walked (well, he walked, I limped) across the small six-berth car park to the service lift where he inserted a key. The doors grated open and we stepped inside. The lift specification said six persons maximum capacity, and Nick took up the space of five. I turned sideways so as not to get squashed by his shoulders.

'So we're "friends", are we?' he asked.

I watched the lift lights as we shot to the third floor.

'Well … in a way,' I said, suddenly nervous. I could smell his aftershave and the perspiration underneath it. But more than that, his proximity was like pin pricks on my skin. It was a pleasant, if unsettling, distraction from the throb of my blisters.

He stared down at me. Not many people got to do that and I hated it. But before he could respond, the lift opened into an open-plan office and twenty sets of eyes fixed on me.

Nick encompassed them all in one sweeping glance. 'This is Tara Sharp. A friend.'

Curiosity rose from them like steam from a kettle, floating towards me and coating me in a moist film.

'Um, hi,' I said with a limp wave. I resisted the desire to look down at my bare, filthy feet.

Nick ushered me into the one enclosed office on the floor and called out, 'Jenelle!'

A smart-looking redhead appeared and he closed the three of us inside.

'Yeah, Nick?' Her blue eyes were wide with interest.

'Get the first-aid kit and show Tara the bathroom.'

Jenelle stared at my feet. 'Oh, you poor thing! Sure.'

'Then go down town and pick up a pair of sneakers for her.'

'No—' I began to protest, but Tozzi's frown silenced me.

'You need shoes, Tara,' he said.

'Thank you.' I sighed then looked at Jenelle. 'I'm size eleven.'

She nodded. 'I'll do my best. This way.'

'Come back in here when you've finished, Tara,' Nick ordered. 'Do you want tea?'

I nodded, and to my embarrassment, my eyes started to fog. 'Please,' I said huskily.

Jenelle showed me to the ladies—a bright, lacquered room with a paper dispenser and a deep basin—and left me to it. No questions.

I washed my feet as best I could and cleaned down the basin afterwards. Then I slunk back into Nick's office, pretending not to notice the murmurs from across the open plan.

Nick had a mug of tea waiting for me.

I sat on a comfy couch, thinking how different Nick's office was from Peter Delgado's—despite containing similar objects. They both had leather couches, but Nick's was a casual soft-pillowed style, not a stiff-buttoned Chesterfield. They both had large desks, but whereas Delgado's was heavy, dark jarrah wood, Nick's was glass and modern, and his wall hangings weren't early Australian watercolours but basketball photos. The best one was Nick in his NBA gear sporting a sensational mullet and standing between Michael Jordan and Scotty Pippin.

I pointed to it. 'Wow! You met them?'

'Yeah. Big moment for a twenty-year-old basketballer from Oz.'

'I'm jealous,' I said. 'Not of the haircut though.'

He grimaced. 'You really do say what's on your mind, don't you?'

I shrugged. If I said what was on my mind right now he'd probably throw me out. I mean he was a very attractive man whose aura was so magnetic it made me feel like a pile of iron filings: little bits of me wanted to stick all over him. 'I'm guessing people aren't very direct with you?'

He sat down behind his desk in the biggest chair I had ever seen. 'Not so much that. It's just that people aren't always *natural* with me. Especially my players.'

'Aaah ... the trials of being *the boss*.' I knew I was being stupid but I couldn't stop my nervous mouth.

He gave me a shrewd look. 'Tara, why do I get the feeling you're trying to distract me from something. Now tell me, why did you visit my mother?'

I swallowed some tea and looked out the window. His view was typical inner city; rooftops and antennae. It was a generous window though.

Like Nick, I suspected.

I sighed. 'I'm not stalking you, Nick. I had a visit from the police. They hinted I might become a suspect in the robbery at your mum's. I ... resented that. Lately I just seem to have a bad habit of being in the wrong place at the wrong time.'

'I'd call it a talent,' he commented. His body language relaxed as we spoke, his arms unfolding.

'Whatever. Anyway, the cops told me that the guy they'd caught, Sam Barbaro, had been bailed by Peter Delgado. It all seemed like too much of a coincidence not to be related. I figured that he—the burglar—must have been looking for something on you.'

'And you don't think the police might have thought of that?'

'Depends on what you've told them. Besides, I bet I know basketball better than any of those cops. I thought I might pick up on something that they'd missed.'

'And you expected my mother to just let you in and tell you anything you wanted to know?'

'Well, not exactly. My mother knows her. I just prompted a re-acquaintance.'

'And how did that go?' I could see him struggling between annoyance and curiosity.

'I'm going over to her house tomorrow to help her clean up the mess. She didn't want the hired help poking around in your things. And...' I paused to take a deep breath, 'you didn't have time to help her.'

Nick squeaked forward on his chair, slapping the table with his hands and sending me instinctively retreating into mine.

'She said that?'

I nodded and gulped more tea.

He slumped back in exasperation. 'Of all the—what time are you going over there?'

'Errr … three-ish, I think.'

He rubbed his forehead in a gesture of frustration. Then he got up and walked over to the couch and sat down beside me. One huge hand took hold of my wrist.

'If you can find—if there *is*—a connection between Johnny Vogue and the burglary at Mum's, Tara, then I would owe you the world.' His gaze was like a chemical peel. 'And I'll make sure you get it. A job, a holiday … whatever you want.'

The change in his mood and manner made me dizzy. I tried really hard to stay sensible. 'I don't want anything from you, Nick, and actually, I'll owe you a pair of sneakers.'

He froze, as if my answer was totally unexpected. Then something weird happened. There was a slight eruption in his aura like a solar flare. A thin strand of it shot out and hit me high in the chest, around the base of my throat. I could see the line of it as clearly as if a red rope tied us together.

I jumped up to get away from it, batting at it with my hands.

micro-
top.
g

.g?'

...ew paces until I was leaning against
...ass desk. The strand stretched. 'Uhh?
err ... just ... I suffer ... panic attacks
...on't worry; it's just a reaction to today. It'll

...ern filled his face; *real* concern. It poured along
...ergy strand to my throat like I was a blotting paper
...spilled ink.

Jeez he likes me. He really likes me.

There was a knock at the door.

'Come in,' he called.

It was Jenelle, carrying a plastic bag from Athlete's Foot. She was flushed from rushing, curls of red hair sticking to her forehead. They complimented the fiery red of her aura. Mr Hara said red auras meant the person was high on materialism. 'Only one size eleven in the whole of the city, I think.'

'Thanks, J.' said Nick.

He looked cool and relaxed, unlike me who was attempting to stand on jelly legs.

'No problem. Anything else I can do?' she asked.

Nick threw the car keys to her. 'Run Tara home for me.'

'In the Cayenne?' That was almost a whoop.

'I can't do it. I'm meeting Tony here in half an hour,' he said.

Jenelle screwed up her face. At least, she didn't as far

as most people would know, but I could see th
expressions that pointed to distaste.

'Wouldn't want to miss that, bosso,' she said.

Nick grunted and turned his attention to his la
'Bye Tara,' he said. 'Stay out of trouble.'

I opened my mouth but couldn't think of a damn th
to say.

Chapter 30

Jenelle drove the Cayenne like several bats fleeing several hells. As the speedo hit one hundred and ten k's around Riverside Drive, I was forced to speak up.

'Err, Jenelle,' I squeaked. 'Think it's only sixty along here. How's the boss about speeding tickets?'

She reluctantly braked back to seventy. 'I always wanted to race cars. Can't seem to control myself when I get in one as fast as this.'

'I'm the same,' I said. 'I've got a vintage Monaro. Cost me a fortune in tickets when I first got it.'

'A Monaro? Lucky you! I drive a tinker toy; economical but boring as...'

We sat in an amicable silence past the university and down through Nedlands. She'd had some tasks to do for Nick before she'd been free to drive me home, and I'd spent the time on my phone, Googling her boss and his business.

'So who is Tony?' I asked.

Jenelle braked for traffic lights and swivelled to give me a good old-fashioned stare. 'Uh?'

'The guy he's meeting with,' I said, playing coy.

'That's Toni with an "i". His wife, Antonia.'

'Oh,' I said. 'I only recently met Nick. Haven't had the pleasure of actually meeting his wife yet.'

'It's no pleasure,' said Jenelle bluntly.

'Oh?'

'You'll see. Or at least, you might. He doesn't usually introduce his other … friends to her.'

'Friends?'

Jenelle blushed. 'I'm talking too much. Sorry.'

The dollar coin dropped. 'Oh, you mean *girlfriends*. Well I'm not that,' I said bluntly. 'I'm just helping him out with something; sort of a working arrangement.'

'Well that's good. You seem nice, Tara, and Nick— much as I love him—doesn't always pay attention to his girlfriends.'

'So he's a player, is he?'

'He wouldn't be if SHE was nicer to him. But don't get me wrong,' she added hastily. 'He'll never leave Toni. Not in a million. He married well. Her old man's worth squillions.'

Wonderful.

She dropped me at home a while later and drove off with a flash of red curls, careering around the corner like Speed

Racer. I hoped Nick got the Cayenne back in one piece or it would be another thing on my conscience.

First thing I did was feed the birds. Hoo was snippy, trying to bite me as I filled the seed container, and Brains was stand off-ish, refusing to come over for a scratch. I felt vaguely guilty about their moods. JoBob had been out since early afternoon and the birds clearly hadn't had their walk. But it was almost dark now—maybe tomorrow morning before I went to Eireen Tozzi's.

I suddenly felt incredibly tired. The day had been long and crappy, and now I just wanted to have a hot, hot shower and lie down.

So I did just that, nibbling the last of JoBob's brie and biscuits in bed; wondering who the suit with Johnny Vogue was, and watching *Scrubs* re-runs on Netflix until I fell asleep.

I slept until well after midday, at which time I staggered out of bed and up to JoBob's to borrow some bread.

And milk.

And sugar.

And toilet paper.

And soap.

And teabags.

And...

'Tara, can't you shop for yourself?' asked Dad, making me jump. He was seated in his favourite chair and his eyes never shifted from the pro golf replay on his plasma.

Now Dad was semi-retired he had two passions in life—sport and the news channel.

'Didn't see you there, Dad. Sorry, been busy. Will replace it tomorrow. Promise.'

I escaped with my armload of food booty, making a mental note that I needed to buy a laundry basket to make it easier to carry my food back to the flat.

Breakfast, shower, rummage for clean clothes, iron crumpled clothes and straighten hair—in that sequence.

I could hear the birds fighting in their cage, Hoo chasing Brains around and around. I took toast and a mug of tea outside and opened the cage door. They both climbed out immediately, as if to say 'about time'. I watched them crawl around the outside of the cage, and up and down the lattice, until I remembered I had no car. A glance at my watch told me it was 2.30PM. I lured the birds back into the cage with a piece of toast and honey, and snapped the gate shut.

Eireen Tozzi wasn't the sort of person you kept waiting.

As I walked the back way to her house, Bok called me.

'Sorry, T. Been so busy with these wankers, but they're leaving tomorrow. What's been happening?'

I told him a version of yesterday's events and could almost hear his teeth grinding.

'Who do you think trashed your car?' he asked.

'Either Barbaro or someone else. I'm thinking someone else.'

'That narrows it down.'

I sighed. 'I know.'

'What are you doing now? How about coffee?'

'Err … maybe not. I'm going to Eireen Tozzi's to look through the things the burglar turned over.' I waited for his disapproval but it never came.

'That's not a bad idea. I'll call you. Later.'

I tucked my phone away in my shoulder bag. Somehow, Bok saying 'that's not a bad idea' scared me. It was like he'd left off the subtext, 'You're in deep trouble and you're going to have to start doing something to get out of it.'

I took that thought to Eireen's front door, past a snazzy, gold Mercedes convertible parked next to the fountain. It seemed a rather sexy number for a lady of seventy plus. Maybe she had visitors.

I was right.

Antonia—Toni—Tozzi answered the door wearing a silk mushroom-pink Alannah Hill shift and a violent red aura. Jenelle's aura had been red too. But there was red and then there was 'red'. Toni 'Falk' Tozzi was the latter. Not like Jenelle's fleshy pink tones; more, drowning-in-fresh-blood.

I recognised her straightaway from the other night, and the social pages. Her sandals matched her clothes, and the colour set off the amazing lush blonde hair which swept around her shoulders. Some women do the tousled chic look so well it's nauseating. Why can't they just look messy?

'Are you the cleaner? Reeny said she had a girl coming

over to help her,' she said in a voice that sounded like she'd swallowed a plum and then regurgitated half of it.

I squared my shoulders. 'Yes, I'm the girl. Could you tell Eireen that Tara is here?'

'Wait here.'

I did as I was told until Eireen Tozzi appeared in an emerald green sheath dress, pearls and pink fluffy slippers.

'Tara Sharp. I wondered if you'd remember. The young can be so irresponsible.'

'Ready and raring to go, Eireen. That is, if you still want me. I see you have ... err ... relatives here.' I stared at Antonia's retreating back.

Eireen tossed her head. 'Psssh. That one is too lazy to lift a hand.' She crooked her finger.

I followed the diminutive figure, made shorter by lack of high heels, through the foyer, past the sitting room and down a long corridor. At the end of the corridor we climbed a set of elegant spiral stairs and entered the first grand door.

Chapter 31

Young Nick Tozzi's bedroom hit me hard psychically—like a piece of furniture dropped on my head from a great height. It wasn't the first time I'd been affected by someone's intimate possessions. There's always residual energy from loved things. Compared to their personal aura, though, it's more like a dull background radiation; how I imagine the Hubble telescope views the backdrop of the universe.

To me, Nick's room was more like a theme park at night. Certain objects glowed brightly. This told me two things: either Nick Tozzi was spending a lot of time in his childhood bedroom, or I'd developed an unnaturally strong connection to him.

I glanced down at my chest. The cord from yesterday had disappeared but there seemed to be a slight distortion in my vision right at the spot where it had joined the top of my rib cage.

'See what he did to my Nick's room?' Eireen waved

her hands in despair. 'I'd kill him with my bare hands if I could.'

I surveyed the emptied carton and overturned chest. 'Well, don't say that to the police, Eireen,' I said. 'They don't take those comments lightly.'

She turned on me, a miniature schnauzer in pink fluffies. 'You think I'm joking?' Her eyes blinked fiercely and her aura swelled and brightened, just like her son's. I'm glad I'd never been in the room when the pair of them were having an argument.

'Hi, Tara.'

Damn!

Nick leaned against the door frame, wearing shorts and a t-shirt. His legs were like massive, sculptured pylons. I dragged my eyes from his thighs to his face and his warm, caramel aura.

But not before he'd noticed me looking.

And so, unfortunately, had his wife, who tottered around the expanse of his wide body holding a glass of champagne with a strawberry bobbing in it.

She gave Nick a sharp look in the suspicious manner of wives who were used to women admiring their husbands; or perhaps more than admiring. Jenelle's comments had made me wary of Nick Tozzi.

'Shouldn't you be at work?' I snapped.

'We're staying here at the moment—in the guest room—until our new house is ready. Didn't I tell you?'

Staying here? Well, that explained the packing carton.

'What's the cleaner speaking to you like that for, Nicky?'

'Tara isn't the cleaner, Toni. She's here to help us sift through this mess. She does this kind of thing for a living.'

'Maid hire?' she asked, innocently.

My hackles rose. 'Actually, no. I'm not a maid or a cleaner. I'm a businesswoman, specialising in communication analysis and kinesic investigation. Kind of like a private detective. Graduated from Harvard.'

'Harvard? I didn't know they had degrees in such things.'

'Yeah. Three years it took. It runs complementary to their law degree.'

Nick frowned at my preposterous lie but I didn't care. His wife was a snobby bitch.

'What is all this talk about,' piped in Eireen. 'I didn't hire Tara—she's a family friend. Her great-grandfather was lord mayor.'

Toni peered at me closely. 'You do look familiar. Where did you go to school?'

'Toni!' said Nick in a warning tone.

'Shotske State High in Bunka,' I lied again. Was there even a place anywhere called Shotske?

'Oh...' Her interest faded again, and she looked like she'd tasted something bitter.

Nick spoke up to forestall any further interrogation. 'Pleasant and all as it is chatting, we have a lot on today.

Remember, Toni? Could you excuse us while Tara and I get this done?' He bent over and righted a chair. 'Mum, would you like to sit?'

Eireen's eyes glinted with sudden mischief. 'Seeing as you're already acquainted with Tara, I'll leave you both to do this tedious and painful job. Antonia, come with me.'

Toni wavered, not wanting to leave us alone, yet knowing that she couldn't refuse her mother-in-law's imperative. Duty and fear of Eireen won out, and she followed Eireen from the room.

Nick sagged a little with tension release. 'I'm sorry, Tara. Toni can be a bit rude.'

I nodded. 'Oh well. Your problem, not mine,' I said cheerfully.

His mouth pursed. 'Yes.'

'Let's get to it then. Can I touch things? Or do I have to wear gloves or something.'

'The police have finished here. They've taken their pictures. I thought we could start with the chest and then move on to the carton.'

'No need for system,' I said, standing in the centre of the room and letting my eyes defocus. There were several bright objects. I walked from one to the other. First was a tangle of ribbons and pennants proclaiming various season wins then came an autographed basketball. I couldn't read the name on it.

A pair of huge size-sixteen boots stood in the foot of the open closet. I bent over to them. They had the faint smell of mould and an eyelet had pulled out.

'Haven't worn them since I left the States,' he said.

I smiled. I could understand that. Wearing them again would somehow dilute the memory.

Each thing was significant enough to Nick to glow with his energy, but none were the thing I was looking for.

Then I noticed something next to the overturned carton, covered by some clothes. The energy around it was bright but disturbed.

I lifted the clothes off it. 'What's that?'

'It's an antique writing desk; a portable one. My grandfather left it to me. He fancied himself as a poet.'

'What do you keep in it?'

He thought about it. 'Some special things. Odds and sods.'

'Do you mind if I have a look through it?'

'Sure. I guess.'

I sat down cross-legged and gently turned the writing desk up the right way. It was like a small drawer with a lid, shaped for writing on your lap. The wood was scarred and inexpertly restored, but the leather insert was in quite good condition. I ran my hands over it and felt a little charge. This piece had been owned and cherished by many people and somehow their lives were all still evident in the energy. Mr Hara called it 'living memory'. Natural materials were like that—wood, especially. I couldn't tell who or what, just that it was there.

Some of the contents had been tipped out and spread

around; some were still inside. A tingle spread across my body. This was significant, I was sure. Something in this little desk was important. I scooped it all into one pile. 'Nick, can you come over here please?'

He came over and knelt down next to me. 'What is it?'

I passed him the papers. As I did, the thread between us reappeared; from his chest to mine.

'Could something here be important?'

He looked at the first item, an envelope with an old stamp on it. He didn't need to look inside to know what was in it. I noticed a slight flush rise up his neck.

'Love letter?' I joked.

'Jenny Baracas. She races supercars now.'

'Lucky her,' I muttered with genuine envy.

He set it aside and picked up the next piece. 'Ticket stubs to my first game.'

I shrugged. 'Can't see much importance in that ... err ... other than to you, I mean.'

He discarded them and picked up the next thing: a glossy brochure with a windsurfer on the front. 'The place we went to on our honeymoon.' Instead of putting it on top of the letter and the stubs, he threw it towards the bin.

The next thing was a manila envelope, slightly crumpled. He drew the papers out of it.

'These are lease documents,' he said.

I raised an eyebrow.

'Toni's father gave me a Pilbara mining exploration lease for my birthday a while back.'

'Novel present.'

'He's a Falk,' he said, by way of explanation.

I sort of got what he meant. The Falks had been involved in the West Australian mining industry for a lot longer than I'd been around. They reputedly owned great chunks of land throughout the Pilbara and Kimberley, and goldmines near Kalgoorlie.

'Why is the document in here?' We were sitting facing each other, our knees almost touching.

'This carton had all my private documents that I keep at home. But the lease is worth nothing. The assay report said there isn't enough of any particular mineral to make it worthwhile mining it. Fifty acres next to a national park and not a damn speck of anything to get excited about. I can't understand why he leased it in the first place. Guess he made a mistake, and thought he might offload it on his beloved son-in-law.'

I heard the sarcasm. 'You don't get on?'

Nick shrugged. 'No one was ever going to be good enough for his little girl, especially someone who works in sport. It's not a real man's job, you know.' He gave a bitter smile.

'Why didn't you tell me that you were living here?' I asked, suddenly.

'Does it matter?'

'Of course it matters. It makes the connection between Barbaro and Johnny Vogue even stronger.'

He looked me straight in the eye. 'What exactly are

you hoping to find? I mean, nothing's been stolen, thanks to Mum interrupting him. How can you possibly tell what the burglar was after?'

'It's hard to explain. Sometimes I n-notice things that other people don't.'

He frowned. 'What sort of things? Are you saying you're a clairvoyant?'

'No,' I said, shaking my head emphatically. 'I don't believe in that crap.'

His tone had been so disparaging there was no way I could tell him about the energy disturbance around the writing desk. He'd think I was crazy. I had to find some tangible connection to one of the items first.

I leaned back, palms on the floor. 'Look, maybe you're right. There's probably nothing to find.' I uncrossed my legs and went to get up.

One giant paw shot out and grabbed hold of my hand, pulling me back down. 'Whoa! You can't just bail like that.'

The cord between us thickened and began to pulse. Where our hands touched, our auras mingled and turned into the colour of fire. I jerked back from it.

'There!' he said. 'You did the same thing in my office.'

'What?'

'Jumped. Like you'd been stung or—'

'Burned?' I offered.

'Yeah.'

I felt the heat rush into my face. 'I can't explain that

either, without sounding weird, so I'm not going to.'

'Have I offended you?'

I saw the confusion on his face and sighed. I touched his arm. 'No Nick, it's just—'

'Tozzi, darling? What are you doing?' Toni's voice cut between us like a diamond drill.

I dropped my hand and turned to face her. 'Finishing is what we're doing.'

'But the mess?' She frowned, and not just at the mess. Toni had sharp antennae for a messed-up coke addict.

'Nick said that he'd tidy it up.' I glanced back at him. 'Right?'

Nick opened his mouth and shut it again, then nodded mutely.

I went to walk out past Toni but she planted her feet astride and blocked the doorway. 'Harvard doesn't run courses in communication analysis and investigation. I just checked on the internet.'

'Oh,' I said. 'I meant Cambridge. Harvard's where I did my undergraduate.' I barrelled on out the door, knocking into her shoulder as I went.

She tottered backwards.

The words, 'how rude' followed me to the front door.

I didn't care. Nor did I stop to say goodbye to Eireen. Truth is I couldn't bear to be in the house with Toni or Nick Tozzi a second longer.

Chapter 32

I got home and gorged on a tin of cold baked beans to raise my carb levels and because it was all I had in my single-drawer pantry.

Then I decided I'd go for a run to work off my stress. It was only a few days until the triathlon and I needed to get in a little fitness work to make the distance.

Make that a lot of fitness work.

I tossed on my daggiest shorts with the flapping pocket (they were clean at least!), joggers and a Lorna Jane crop top, and hit the pavement. My feet were still sore from the Bunkas fiasco but not enough to stop me. The first two k's were easy, down Lilac Street and into Peppermint Street, past Smitty's parents' house. Instead of running west towards the highway, though, I turned left at the end of Peppermint and headed towards the river.

The river-end of Euccy Grove was one beautiful little suburb, full of magnificent old paperbarks and pepper trees. The block sizes were enormous and the houses mostly grand, if a little dated. These were occasionally interspersed with uber-modern, white block houses with lots of glass and embassy-type security.

I'd always fancied myself ending up as an eccentric old lady living in one of the grand old houses, feeding the wild birds and forgetting what day of the week it was.

Not sure how I was going to get one of those houses exactly, considering my net worth was zero dollars, a laptop and a reconned Monaro.

By the time I made the downhill stretch to the river, I was puffing hard but feeling good. Four k's and no problem. I was fitter than I thought.

I turned left at the Freshwater Bay Yacht Club and began the arduous climb up to Devil's Elbow.

Joanna, on the rare occasions we were in a car together, sometimes drove me around Devil's Elbow and pointed out the house her grandfather used to own.

'He gambled away all their money, you know.'

'Uhuh.'

'Broke my grandmother's heart. They had to leave the house and move down to Lilac Street.'

'What's wrong with our house?' I'd say defensively.

'Oh Tara,' she'd say, and roll her eyes in despair.

As I puffed my way towards dear old gambler-holic Great-Granddaddy's home, I admitted to myself that Mum was right. The view was spectacular: a crow's eye view of the Swan in all its sapphire, sandbar-dotted, boat-busy, sunlight-glinting glory. It was something else.

Come to think of it, the house I imagined growing old and feeding the birds in looked a lot like this.

Right about the end of that thought, things started to go very wrong. Yesterday's blisters grew new blisters and the mild air became like sandpaper on my windpipe. My legs developed a serious wobble, and the jog became a walk, became a shuffle. My stomach boiled with the exertion.

I spotted a lane between Great-Granddaddy's house, and the next, and staggered up there to find a discreet something or other to throw up in.

With immaculate timing, I began barfing my baked beans into a small jade bush just as a removals truck roared into the lane, tooting his horn and scaring the decorum out of me. I jumped back into the jade bush to avoid being flattened.

As I shook my fist at the truck's rear-view mirror and let loose with my most alliterate profanity, a sleek grey Lamborghini cruised up behind it and the batwing door popped open.

Not any old Lamborghini, mind—a *Reventon*, the most bad-arse sports car ever made.

'Tara, are you alright?' A Hugo Boss-suited Nick Tozzi enquired from within.

Fuck. 'I thought you drove a Porsche,' I stormed to combat my embarrassment.

'I do,' he said. 'Most of the time. But we're moving house today. I had to bring the Lambo over.'

I looked helplessly after the truck as it turned into the back entrance of Great-Granddaddy's house. 'You're moving in *here?*'

'I wasn't aware I needed your permission,' he said dryly.

Somewhere, someone was laughing at me. Nick Tozzi drove a Reventon *and* he'd bought *my* house. *Have I really been so bad, God?*

I suddenly stopped feeling sorry for him.

'May I give you a lift home?' he asked. 'I think I have a towel in here that you could sit on.'

I looked down at my bare legs. They were spattered with something I'd rather not name. I drew myself up to my full height and stepped out of the bush. 'Not if yours was the last Lambo on earth.'

Real smooth, Tara. And what was I saying anyway? Naught to one hundred kph in three point three seconds. I'd kill for a ride.

Without a shred of dignity left, I strode off.

A few houses over the crest and thankfully on the downhill, my phone rang. I pulled it from the strap of my crop. 'Yes,' I snapped into it.

'Tara?' asked a deep, masculine voice.

'Er, yeah.' I didn't know any deep masculine voices other than Bok and Tozzi, and it wasn't either of them.

'It's Edouardo.'

I sucked in a breath. *Edouardo. Club Eighteen. Gorgeous tight bum.* 'Hey dude.'

'Hey.'

Silence. I mean I hadn't really expected him to call and I was plastered in sweat, vomit and envy.

He jumped in. 'I … err … wondered if you wanted to catch a bite tonight?'

'To eat?'

'Yeah.'

My mortification began to ease. 'Sure. Where?'

'I'm working until eight.'

'I'll come by after that if you like.'

'Great. Pick a place.'

'You like Indian?' I asked.

'Onion bhaji is my muse.'

'Mine too. Later.' I hung up.

My day was looking up.

Chapter 33

I arrived at Club Eighteen as the afternoon shift swapped over with the evening bar staff, and had to wait while Edouardo pried himself away from a fresh lot of gym junkies. At least Mrs Honey-to-be wasn't one of them.

'You must get tired of that,' I said to him as we ran out to the car park before they could follow him. 'My friend Bok has the same problem. Though not as badly as you do.'

'I didn't think he looked like your brother.'

I grinned, though I doubt he could see it in the dark.

My phone rang as Edouardo unlocked the car. It was Wal.

'Bog called me. Your car's ready. He wants it out of there tonight,' he said.

'Tonight?' I gasped.

'He's got a load coming in. Needs the space.'

'But it's 8PM.'

'Load's not in till midnight. He'll be there all evening. Can you do it?'

'What if I can't?'

'He'll likely park it outside the compound. Course it might not be there in the morning.'

I thought of Bunka. 'Tell him I'll be there before midnight.'

'Right. Ahhh. Take some company. Not the place for wimmen at night.'

That so?

I got inside Edouardo's 2002 Subaru, and we sat with our knees pushed up around our ears. 'Nice car,' I said. 'Cosy.'

He laughed. 'Got it for my eighteenth birthday. Then I grew eight inches.'

'Wow!' I said. 'You must be from the same gene pool as Bok. Happened to him too. Scrawny little punk at seventeen; major tall hunk at twenty.'

'So where are we going?'

I fixed him with my best smile. 'Actually, Edouardo, I have a favour to ask.' I gave him a lean account of the abridged version of Mona's plight, leaving out the nature of the graffiti, how I knew Bog, and that I had a little scouting in mind.

'Sure, no problem, Tara. Haven't been out to the east side. Time I learned my way around Perth. Mind if we eat first though?'

'Sounds like a plan. You know Northbridge?'

'Sure. My modelling agency's got their office there.'

'Well there's a great Indian restaurant in James Street

and it's kind of on the way to Bunka.' In the way that following the North Star is the way to Jesus in the crib!

Edouardo drove into the city and we found a lucky park on busy William Street. 'My modelling agency is right over there.' He pointed across the road to a shop window full of black and white photos on easels.

We ran across when there was a break in the traffic and I ogled the male models.

'That *you*?' I asked, pointing to a particularly hot body wearing only a mask and a pair of boxers.

'That's me,' he said. 'Advertisement for Bonds.'

I swallowed hard, taking in the silky skin, and abs like rippling sand dunes. His curly hair had been straightened and he looked like something from Man Power only much, much more gorgeous. And tall!

'You like it?'

I stuck my fingernails into my palms to help collect myself and shrugged. 'Not too shabby for a country boy.'

He laughed again. 'Anyone ever tell you, you're pretty cool? Most girls I show this one to come over all man-eater.'

'Uh?' My ego detector began to swivel. 'So I've passed the test then?'

He flushed. 'Yes … no … what I m-mean—'

I punched him in the arm. 'Let's eat.'

We chatted our way through two serves of onion bhaji, a madras curry and cucumber raita. Edouardo was a witty conversationalist—interested in everything. In fact, he seemed so sweet that I was beginning to feel guilty about dragging him out to Bunka. Then again, maybe he needed to pass a couple of my tests too.

We split the bill and walked back to the Subaru.

I directed him onto the bypass and out east, remembering my last trip on this road in the Cayenne. I wondered if Nick was enjoying his first night in *my* house.

'Take the next exit,' I said.

We left the highway and merged into the local traffic doing their perennial laps around the streets of Burnside. A crowd of people were street drinking on the embankment near the station. I wondered if Cass and her gang were there.

'Can we take a short detour? I just need to check out a place close by,' I said.

Edouardo shot me a quizzical look. It was amazing how handsome his face was at any angle in any light; even the sulphur yellow of the Bunka street lights.

'You thinking of buying property out here?' he asked.

I peered out the side window looking for something familiar. 'Not unless I can afford a full-time security guard. There! Slow down and turn into that lane.'

He did as I asked, and the Subaru bumped up the laneway alongside Johnny Vogue's compound. There were no lights on and everything seemed quiet.

'Stop the car and kill the lights,' I whispered.

Edouardo complied, then slid his arm along the headrest of my seat and leaned towards me. 'Tara?'

Oh my god. Asking him to pull over in a dark place had given him totally the wrong message. Trust a man to think a back alley in Burnside could be sexy.

Then again…

Edouardo's lips brushed my hair and his breath fanned warmth on my ear. He smelled of garlic and Indian spices. 'We didn't have to drive all this way to—'

I grabbed his hand in a very un-sexy manner to jerk him out of his hormone surge. 'Edouardo, this is going to sound a bit demented. But I just have to check something out in this warehouse. Nothing illegal. I just need to have a look inside. Can you sit tight and wait for me?'

He sat back in his seat surprised. 'Wha-at?'

'Look, it's a really long story which involves too many people you don't know and questions I can't answer. So I can't go into it all now.'

I flipped off the seatbelt. 'I just want to look in the window and then we're out of here. OK?'

It was a bit dark to see his face now, but I guessed he was looking dubious, and a little offended. I would be too, if someone had knocked back my perfectly good sexual advance. I was guessing it didn't happen to Edouardo too often.

'I s'pose so. But I don't want trouble with the police, Tara. I'm trying to get a career going. My agency would drop me in a second if they—'

I traced my fingers across his chest. 'Cross your heart. No trouble.' Then I uncrossed my legs. 'Back in a jiffy.'

I jumped out of the car and surveyed the options for climbing the eight feet-tall fence. At least there was no

razor wire.

I stuck my head back in the window. 'I need a leg over.'

He climbed out of the car and joined me on the bonnet. 'How will you get back?'

'I'll find something on the other side to stand on.'

'You sure? What if you can't?'

'I will,' I reassured him. 'It's a warehouse. Warehouses always have things lying around that you can stand on.' *Hopefully*.

The hoist over was ugly but effective and I crashed down the other side like a cat with no legs.

'Alright?' Edouardo asked anxiously.

'Dandy,' said I, picking myself up. Now I was in here, adrenaline was shooting out through my toes. What if I'd missed noticing guard dogs? Or a security person?

I sprinted across the crumbling bitumen yard to the building.

Chains and padlock on the door, chicken wire over the dirty glass windows. I spent a few minutes locating a broken crate to stand on to look inside. Edouardo's little torch worked a treat but the dust on the windows might as well have been curtains. If I could find a little gap to peer in through...

Before giving it deep amounts of thought I reached down and slipped off my heels. Positioning the heel spike inside a loop of chicken wire, I hammered down on the shoe with the palm of my other hand. A chunk of glass cracked off and fell in.

The alarms went off as I flashed my phone torch around and got a good look. The building was wall-to-wall machinery. Huge scraper extensions and excavator buckets lay on the ground between the machines like giant discarded shoes. Most of them wore the Caterpillar brand emblem. What was Johnny Vogue—drug baron of the west—doing with a warehouse full of heavy equipment? Was it his?

Dragging the broken crate behind me I dashed back to the fence. The dogs across the lane in the refrigeration yard were going crazy, baying like hellhounds. Edouardo was pacing up and down next to the car.

'Hurry *up*,' he cried.

The crate collapsed on my first go and I had to reassemble it and prop it against the fence. This time I got up and over, leaving a good scraping of my skin behind. Hopefully the Burnside cops didn't stretch to DNA testing.

I fell into the car and threw Edouardo the car keys. He put the pedal to the metal and we were back in traffic before I could do my seatbelt up.

'What happened?'

'Accidentally broke a window,' I said.

He took a deep breath and I noticed his hands were shaking on the steering wheel. 'Let's get your car and get out of here. Then you owe me an explanation and a lot of vodka.'

He seemed to be taking it well.

'OK. Deal,' I said.

Chapter 34

We arrived at Bog's yard five minutes later. Bog was sitting on the bonnet of my car drinking beer straight from the carton—no esky in sight—under a spotlight.

He waved and slid off the bonnet when he saw me. Edouardo drove the Subaru up alongside.

I lowered the window. 'Evening. Got your message.'

Bog didn't answer but he stepped out of the way so I could see Mona. She was clean as a whistle, shiny orange but...

'What's that?' I gasped staring at the black swirls across the bonnet and down the side.

'Flames,' said Bog. 'You said you wanted to race her. Thought I'd throw in an extra for you. Had a set of transfers hangin' around.'

'N-i-ce,' I managed to get out. My car looked like a hell-beast Transformer.

In the seat next to me Edouardo sounded like he was choking.

'Don't you think it might attract attention?' I asked Bog.

'That's the idea.' He tossed the can away and ripped open another. 'We got a deal though. Remember? You race, I wrench.'

'But you're a spray painter,' I protested.

'Yeah, only cos … well I got my reasons. But I got my trade as well. As good a mechanic as you can find.'

'Oh,' I said, stumped. 'Fair enough. I'll keep it in mind.'

Bog cocked his head as a truck turned into the street, headlights off. He flicked us a salute. 'Time you folk went.'

I got a cold, shivery feeling. If Bog was up to something illegal I didn't want anything to do with it. I'd pushed my luck enough for one night. 'Sure.' I glanced at Edouardo. 'Follow me home. We'll have that drink at The Cocked Dog.'

Edouardo nodded; a tight jerk of his head that told me he was thinking the same thing as me. It was time to go.

I jumped out of the Subaru and into Mona. The engine fired up sweetly—so sweetly, I swear Bog had tuned her as well. With one slight depression of the accelerator, and a swing of the steering wheel, I flew out of Bog's yard and headed down the street towards the incoming truck.

A quick glance in the mirror told me Edouardo was sticking tight to my tail.

As we crossed paths—two innocent cars happening to be on the same street as a dirty-great-big unmarked truck—two police cars screamed around the corner, sirens blaring.

Before I took the same corner, I glimpsed the truck being pulled over to the side of the road at the gate of Bog's yard.

The rest of the trip home was uneventful apart from my thumping heart, clammy hands, and the hoons that tried to drag me at every set of traffic lights.

Flames. My flipping car's got flipping flames.

How was I going to park it in Lilac Street?

Worse! How would I tell Bok? Bok loathed all things bogan.

By the time I turned off Stirling Highway into the car park of The Cocked Dog, I'd pretty well justified myself to Bok in my mind, by deciding the whole thing was his fault anyway.

Edouardo ended up buying the bottle of vodka and drinking most of it—among other things—and I ended up driving him home. Not before he accidentally tossed a flaming Drambuie over his shoulder (instead of into his mouth) and nearly set fire to the barman's dreads.

About then the management decided it was time for us to go, and possibly not return for some time.

I saw Edouardo to the door of his ground-floor unit in a salmon-brick apartment block in Graylands.

'Thanksh, Tarah,' he slurred. 'Never hadda night witha girl like that befoe.'

I put his key in the lock and opened the door.

'Yeah, well,' I said, feeling guilty. 'Sorry.'

He threw his arms around me and hugged me tight. 'Don' 'pologise. 'S'fun,' he mumbled in my ear. 'Scary but fun. Like you.'

I laughed, pushing him away. 'You're a cool dude, Edouardo. Take care.'

His face dropped as he grabbed the door jam. 'Don' you wanna mess around?'

I leaned forward and kissed him firmly on the cheek. 'Some other time.'

Chapter 35

I parked Mona a little way up Lilac Street so that it wasn't the first thing JoBob saw when they looked out of their bedroom window in the morning. Then I crept down the driveway into my flat, past the sleeping birds.

I was still churned up, so I got on the internet and surfed. By about 3AM I'd established that the machinery I'd seen in Johnny Vogue's warehouse was mining plant: wheel loaders, dozers and excavators.

Weird.

I fell asleep on that thought and woke up six hours later with another.

Nick Tozzi's exploration lease.

There had to be a connection.

I rang Nick before I got out of bed.

'Tozzi,' he answered.

'Sharp,' I replied.

He paused. 'Yes?'

'We need to meet. I have some … information for you.'

Another pause. 'Important?'

'Maybe.'

He sucked in breath. I couldn't tell if it was in annoyance, or out of concern for what I might have found out. I ran with the latter.

'I'm having drinks with some business associates at 7PM tonight. The Cocked Dog. Come along and we can talk there,' he said.

'Oh,' I said, thinking of Edouardo and the flaming Drambuie.

'Is that a problem?'

'Err … well. Can we meet outside?'

'OK. But why?'

My turn to sigh. 'I was there last night with a friend. We kinda got … kicked out.'

'Don't tell me … you vomited into a pot plant.'

He hung up, laughing, before I could spit out an indignant reply.

I spent the rest of the day washing my clothes and moping around the flat wondering what to do with what I'd learned. Did it mean anything at all? I mean, it's not illegal to own mining gear. Yet the disturbance around those lease documents had been strong.

By late afternoon I was feeling antsy so I threw on my runners and went for another jog. Things went better this time. I stuck to the fairly level route towards the highway and got through four k's without any ill effects.

Feeling cheered up by that, I showered and nibbled on some dry crackers and the last corner of brie. Then I read the daily news on my computer before I got ready to meet Nick.

Bok rang as I was hunting out one of my old handbags.

''Lo babe. Where were you last night? I called around.'

'Had a date,' I said smugly, shovelling things into a worn but still stylish Mandarina Duck satchel.

'You? A date? Who with?'

'Not telling. How're things at the mag?'

'One minute I think we're going to make deadline and then the next I lose my lead story.'

'Huh? Really?'

'My major celebrity interview's fallen through. They've coughed up the withdrawal fee but I still don't have a cover. I don't think I'm cut out for this type of stress.'

I grabbed my keys and handbag, and headed out of the flat. 'Course you are. You thrive on stress. Can't you get an interview with someone else?'

'I'm trying. No one of any significance wants to do this sort of thing on short notice. They want photo shoots in Bali and blah blah.' He sounded bone weary.

'Crapski. Sounds like we need a pizza and DVD night.'

'Yeah. Anyway, how are things with you? Anyone tried to run you down since we spoke. Or shoot you?'

'Very funny,' I said as I left the driveway and walked down the street towards my car. 'I'm fine. That is … oh, bugger … I'll call you back.'

There was a cop car parked behind Mona, and two cops were looking in the windows.

As I got closer I recognised Greg Whitehead and his partner, Tony, both lit up by a street light.

'Whitey?'

He glanced up, smirked, and came over to me. 'Your car been pimped, Tara?'

'Some nut case graffitied it. I had to get it painted. Nice, huh?'

Tony looked me up and down. 'You're the girl without her pants.'

I gritted my teeth. One little slip-up and they couldn't let it go. *Men.*

'Leave this one to you, Greg, my Big Mac's getting cold.' Whitey's partner retired to the car and proceeded to bury his face in a Macca's bag.

'What's the problem, Whitey?' I asked impatiently. 'I'm in a bit of a hurry.'

'Got a report of an abandoned car in Lilac Street. Might have guessed it was yours.'

'It's not abandoned. I just parked it up the street a bit because—'

'Hey, you look hot.' Whitey stepped up closer and leered down my cleavage. The way things were between me and the local constabulary I didn't want to punch a cop, but surely a little shove couldn't—

My hand shot out and contacted Whitey in the chest,

but he grabbed my wrist and held onto it to lessen the impact. We stood there for a frozen few seconds, me glaring, him leering, until the blue BMW roared around the corner and swerved dangerously close to us.

We both leaped back onto the pavement, the beautiful moment between us broken. Then Whitey dropped my hand and pelted back to the squad car shouting, 'Park your car in front of your own house in future.'

With those pearls of wisdom he, Tony and the whopper were gone, chasing the BMW.

I drove well under the speed limit to The Cocked Dog, not trusting my nerves or my current run of luck to not lead me into a speed trap. I parked in the same car park as the previous night and checked my watch. Five minutes early.

I sat in the car and fiddled with my hair using the rear-view mirror. It was shoulder-length and dark at the moment and didn't take much work, which was just as well. I studied my face.

'You have a strong face, Tara,' Aunt Liv liked to say. 'Strong and handsome.'

'What? Like a guy?' I'd retort.

'A character face. Perfect for that physique of yours. You'd look silly if you were too pretty.'

Oh. OK, thanks, Liv. I think.

Right now my reflection told me that my 'strong, handsome' face looked slightly harassed. Wild even.

It also told me that the mysterious blue BMW was

parked behind me, wedged under a street light between a slightly bashed-up, old diesel Pajero, and a 300 series Mercedes Benz.

I flung the door open. This is Australia, the only weapon women carry here is their handbag. Totally effective when it's weighed down with half a bottle of orange Powerade, breath mints, too many loose coins, and a trashy novel.

I advanced on the BMW with my Mandarina Duck satchel and lethal intent, but halfway across a hand grabbed my elbow and swung me around—Nick Tozzi looking altogether too damn fine to be alone in a car park.

'Tara? Where are you going? You look like you're about to murder someone.'

'Th-the car that tried to run me over d-down at the jetty, and then again a few m-minutes ago, it's over th-there,' I stuttered.

I pointed.

He swivelled and looked across. 'Are you sure?'

I nodded.

'Stay here,' he said. 'I'll check it out.'

I went to follow him, but he turned around and stopped me with a ferocious look. 'Stay! Jazz, come with me.'

I suddenly realised he wasn't alone. There was a guy standing a little behind him, almost as tall but younger and slimmer, and wearing a cap despite the fact that it was dark; Jazz Broad, currently the best power forward in Australia.

My knees went weak.

I watched the two giants walk over and around the car, looking in windows the same way Whitey had checked out Mona.

A few minutes later they returned.

'No one in there,' said Tozzi. 'What do you want to do?'

I patted my handbag. 'I've got the plate number. I'll take it down to the police station when I leave here. I've got a copper who'll help me.'

Tozzi smiled; pale giant's teeth. 'That's a relief. I thought they all wanted to put you in jail.'

'Woah!' exclaimed Jazz. 'Who pimped that bitch?'

For one horrible moment I thought he was talking about me, and that I was going to have to punch Tozzi's best player. To my relief though, I realised he was looking at my car. The flames on the bonnet were glowing fluorescent in the dark. I hadn't noticed before.

Bog, what were you thinking?

'Is that your—Tara, is that—' Tozzi couldn't seem to get the words out.

'Someone trashed my car. I … err … got a cheap … paint job. The guy got a bit carried away.'

Tozzi and Jazz exploded in fits of laughter.

When they finally stopped, Tozzi wiped his eyes. 'Jazz, this is Tara Sharp, a work colleague. Don't go jogging with her.' His last comment sent him off into fits of laughter again.

I stuck my hand out to shake Jazz's, and rolled my eyes. 'Is he always so rude? Nice to meet you.'

Jazz nodded. 'You too.'

Nick collected himself again, and patted my shoulder. 'Come inside and have a drink. I insist.'

'But—'

'I'll square it with the manager. The owner and I are good friends.'

I looked up at him doubtfully. I could do with a drink but I felt embarrassed going in there under Tozzi's guarantee. And knowing that the person who'd tried to run me down was close by made me want to camp by the blue BMW with a crowbar.

On the other hand, no one was likely to try to hassle me while I was out with two man mountains. And the truth was, any excuse to be around Nick Tozzi was a good excuse. 'OK. Just one.'

One drink turned into two, and a lively discussion at the bar about the impending NBA finals and the latest changes in the AFL rules. Most of the team had joined us, and I was feeling pretty damn good. I mean, it wasn't often I was the centre of attention with a bunch of guys who were all bigger than me and equally keen to talk trash and sport.

Nick dragged me away from an argument with Jazz over who'd win MVP for NBA for the season, and ushered me over to a booth.

'What did you want to tell me?'

My mood sobered instantly. It had been a good hour of fun and distraction, and now it was over.

'I accidentally saw inside Johnny Vogue's warehouse in Burnside.'

He scowled at me. 'What warehouse? What do you mean "accidentally"?'

'When I went to pick up my car from the spray painter.'

'How did you get out there?'

What was this? Twenty questions? 'I had a date. He took me.'

'You talked your date into taking you to *Bunka*?'

'He's new to Perth and he told me he had a fun time,' I said, defensively. 'Anyway, that's beside the point. The warehouse is full of mining equipment: small plant.'

He stared at me calmly but I could sense his mind jumping, and his aura began to glow. 'And you think what?'

'Well it seems like a kinda odd sideline for someone like Vogue. I can't help but think it might somehow be related to that mining lease of yours.'

Nick had probably made the same connection but his sceptical side wouldn't let him agree with me. 'Hold on a second. There could be a thousand reasons why Viaspa has a shed full of dozers. Maybe he's going into the building industry.'

'It wasn't just dozers. There were loaders and excavators too.'

'Still a weak connection.'

'OK.' I scowled at him and swirled the ice cubes around in my glass, clinking them annoyingly. 'It was just a thought. No need to be condescending.'

His hand shot out to stop me, fingers curling around my wrist. 'Don't be childish, Tara.'

'Tozzi?'

Antonia—Toni—stood only spitting distance from us, teetering over the edge of her heels and a fair dose of whatever. Her beautiful eyes were bloodshot.

Nick slowly released my hand and leaned back against his booth seat. 'What are you doing here?'

'I thought you were drinking with the boys tonight. Then I got a phone call that you were entertaining a woman.'

'A phone call?' He frowned. 'Who from?'

'Does it really matter?' said Toni. From the way her lip was quivering, she was working up a storm of emotion.

I grabbed my handbag and got ready to abandon ship. 'Well, Nick, I'll leave it with you.'

'Tara and I were talking about the burglary,' he explained to Toni.

'Does that require holding her hand?' Toni's quivering lip was joined by brimming eyes.

Waterworks alert.

I stood up. 'He wasn't holding my hand. He was trying to stop me throwing ice cubes at him for being such an arrogant, narrow-minded, ungrateful prat.' I smiled sweetly. 'But I guess you only see his best side.'

With that, and the quickest of waves to the Western Thunder boys who were watching proceedings with sly grins, I left.

Who the hell had phoned Toni Tozzi?

Chapter 36

Deep in indignation, it took me a few moments of standing in the car park to realise that the BMW had gone. I stood staring at the empty car space.

Well, I guess there was one thing I could achieve today.

I hopped into Mona, and drove the three blocks to the Euccy Grove police station, stuffing two mints in my mouth before I went inside.

The copper on desk duty looked like a newbie.

I asked for Fiona Bligh.

'Gone home, love,' he said.

'Can I leave a message for her?'

He handed me a notepad and a pen. 'Go for it.'

I copied down the licence plate number and told her it belonged to the blue BMW that had been following me. I finished with my mobile number.

I gave the young constable a firm look. 'Make sure she gets it, won't you?'

He raised an eyebrow and turned back to his computer.

I called Bok from outside the station. 'You still at work?'

'Where else?' he said.

'Feel like pizza?'

He gave a sigh. 'Why not? Meet you outside Kimmy Koo's in fifteen minutes.'

I was only five minutes away, so I killed time by wandering up to Club Eighteen to see if Edouardo was working.

'He phoned in sick,' said one of the other barmen. 'Said he ate something crook at an Indian restaurant.'

I nodded sympathetically. 'If you think of it, can you tell him Tara called in?'

'Wait on,' he said, and added my name to a list with half a dozen other names on it. 'There. Now I won't forget.'

'His fan club, huh?' I said.

'The rest of us should be so lucky,' he sighed.

I walked back to Mona and drove sedately to Kimmy Koo's. The streets were pretty quiet. Traffic hadn't really caught up with Perth. I wound down my window to let the balmy night air in. Early autumn was my favourite time of year. Short sleeves and brilliant days; long sleeves and brilliant nights.

But even the luminous night couldn't negate Nick Tozzi's casual dismissal of my theory.

By the time Bok and I sat down to eat a family-size cheese and pepperoni at the tables in Kimmy Koo's courtyard, I was fit to burst about it.

Bok sat patiently through the whole tirade, eating, and playing with bits of mozzarella. 'Aaah, it's good to hear about someone else's problems,' he sighed when I'd finished.

'He thinks I'm a space cadet,' I pronounced, crunching a piece of extra-thin crust angrily.

'Well, let's face it, T. You do act kooky. Only those of us who know and love you understand that you see through entirely different eyes from the rest of the world.'

Bok never judged me on the aura stuff. Sometimes it's like that when you've known a person as a kid. You accept things about them that you'd never allow if you met them as an adult. 'I'm not sure about that anymore.'

''Bout what?' he asked, scraping the fallen mushroom from the base of the carton.

'There's got to be other people out there in the world like me. Look at Mr Hara.'

'Yeah, he's kooky too.'

'Hasn't stopped you conning food from his wife,' I retorted.

'Aahhh, meatballs.' He licked his lips. 'Shame they had to go on holidays.' He brightened. 'They must be back soon?'

I rolled my eyes.

'Don't give me that look. She loves cooking. Besides, I was just keeping an eye on you.'

'That the real reason?'

He sighed. 'Do you know how often I get a home-cooked meal, T? At least you can raid your parents' fridge.'

Bok's dad had died a few years ago when Bok was still living in Sydney. After the funeral his mum had gone back to the Philippines to live. There was a bunch of guys and gals out there who would gladly move in and play cook for him, but Bok was flying solo at the moment.

'Maybe we should live together?' I offered.

'What, so you could open the tin of baked beans and eat it before me? Maybe not!'

I shrugged. 'What am I going to do, Bok? About Nick Tozzi and Johnny Vogue.'

This is where my pragmatic friend dragged me back into reality, and metaphorically smacked me around the face. 'Trust your instinct,' he said.

'What?' I wasn't expecting that. Maybe, *Get a grip, Tara*. But ... *trust yourself?*

He grinned at me. 'Maybe I've been spending too much time with oily magazine execs, but I'm sick of other people's agendas running my life. Don't let that happen to you. Next thing you know you're just a whipping boy.'

I reached across the table and gave him the last glob of mozzarella. 'Hang in there,' I said. 'Things'll get better.'

We talked about the magazine then until Kimmy Koo kicked us out of the courtyard about midnight.

I hugged Bok in the car park and drove home.

As I fell asleep, anchored to my bed by a kilo of cheese, an idea had well and truly planted itself.

Chapter 37

'Can I help you?' asked the guy behind the desk at SUP Assayers Inc.

'I want to enquire about getting a mineral sample analysed,' I said. I was dressed in my best anonymous clothes, wearing my hair in a ponytail. *Olga Ordinary*, I hoped.

'Sure. Fill out these forms about what you want. There'll be a charge of thirty dollars per two hundred grams.' His aura looked thin and miserable like an animal that needed to be stroked. Its colour was almost indistinguishable from the bone-coloured walls and toning carpet. Unhealthy.

I took the paperwork. 'Kinda breathtaking decor, isn't it?'

He stared at me for a moment, wondering if he'd heard right. Then suddenly he burst out laughing, and his aura flickered alive and became distinguishable from the surroundings. It turned a lovely soft green colour like spring grass.

I grinned madly at him.

'Here, I'll help you,' he said. 'Some of the questions can be ambiguous.'

After I gave a fake name and address, I found out that James-of-the-soft-green-aura was just doing sick relief for a woman who'd had a breakdown, and that he normally worked in the company's other office.

'So what happens to my little sample bag now?' I asked, bringing out some of JoBob's best garden soil from my Mandarina Duck and dropping it on the counter.

'We courier it out to the lab and they do their thing. Takes about two weeks to get the result.'

'That long?' I got all wide-eyed. 'Does it have to go to Neverland and back?'

He chuckled. 'No, Burnside.'

'Burnside?' My psychic sensitivities began to smoulder. 'I thought Burnside was just spray painters and refrigeration storage places.'

'There's a lab out there that does the analysis.'

'In Burnside?

'Yeah, right near the government land alottment.'

'Government land? Sounds like the state housing in Euccy Grove.'

James rolled his eyes. 'Major difference in the council rates though, I bet.'

We exchanged understanding looks, the way people do when they know a city, and all the nuances of wealth and poverty that exist there.

Then the door opened and another customer entered

the office.

I smiled warmly at him. 'You've been wonderful, James. I hope you get back to your other office soon.'

He smiled back and, if nothing else, I was pleased to see that his aura stayed bright.

'Say, you wanna get a coffee later?' he said.

Crap. 'Sure thing. Got a few things happening at the moment. Maybe when I come back in to collect the report.'

His face fell a little. 'OK.'

I caught the lift to the dimly lit basement car park and wandered around looking for my car. When I found it (that's right, I parked in one of the 'Reserved for SUP Employees Only' bays), I threw the receipt and SUP pamphlet on the passenger seat and slumped in behind the driving wheel, resting my head on the sheepskin cover. *Form 1a–f* had severely taxed my Thursday morning brain.

Thursday morning!

I banged my head on the steering wheel. That meant two days until my meeting with Peter Delgado. I had to run in the triathlon before that. I wondered which was more likely to kill me—the triathlon or Delgado?

Stop being hysterical, I told myself severely. *And get moving.*

I sat up and put the key in the ignition. 'Aaaagh!'

A dead bird lay squashed under my windscreen wiper; neck broken, beak wide. And not just any bird: a pink and grey galah. For one shocking moment I thought it was Brains or Hoo.

Get out of the car, Tara. Go and look. Identify the body, ordered a bossy voice in my head.

Operating under its command, I got out and examined the corpse. The bird was neither Brains nor Hoo and had been dead a while. It was stiff and crawling with ants.

I reached into the car and grabbed the SUP pamphlet. Then I pulled back the wiper blade, wrapped the bird up in the paper and took it to the nearest rubbish bin.

'Uuugh.'

I ran back to the car, slammed the door and squealed out of the basement. When I was back in the sunshine, and a reasonable distance from the city centre, I let out a scream.

I did that intermittently down Stirling Highway, stopping only when I got to the corner of Lilac Street.

I parked and ran down the driveway straight to the bird's cage. They were busy shagging and looked quite annoyed at the interruption.

The pain in my chest eased enough for me to catch my breath—then I saw a photograph pegged to the food gate. It had been taken with an instant Polaroid; a picture of the dead bird under my windscreen wiper.

A sweet little message from some sweet little psycho.

I snatched the photo and jammed it in my pocket, then

I grabbed hold of the cage and began to wheel it up the back of the driveway towards my flat.

The birds started screeching and flapping.

Dad came out to see what the commotion was all about. 'Tara?' He peered down from the pool verandah.

'Hi Dad. Just moving the birds outside the flat. You're away a lot. I thought they might like the company.'

'Ohh.' Dad looked nonplussed. 'Have you checked with your mother?'

'Uh,' I grunted with the weight of the cage up the incline. Water sloshed onto my feet from their drinking bowl. 'No—but—I—will.'

Joanna appeared on the verandah beside him. 'Will what?'

I repeated myself.

My mother frowned while I pushed the birds over a hump in the pavers and into a nice shady spot under the eaves near my door. 'There,' I said. 'Perfect.'

'Well, if you're suddenly feeling so responsible, Tara, you can feed and change their water every day as well, cover them at night, exercise them regularly and give them treats. Otherwise you can *put them back where they were.*'

Joanna wore her most formidable expression.

What could I say? Someone was threatening to kill the birds because of something illegal I'd got mixed up in and now I had to protect them? 'OK,' seemed so much easier.

We chatted for a few minutes about other things and

then I excused myself. As I did, their voices floated down to me. 'Will she ever grow up, Bob? She's so … careless and impulsive.'

'Don't worry, Jo. She's a good kid. She'll get there in the end.'

'You're too soft on her, Bob. I've been telling you that for years.'

'Yes, dear. You have.' Their voices trailed off as they moved back inside.

Good kid? I sighed. I was neither of those things. When would they ever realise?

I sat and pondered my miseries over a back issue of *Marie Claire for a while. Then I brought up Google Maps on my phone and began to examine the Burnside streets.*

Much to my annoyance, I realised that I needed information from Garth. He didn't answer his mobile when I rang it, so I tried his work number.

'Wilmot & Associates,' he answered.

Garth had never had a full-time PA. He was too tight.

'Where's your mobile?' I asked.

'Right next to me,' he answered, surprised into the truth.

'So you're ignoring me?'

'Tara?'

'Who else?'

'Yes, I *am* avoiding you. When you're not being abusive, you're asking me crazy questions. Why wouldn't I avoid you?'

'Because your life is so boring that my presence in it actually livens it up. And you owe me for the Whitey thing.'

'I told you it was a joke. I never thought he'd ring you. I was mad at you because you laughed at me about the break-in.'

I didn't let him distract me. 'You also blabbed to the cops.'

'I kept it as general as I could, but I had to tell them something about you. So I chose things anyone would say.' He sighed. 'Come on then, what is it?'

'Where's the government land in Burnside?'

'Wha-at?'

'You heard me. I've got my street directory open, I just need some landmarks.'

'Why would I know that?'

'Because you drove taxis to put yourself through uni. Perth's not a very big city.'

He sighed again. 'I always forget you know so much about me. Look north of the railway line on your map, right on the border of the next suburb. There's a triangular-shaped wedge of land. The north-east freeway runs along one side of it, and … I don't know … Lucas Road, I think, runs the other side.'

Lucas Road. I flipped quickly to the index and back. 'Got it. Thanks Gartho.'

'Tara,' he said quietly. 'What sort of trouble are you in?'

'What do you mean?'

'When did you last call me Gartho?'

He was right. Knowing someone well worked two ways. It seemed anxiety was leaking out of me in endearments. 'Gotta go. Talk to you later.'

I hung up and glanced at my watch. My meeting with Delgado was on Saturday morning. That gave me about forty or so hours to work out what was going on and how to handle it.

I rang Wal. 'Wal, it's Tara Sharp. I need you to ride shotgun with me to Bunka.'

'When?'

'Now. This afternoon.'

'No can do. Gotta set up for a gig at the Subi.'

The Subiaco Hotel was only a fifteen-minute drive away from Lilac Street. 'What time will you be finished?'

'Around 4PM.'

'I'll pick you up then.'

'Gotta be back by midnight to pack up.'

'No problem.'

'Ah … should I bring any … deterrents?' he asked with a hopeful note in his voice.

I thought about the dead galah on my windscreen. 'Yeah. Please do.'

'Sweeeeet,' he said.

Chapter 38

I dressed for Bunka in jeans and runners then snagged a jacket over my shoulders. Then I added a cap that I could pull down over my hair.

I took a look in the mirror. Too designer still, I decided, and swapped the jeans for some worn but fitted track pants. The tracks clung too closely to my legs but at least they didn't scream money.

Satisfied, I locked up the flat, and tipped the birds' crunched seed husks into a dead pot plant. The birds were still a little flustered by their change of location and Brains tried to bite me when I reached in with fresh seeds.

'Silly bird,' I said sternly.

She took another swipe and nicked the tip of my finger.

'Owww!' I snatched my finger away but Hoo sidled up against the bars, clicking at me. He wanted a cuddle.

I scratched him with my non-injured finger and he purred like a cat, cocking his head at an impossible angle so I could get under his chin. Brains kept a baleful distance, attacking the sunflower seeds.

Why did they remind me of Fiona Bligh and Bill Barnes?

It was still a bit early to put on their night cover so I slung the canvas over one corner of the cage and left them fighting over a peanut.

I pulled into the car park of the Subi just after 4PM. My phone rang as I undid my seatbelt.

'Tara? It's Ed.'

'Edouardo?'

'Yeah, him too,' he laughed.

'Are you OK?' I asked. 'They said you had food poisoning.'

'Must have been the Indian food,' he said innocently.

'Must have,' I agreed. 'Listen. I'm sorry. That was a lousy date.'

'I wouldn't call it lousy…' he said. 'More … interesting.'

'Yeah well… I'll make it up to you some time.'

'How about tomorrow night?'

Yikes! He actually wanted a second date. 'Err. Got some work on.'

'Saturday night?'

'Su-ure.'

'You don't sound certain?'

He was right on that score. I mean there was Delgado to think about, and the triathlon. And then there were my mixed-up feelings for Nick Tozzi. 'What are you like at body massage?'

'S-say again?' he spluttered.

'I'm running in a team triathlon at Perry Lakes on Saturday morning. I might need reviving.' For all sorts of reasons.

'I can't think of anything I'd rather do,' he said in his sexiest voice.

My mouth went totally dry. I mean … I'd been joking. Was he? My turn to splutter. 'T-talk to you l-later then.'

'I've got all of Saturday off, so I'll come and cheer for you at the finish line,' he said, and clicked off.

I got out of the car and walked into the band lounge of the Subi, sporting a blush that could have lit up half the brothels in Northbridge. Fortunately, the place was empty apart from the roadies.

Wal was crawling around on the stage, with a rollie about to burn up his lip, and a bunch of electrical leads in one hand. I watched him connect them through puffs of smoke, and wondered how the hell he could see what he was doing.

When he'd finished, he spat the rollie out on the stage, not even bothering to stamp it out, and stood up. Collecting his jacket and backpack from the back of a chair he headed down towards me.

We didn't speak but, as we reached the door, a bunch of cat whistles pierced the air from the roadies over at the sound desk. One of them offered to lend Wal a stepladder.

Wal stiffened and hustled me through the door.

'Next time, wait outside,' he said gruffly.

'Oh?' I said, confused.

'You're killing my rep-u-tay-shun.'

It took me nearly to Bunka to swallow that down. Like before, when we'd been having coffee, part of me wanted to giggle. Then there was the other part of me that wanted to kick him in the kneecaps.

He broke the silence finally as we cruised past Burnside train station. 'So, what's the story?'

I looked out for Cass, but the platform was full of nine-to-fivers, knocking off early. I wondered if Thursday afternoon was like that everywhere in the world.

'I probably won't need you to do anything,' I said. 'I just want to check out some things in an office out here. Got chased when I brought the car out to Bog.'

Wal took out his tobacco and started rolling another smoke. 'Yeah. Bog heard about it. They reckon you can run pretty damn quick for a chick.'

I gave him a sideways look. 'You heard about it?'

He shrugged. 'Bog's shut up shop for a while. Cops been sniffing around.'

I wanted to ask more but I didn't. Less I knew about 'Wal's World' the better. There was one thing I couldn't resist asking, though. 'What's in your bag?'

He rolled the numbers on the chain lock and unzipped it. 'Just my working kit. Nothing flash.'

'OK, put it away,' I said, after glimpsing the butt of a pistol and a knife sheath. 'You got a licence for that stuff?'

He stuck the rollie between his lips and lit it with a zippo he pulled from his pocket. 'Yeah. Sure.'

I had a moment of complete panic as we turned down Lucas Road. I was driving in a car with an armed and dangerous man. And I'd invited him. What was wrong with me? Then I thought of the galah, stiff and ant-eaten, left under my windscreen wiper. Wal was my insurance.

We cruised up and around the government land strip until I located SUP's lab building. It was an ugly little demountable adjacent to a more solid steel-framed government warehouse. I parked a way back from the driveway, and told Wal to stay put.

'That all?' he asked.

'For the moment. If I can't find out what I want, we might have to hang around for a bit. You know, until it gets dark.'

'Sweet.' He opened the door and stuck his feet up in the vee of the hinge. A bag of sandwiches materialised out of his kitbag. Egg by the smell of it.

I raised my eyebrows at the odour, but he ignored me, so I hustled down the long driveway to the demountable.

The blonde desk-girl had a comb in one hand and was rummaging in her handbag with the other. 'We're closed,' she said without ceremony, pulling out a packet of menthol cigarettes.

'I'm looking for a business, and I've lost the address.'

She frowned, clearly not in a helping mood. 'What kind of business? I've gotta catch a train.'

'Mining,' I said. 'Got an appointment with some bloke called Mitch. I sell diggers.'

Her annoyed look was amplified by the way her aura was zipping around her body like a go-kart on the speedway; a dull red aura with not much going for it other than its speed.

'It's a really important meeting. Twenty bucks in it if you can help me,' I said, waving a note.

'Joey, can you come out here? Someone's lost. I'm late.' She shrugged towards the guy who appeared from a back room. 'Try him.'

I scrambled for an excuse to keep her in the office a bit longer. 'Are you catching the 4.30 to the city?' I asked.

'Yeah. Why?' Her eyes narrowed.

'Haven't you heard? There's a strike. No trains until 5.30PM. I just drove by the station. It's crazy down there.'

She wrinkled her forehead. 'Never heard nothin' about it.' She glanced at the computer. 'I just shut down.' She dropped her bag back down on the desk and started rummaging in it again.

'Might be worth waiting till the worst's over,' I said, helpfully.

'What you looking for?' asked Joey, who looked like one haircut short of Cousin It. A wookie compressed into a medium-sized white lab coat.

'A mining warehouse. I sell diggers.'

Joey grunted and shrugged. 'I can drive you around, to look, if you like?' he said, hopefully.

I ignored the offer. 'You got anyone else out the back there who knows the area?'

Joey went over to the back door. 'Hey, Zach. Girl needs help out here.'

Zach emerged a minute later. Slim, white lab coat, dark, oily hair and small scar on his chin. His aura was the colour of a pair of tan boots I used to own, and sprinkled with black dots.

'What is this place anyway?' I asked, looking around. 'Pathology lab?'

'Assay,' said Blondie, texting on her phone.

'Assay lab? Think there'd be more of you.'

'We've got another guy,' said Joey. 'His wife's just had a baby though.'

'Uh. Oh.' I looked at slim Zach. 'I sell mining equipment. Got an appointment with a guy—lost the address though.' Now I had them all together, I dropped the bomb. 'Think his name was Viper ... no ... Viaspa.'

Bang. Zach's aura expanded like popcorn. The other two didn't change.

Zach shook his head. 'Never heard of him.'

'No sweat. Thanks.' I headed to the door as a text message chimed on Blondie's phone. 'Hey!' she called out after me, 'There's no stri—'

I slammed the door and high-tailed it down the driveway.

Wal tucked his leg in and shut his door as I pulled away from the curb. 'So?'

I turned off Lucas Road at the nearest street, and pulled in between two parked cars. 'I need to tail someone.'

Wal looked at me. He'd been cleaning his teeth with dental floss and it hung out the side of his mouth still. 'In this car? Thought you was smart.'

'No choice.' I peered out of my back window towards the SUP building.

'You need a white car, or blue. Like that one.' Wal tapped my shoulder and pointed to the car in front.

'What do you mean?' I said blankly.

His hand fell to his backpack. 'I got the gear here. Could wire it in a few minutes.'

'You mean "steal" it?'

Wal tongued the dental floss. 'Borrow.'

'Absolutely NOT! And too late anyway,' I said, as a red SUV pulled out from behind the demountable. It turned left onto Lucas in the direction of the train station. From what I could see, Blondie was in the passenger seat and Zach was driving.

I swung Mona out and followed at a fair distance. 'He's dropping her at the train station,' I muttered to Wal.

But he'd already settled his head against the door and closed his eyes.

Chapter 39

I found the last space in the Burnside Station car park and slotted in there, craning my neck out of my window to see the SUV, standing illegally in the taxi bay near the steps to the platform. Zach and Blondie must have been having a deep and meaningful.

'Hey, that you Tara?'

I glanced around. Cass was leaning against the car park railing, bathed in her freckly cinnamon aura; not sickly, but not quite healthy either. She wore thick purple eye shadow, a plain black shift and some tatty platform Goth boots. My handbag hung off her arm like a trophy. Her peeps ambled up behind her, smoking and sharing coolers.

'Cass?'

'Watcha doing out this way again?' She ducked under the railing and came closer, staring in the window at Wal.

He was breathing heavily with snoring imminent.

'I prefer Nick,' she said with a curl of her lip.

'So do I.' I grinned. 'Wal and I ... work together.'

Wal gave a little snore.

'Oh. OK. He looks kinda familiar.'

'Roadie. Hey Cass, you know a lot of people around here?' I asked.

She inclined her head and fiddled with her nose-ring. 'Sure, I guess.'

'You know the guy driving the red SUV over by the steps?'

Lifting her head, she squinted over the top of the parked cars. 'Seen the wheels before. Lemme go look closer.'

I lifted Wal's tobacco packet up off his lap and passed it to her. 'Be discreet, huh?'

She dropped the tobacco into her bag. 'You mean, like in the movies?'

I nodded.

A light came into her bored face and she turned to say something to her peeps.

Her boyfriend, Danny, came over obediently and slung his arm around her. They walked towards the SUV, entwined like they were totally engrossed in each other. When they got parallel to the car, they stopped, and started kissing.

They stayed there, lip-locked, for a bit. Then Cass pulled away and rolled a smoke. She knocked on the SUV window.

The window glided down the way electric ones do and she bent in, cigarette on her lips. Blondie extended an arm, lit the cig and the window went up again.

Cass and Danny boy shared the cig in a slow unhurried way and then wandered slowly back into the car park. Cass sent Danny back to the peeps and sauntered over to Mona.

'Slick work,' I said.

She gave a grin and shook her head in a way that made all the piercings in her ears shake. 'I know 'em both.'

I held my breath.

'Karnie Foster. She wuz two years ahead of me at school. We did Saturday Ds together a few times. She finished school though. Got a job.'

Detention. *Why was I not surprised?* 'And the guy?'

Cass's lip curled. 'She could do better. Sleaze bag. He's name's Lupi.'

'Zach?'

'Yeah, that's it. Zach Lupi. Thinks he's got some kinda big dick because he got connections to Sammy B and Johnny Vogue.'

My body went cold. 'You mean Sam Barbaro?'

'Uhuh.'

'You sure about that?'

'Course. Sammy and Zach fixed my sister up with some amps. Turns out it wuz cut with baby powder or some shit. Put her in hospital. They never told her not to inject it. If I wuz a guy I'd smack 'em both down.'

I screwed up my face in sympathy.

'How come you know Sammy B?' she asked. 'You use?'

'No. Just acquaintances,' I said. 'Listen, thanks. That helps me a lot.' On impulse I fumbled in my glove box and found a card. 'If you're ever in trouble … I'll help if I can.'

Cass stared at it, frowning in concentration. Her aura flattened and I realised she couldn't read.

'It's got my phone number on it. You can call me.'

Her face relaxed a little. 'Wot's yer job?'

I ran through a few definitions in my mind. 'Sort of like a private investigator.'

Her face tensed. 'You work for the cops?'

'No. Definitely not,' I said.

She relaxed again. 'I don't do cops, Tara. Get it?'

I nodded. 'Completely.'

Danny called out something I couldn't hear. She sent him a scowl. No prizes for guessing who wore the pants.

'Later,' she said to me and walked off.

Shortly afterwards, the SUV pulled away from the curb minus Karnie Foster. As she wobbled up the platform steps in her high heels, I eased Mona out of the parking lot and followed Zach Lupi.

Most of the traffic was heading towards the highway, so it was easy enough keeping him in sight as he doubled back through Burnside. Just on dark, he pulled into a shabby duplex in the next suburb over; one tree in the yard, no lawn, no fence and a gravel driveway.

280

I drove past without being noticed. *I think*.

Wal continued to sleep: three heavy breaths, nothing, and then a deep snore. With that symphony as my companion, I parked around the corner from Lupi's house and settled in to wait.

By about eleven, I was starving and desperate for a toilet. Wal had stirred once or twice to change positions. I considered waking him up for conversation's sake then thought better of it.

Instead, I pondered—again—on the identity of the suited man with Johnny Vogue at the warehouse. It was really bugging me that I couldn't remember where I'd seen him.

When I got tired of coming up with nothing, I moved on to an entertaining fantasy about who I'd choose between Edouardo and Tozzi if they both fell at my feet and begged me to have them. Edouardo was so sweet and so gorgeous but a little too eager, even when he was trying not to be. Tozzi had everything, including the attitude that goes with it. He was also married to a goddess.

I glanced at my watch: 11.15. Wal had to be back at the Subi by midnight. I reluctantly admitted to myself that I'd just wasted four hours of my life. Then Zach Lupi emerged from the duplex and drove off.

I followed at what I hoped was a fair distance, and in five minutes we were back in Burnside and Zach was turning into the street that harboured Johnny Vogue's warehouse.

Lupi stopped at the gate and got out to grapple with the padlock.

I drove past, heart thumping, around the block, and cut into the laneway with my headlights off. But by the time I reached the spear grass I'd previously fallen into, Lupi's car had gone.

Damn. Was he inside? Or had he driven off? I wound down my window and peered out into the dark.

I couldn't see much but the alley smelled of Davidoff aftershave. I recognised it because it was one of Garth's favourites.

'Hey Wal,' I whispered. 'Do you smell something?'

Wal didn't answer.

But someone else did.

'You know what I do to nosy bitches?' said Lupi, dressed in black and hugging a baseball bat.

I reached for the ignition, but an arm pinned me back against the seat. The hand that belonged to the arm held a pistol.

'You know what I do with fancy smellin' wog boys who like to bully wimmin?' said Wal in an expressionless voice. 'I like to blow their fuckin' heads off, and watch their body flop around like a chook.'

Lupi dropped the baseball bat and held his hands up. He knew crazy and dangerous when he heard it. 'Steady Eddie, mate. Mistaken identity. S'all. Chill. Chill.'

'Yeah,' said Wal pointing the fingers of his free hand to his face. 'Well look close, mate. Don't mistake this identity again. It'll come after ya. Now piss orf.'

Lupi went back down the alley in a flash.

Nearly as quickly, I started Mona and drove out of Burnside, not sure whether to cry from relief or horror.

We were speeding down the Eastern Highway into the city by the time my terror had settled enough to let me speak.

'Thanks Wal,' I said, thickly.

All I got was silence and a lolling head in return.

I woke him up when we got to the Subi car park.

'You been doing this long?' I asked.

Wal stretched and burped out something that smelled like eggy fish cakes. 'Doin' what?'

I leaned as far away from him as I could, and cracked the window to let in some air. 'Sleeping all the time.'

He scratched his head and looked around. 'What's the time?'

'Near midnight.'

He blinked at me. 'Yeah? True? Well, usually I sleep days. Lately though…' He shrugged and bent down to zip up his bag of goodies, dismissing the conversation.

Wal was a roadie who worked nights, so I guess that made sense. But there was something about it, the suddenness, and how deeply he fell, that didn't seem right. I wasn't going to let it go at that. 'I think you need to see a doctor.'

'Say wha-at?'

'I'm serious, Wal. No one sleeps like that; sudden and deep with stuff happening around them.'

He nodded, taking in what I'd said. I think.

'And thanks again for tonight. That guy … well … I owe you a bunch of free classes,' I finished.

'See you Saturday morning, Teach.'

He got out of the car and ambled towards the back entrance; a short, brawny, crazy, black-jeaned roadie who was scarier than any tall, brawny, crazy guy I'd ever met.

Chapter 40

I tossed all night, fretting about a bunch of things. Should I ring Nick and tell him what I'd learned? What *had* I learned? A guy at the assay lab was connected to Johnny Vogue and Sam Barbaro. How did I know that? I'd seen his aura flicker, and a young scrubber from Bunka had confirmed my suspicions. Yeah, right!

Then I moved on to my next set of worries. Had I trained enough to not embarrass myself in the triathlon? What was I going to say to Peter Delgado? Who'd threatened the birds? Was the suited guy important?

Somewhere around 4AM I drifted off, only to be woken by Hoo and Brains screeching for proper daylight and attention. My phone told me it was only 7AM. Why were the damn birds always up with … well, the damn birds. I stumbled outside and uncovered them, topping up their food and water.

They both scowled at me and got busy with their morning antics. Mating season was supposed to taper off in about March—which was now—but I couldn't see any signs of it. That reminded me, I'd been back living at JoBob's for almost three months and I still only had a little under two hundred dollars to my name, plus considerably more aggravation than I'd had when I arrived. I hadn't touched Delgado's retainer and I wouldn't. Not in a million.

I decided to go for a run to fend off a glum attack and pulled on my shoes, shorts and a top. Heading towards the river, I was determined to make a better job of the hill climb. After all, I hadn't eaten a tin of baked beans.

Encouragingly, I got halfway up the climb towards Nick Tozzi's new house before I was forced to walk. I toyed with the idea of knocking on his front door to discuss the Barbaro–Lupi connection, but images of Toni in a mushroom silk negligee melted the whole idea away.

Instead I trudged to the top of Devil's Elbow and looped back towards Lilac Street. The return leg was mostly downhill, and I recovered enough to jog the last few streets to home.

My phone rang as I limped down the driveway, and I pulled it out of my sweaty crop strap. I used to wear a bumbag until Bok pointed out how tragically eighties I looked. It's alright for him—he never jogs!

'Tara Sharp,' I said.

'Bligh here, Sharp.'

'How did you get my number?' I asked.

She made an exasperated noise. 'You filled in the form,

remember? Name, address, contact numbers? You also left it on your note.'

Doh!

'Look, this is a heads-up. We've got an ID on the blue BMW but…'

'But?' I said, listening closer.

'It's a bit delicate and we don't have anything to charge the driver with yet. I just wanted to say, DO NOT APPROACH the car if you see it, and call me right away. You've got my mobile number now, so put it into your directory.'

'Bligh, you're giving me your phone number,' I said after a moment. 'Are they trying to kill me?'

She was silent and I pictured her hair tucked up tight behind her ears, her eyebrows drawn together in their semi-permanent frown.

'Possibly,' she said, at last.

'Shouldn't I be under police protection then?' I squeaked.

'Don't be a wuss, Sharp. And call me if you see the car.'

'*Don't be a wuss!* Is that how the law protects innocent citizens?'

'Bye.' She was gone.

I got into the shower feeling more angry than scared. Obviously I was going to have to take care of myself.

Which led me to make a couple of decisions: I *would* talk to Tozzi, and I needed to cancel tomorrow's Social Skills class. I also had to find out more about Johnny

Vogue and Nick Tozzi's backgrounds.

I towelled off, threw on a tracksuit and t-shirt, and emptied my fridge of JoBob booty; Nutrigrain, milk, toast and Swiss cheese, and a packet of figs. *Yum*.

Then I settled on my couch with my laptop and phone.

First I rang Tozzi's number.

'It's Tara,' I said, when he answered. 'Did you get your assay done at the SUP labs?'

'Why do you want to know?'

'Just answer, please.'

'Yes.'

'Then you should know that one of the guys working in the lab is in tight with Barbaro and Johnny Vogue.'

Silence.

'Nick?'

'I appreciate your interest. But, please, Tara. Stay out of this.'

'Bit late for that,' I said and hung up.

Next I rang Lloyd Honey.

'Mr Honey, it's Tara Sharp.'

'Ms Sharp,' he said, then hesitated. 'Is there something you forgot to tell me?'

'No, nothing like that,' I said, reassuringly.

'That's a relief. Please call me Lloyd.'

'Lloyd, I'm sorry to call in a favour so soon, but you said you might be able to help me on a background check.'

'Yes.'

'I'm looking for information on some people. The sort

of thing you couldn't find from just asking around.'

'Certainly. Who is it you want to know about?'

I gave him the names. To his credit he didn't react. 'I'll see what I can do. I'll call you with my findings. Is there anything you're looking for particularly?'

'A connection between them.'

'Fine.'

'Lloyd, this is … sensitive,' I said in my best PI voice.

'Of course, Ms Sharp.'

'Tara, please.'

'Yes.'

'Bye.'

I sat for a moment, thinking, before I sent off texts to Harvey and Enid cancelling the next class.

Then I rang Wal. I had to raise my voice so he could hear me over the birds' screeching; maybe moving them so close to my door hadn't been such a clever idea.

'I'm running a triathlon tomorrow. Have to cancel class until next week. Now tell me, what's the best way to lose someone who's following your car?'

He answered as if it was the most normal question in the world. 'Simple,' said Wal. 'Traffic lights. Slow down towards them. Pass through late on the orange and they'll get stuck. And don't go places you don't know.'

'Why's that?'

'If you get caught in a dead end or something, gives 'em time to catch up. You still got problems, Teach?'

'Yeah. A little.' Cough.

'Need me?'

'Got nothing to pay you with, Wal,' I confessed.

''Bout that,' he said slowly. 'Went to the doctor this morning like you said to.'

'Oh,' I couldn't keep the surprise out of my voice. 'And?'

'Gotta have some tests, but he thinks mebbe I got narcolepsy.'

'Narcolepsy?' Well that made sense.

'Doc says it's lucky I came to him before I had an accident. Told me not to drive until it's sorted.'

'Oh,' again.

'Shit happens,' he said eloquently. 'Means I can't drive the truck anymore for the band. So I'm thinking mebbe I'll come work for you full time.'

'But I can't pay you, Wal,' I gasped. *Nor do I want a psycho, narcoleptic ex-roadie as my employee.*

'Got that all figured out. I'll get the disability pension now. And you can cash me up on the side when your business builds up. Man's gotta have something to do, Teach.'

'I— I… Look, I've gotta go, Wal. But let's talk about it later on.' *Coward.*

I dropped my phone on the couch and writhed around in horror. *OMG. OMG. OMG.*

'Tara?' a muffled voice called out. 'Are you *alright*?'

Dad was at the door, face pressed to the glass.

I cut short my dramatics and jumped up. 'What's

wrong?' I asked, opening the slider.

He looked flustered. 'Tara, do you have Brains in here with you?'

My heart missed a beat, and I rushed past him to look into the cage. The main door was open. Hoo was sitting over the water container looking slightly bewildered. Alone.

'But she was there when I came back from my run. And then I had a shower and made some calls…' I trailed off as I remembered the screeching when I was on the phone to Wal.

'Dad, you'd better come in,' I said, shutting the cage door.

His flustered expression turned into something much sallower. He came in and sat stiffly on the end of the couch. 'What is it, Tara?' he said, tersely.

'I've got some stuff going on to do with my new work. Some criminals are involved. I'm—I'm working with the police to help catch them.'

He digested this for a moment. 'You're working *with* the police. Are you sure about that?'

'Dad!' I feigned hurt. 'I think one of the crims has taken Brains.' I paused, letting that sink in as well.

'That's why you moved them around the back here. To protect them?'

I nodded. 'Didn't do a very good job of it.'

'But what's it all about?'

'I can't tell you yet, Dad. It's police stuff. But I will

soon. I promise.' Too much. I sounded like something out of a B-grade cop show and the suspicious look in Dad's eyes suggested he thought so too.

He stood up slowly, his brow crinkling into something quite stern. 'You need to sort out your affairs, young lady, and bring our bird back. Is that clear?'

Dad hadn't used that tone of voice on me since I'd broken his lawnmower in high school, racing against Mr Bok's ride-on.

He hadn't finished either. 'If anything happens to Brains, your mother will be heartbroken. And I'm telling you very clearly, Tara, I WILL NOT HAVE IT.'

I don't know what I'd expected him to say, but it sure wasn't that. 'Yes, Dad,' I said meekly.

He turned to leave then stopped at the door. 'I'll padlock the cage door and give you a key. In the meantime I'll tell your mother that you've taken Brains to the vet because she has beak mite. You'll then report that the vet recommended an overnight stay. That should give you time to sort this out.'

'Yes, Dad.'

He nodded and left.

Chapter 41

Dad's visit left a throbbing lump in my stomach. It wasn't very often my saintly father got peeved with me, and the guilt was almost worse than the thought that someone in a blue BMW was trying to kill me. But nowhere near as bad as the thought that Brains had been hurt or killed because of me.

I fished around under the couch until I found my thongs and walked to the corner deli to buy some phone credit and a large bag of clinkers. The clinkers raised my blood sugar level sufficiently to narrow my panic from a gushing waterfall into a fast-flowing stream.

I fell into a Q and A with myself.

Who's taken Brains? I asked.

The BMW driver.

Possibly. But who is that?

The crazy woman who rang me?

Yeah. But who was she?

Whitey's wife?

Hmmm. She had been acting pretty crazy in the shop with Smitty.

Peter Delgado?

Nah. Never get his hands dirty.

A random?

Possible again, but unlikely given the dead bird and the photo.

Sam Barbaro?

He said he'd get me. Plus, he and Zach Lupi could have worked out by now that I was the snooper at the SUP labs.

Barbaro was the most likely.

My head hurt.

Then I had a brain wave. Maybe two different people were threatening me.

If that was true then there were still only two I was likely to be able to locate. June Whitey and Sam Barbaro.

Whitey lived in Mosman Park. That was a cinch. But how did I find out where Barbaro was, while he was out on bail?

It took me the entire bag of clinkers to come up with an idea. I dialled in the credit and then rang Bok.

He sounded harassed. 'Can't talk, T. Major crisis here. I've got a day to find another major profile for the first edition or I might as well give the Louies back.'

Louie was Bok's name for his Louis Vuitton travel luggage. He'd been given it as a sweetener when he'd got the new job.

I wanted to cry on his shoulder, but I sucked it up. Bok had his own stuff going on; I couldn't run to him every time I had a problem.

'You'll find someone,' I said confidently.

'Sure.' After a bit more chitchat, he hung up.

In the time it had taken me to walk up and back to the deli, Dad *had put a padlock on the cage door. Short of carrying the ten-by-eight-feet birdcage off the property, or using a gas t*orch, no one was going to get at Hoo.

Meanwhile the poor darling was busy trying to bite the lock off through the bars. I scratched his head but he was much too engrossed to stop.

I went into the flat and fell on my bed. My feet were sore from running, and I hadn't felt this miserable since my ex-boyfriend, Pascal, had cleared out of our semi-detached with all our furniture and our share-buddy, Janis.

After some long aching moments of soul searching, I did what any desperate woman would do—I called a crazy, narcoleptic, ex-roadie for help.

'Wal?'

'You gonna let me work for you, Teach?'

I hesitated one last time before I sealed my doom. 'Yeah. OK. Deal. Remember, there's no money to pay you with at the moment, but I'll try and cover any expenses.' *As if!*

'Cigs?' he asked.

'No.'

'Booze?'

'No.'

'Bullets?'

'Errr … no.'

'Hmmph.'

'But I'll get you a business card,' I said, thinking of Bok's colour photocopier. 'Now, here's your first job. I need to find a guy called Sam Barbaro, really quickly.'

'Barbaro? Did he used to work at the servo on Forest and Gugeri? No forehead? Aggro?'

I remembered Barbaro's angry surprise when he'd collided with me, his ugly expression. Then later on, Bligh's inquisition.

'He's the one.'

I waited for Wal to continue, but all I got was the sound of heavy breathing.

'Wal!'

'Yo!' he sounded startled.

'Did you go to sleep?'

'Who's that?'

'It's Tara Sharp. We were talking about Sam Barbaro,' I said, between clenched teeth. 'I need to find him. Quick. Today. Wal, concentrate, please.'

'Oh that,' said Wal, collecting himself. 'Too easy.'

'What do you mean?'

'He lives in the boarding house behind mine.'

'For real?'

'Yup,' said Wal. 'That mean you'd be coming over here right now?'

'Why?'

'I'm out of baccy. Champion Ruby.'

I gave an exasperated sigh. 'Tell me your address.'

Chapter 42

It should be too ridiculous to be true, but the sad fact was that Perth was so small, as cities go, that it wasn't even weird that a small-time criminal and a big-time crazy had gravitated towards boarding houses in a similar part of town.

East Park to be precise.

I changed into a grey, sleeved t-shirt, black track pants and a cap and joggers. As an afterthought I looked around for something solid. Under the sink I found one of Dad's wrenches. I dropped that in my Duck, which was looking less handbag and more pregnant tyre.

Before I fired up Mona, I rang Nick again.

Jenelle answered this time.

'Hi Jenelle. It's Tara Sharp,' I said.

'Hi Tara. How are the feet?'

'Fine,' I answered. 'How's the Cayenne?'

'Got a speeding ticket but no damage.'

'Good for you.' I grinned to myself.

'If you're looking for Nick he's diverted his phone to

me. He left for Sydney half an hour ago. Not sure when he's back. I'll be the last to know, of course.' She sounded decidedly put out. 'Shall I get him to call you?'

'Just tell him I rang.'

'Okey dokey. Bye Tara.'

I hung up. *Why had Nick rushed off to Sydney?* After a moment's puzzling I put that one away in the too-hard basket. I knew nothing about the man or his life. He could have gone there to play golf. Or visit his bondage mistress.

Instead of wasting time worrying about Nick, I drove Mona down to Croker Street and followed it back towards the river. Whitey lived in a renovated thirties brick and tile along one of the intersecting streets. His mother had left it to him, and June had moved in shortly before the wedding. So Smitty said.

I parked around the corner and did two walk-bys before ducking in the side gate and snooping through the back windows. No sign of Brains, or June, or Whitey; only a fat ginger tabby asleep on top of the agapanthus.

I jumped back in the car and sped out of the western suburbs, cutting across the city into East Park. Remembering the tobacco, I pulled up outside a dodgy looking deli, a stone's throw from Nick Tozzi's office. It was tucked in between a laundromat and a tired junk-and-antiques shop. I scrabbled under the seat of the car for loose change and got just enough to buy Wal's smokes. As I left the deli though, something in the junk shop window next door stopped me dead in my tracks. The ghastly pink and green of the glazing was what snagged my attention, and a second look confirmed it: a Wembley Ware dish. Before I knew it, my feet had taken a sharp left turn in through the door and transported me to the counter.

The shopkeeper was older than most of her merchandise. She sat on a high stool, fanning herself, and gazed at me from under thick blue eyeliner and a curly brunette wig.

'May I have a look at the glazed dish in the window, please?'

Her expression was a rebuke, as if I'd committed a serious crime by asking.

The process of retrieving the ashtray from the display took so long I began to jig.

'Can I help you?' I asked, as she knocked her wig askew for the third time, trying to reach between a four-tiered glass cake stand and a stuffed one-eyed peacock.

'Hold your horses, Missy,' she scolded me.

I gritted my teeth, and counted passing cars until her trembling fingers placed the pottery on the counter.

I examined it closer, and my heart began to race. The plate had a grey marron attached to the edge, complete with pincers and painted-on feelers. This would improve my stocks with Mrs Hara.

'How much?'

'Forty dollars.'

I only had thirty left in my savings account. 'Thirty,' I countered.

'Thirty-five,' she said sharply, 'and not a cent less.'

I took a deep breath. 'Twenty and my handbag,' I said, waving my Mandarina Duck in front of her nose. 'It cost a squillion, you know.'

The old woman scraped the front of her teeth with a yellowing fingernail then nodded.

I did a card withdrawal of the twenty and then tipped the contents of my Duck onto the counter.

She didn't blink at the wrench, just fished underneath her till and found me a plastic bag.

'Don't bother wrapping it. Bit of a hurry.' I scooped my things into the bag, grabbed the marron plate, and ran out the door before I changed my mind.

My Duck. My poor, poor Duck.

I climbed back into Mona and sped past Tozzi's office driveway, turning left at the park. The business district suddenly melted away, replaced by houses that made the streets in Bunka look pretty damn shiny. There were no half-starved, angry dogs, no hoons; just broken fences and boarded-up windows. I kept the doors locked as I sat around the corner from Wal's and went over my plan. It was pretty much the same one I'd had at Whitey's. Snoop around Sam Barbaro's, find my bird, and get out of town—well, out of East Park at least.

I employed a fragment of forethought to ponder what could possibly go wrong. If Wal fell asleep I could just leave him, I mean he lived close by. If Barbaro turned up and got nasty I had my wrench. What else? My phone was charged, and I had Bligh's number. If the car wouldn't start, or something like that, I could run to Tozzi's office.

Bok and Smitty would be proud of me; nothing impulsive going on here.

Before I could put my perfect plan into practice, there was a knock on my window.

When my heart steadied enough for my vision to return, I identified Wal in a once-white singlet, thongs and ripped blue jeans. I cracked the window. 'Jesuus, Wal.'

'There's a lane behind. I'll meet you back there,' he said, sauntering off before I could answer.

I started the engine and drove the short distance to the laneway. As I turned between two large fence posts onto the dirt road, I wondered if there was a connection between back-alley lanes and heading down the wrong path in life.

If so, I was screwed.

Wal's laneway was less salubrious than most. The dirt was covered in a carpet of shattered stubbies, and the backyards were demarcated by piles of plastic meth bottles and burger wrappers. If I looked closer I knew I'd see syringes and various other treats. I made a mental note to wear my hiking boots next time I visited dero's paradise.

Wal was already waiting for me, leaning against a gate. His hair was caught up in a ponytail and looked like something Brains might nest on.

Brains. My heart thumped again.

I pulled in close to the fence, so another car could get

past me if it had to, and got out of the car. As I joined Wal, he shot his nicotine-stained fingers out to shake my hand and I slapped the Champion Ruby into them.

'Thanks. How do, boss?'

'Uuh. C-cool, I guess.' It was gonna take a while to get used to the boss thing.

'Barbaro's place is over there.' He lifted his head to indicate across the laneway to the back of a house that one time would have been a pleasant enough imitation Spanish hacienda: the pride of the suburb even. Now, though, the arches looked dangerously saggy, and the verandahs beneath them were piled with old clothes and broken things: pushbikes, wasted luggage, three-legged chairs. There was no ferocious dog roaming the backyard, but a mangy-is-too-kind-a-description cat and kittens had set up home in an old car tyre.

Other than that it seemed deserted.

'Tasty.' My stomach began to churn.

'He lives in that room.'

I followed the direction of Wal's nod, to the back corner of the house where the verandah arches had been enclosed with plasterboard.

'There's no window,' I said.

'Small one, round the side. No blinds or nothin'.'

'You had a look?'

'I can see the light at night when I walk around out here. Can't smoke in the house,' he added by way of explanation.

I stared at the narrow gap along the side of the hacienda. It was barely a shoulder's width to the fence. I really wanted to ask Wal to go and look in the window for me, but that was pretty cowardly. Leaning in the car window, I grabbed my wrench out of the plastic bag and tucked it into my waistband.

'Watch my car,' I said with more assertion than I felt.

I hopped over the low chicken-wire fence and stooped down near the kittens. If anyone came out and accused me of trespassing I'd feign being a member of the RSPCA concerned about the welfare of the animals.

As I reached into the tyre, the mother cat spat at me. I pulled my hand back and stared at the babies. Only a few days old, still blind and covered in black mite.

Errk.

Maybe I *would* ring the RSPCA when I got home.

No one had burst through the back door, so I stood up and hurried over to the corner of the house. Now I was closer I could see that the plasterboard had a rough doorway cut in it, giving Barbaro a private alternate back entry to his room.

I stopped for a second or two to steady my breathing, then inched along the side of the house towards the window.

Wal was right. No curtain.

I pressed the side of my face against the window frame and slowly rolled my head around it so that one eye could see in.

A second later I was back to start position, my heart hammering. Barbaro was in there, sitting on his unmade bed. And he wasn't alone.

Johnny Vogue was sitting in a chair in the centre of the room, like a king on his throne, feet up on a dilapidated dresser. He looked surprisingly at home despite his expensive suit and shoes.

Every atom inside every molecule in my arms, legs and torso wanted to run away, but my feet seemed to be under instruction from a different brain, carrying me back around the corner of the house to the door cut into the plasterboard. Barbaro's room was in two parts, I was sure; the built-in verandah and the room I'd just looked into.

The verandah door wasn't locked and with infinitesimal care I eased it open. The only light in the small, dark room was coming from where I stood; enough for me to see the outline of another door beyond the piles of magazines and boxes of electronic gear—play stations, power cords and DVD players. I slid inside, pulling the door over, and waited for a moment for my eyes to adjust. In the quiet I could hear the murmur of voices in the next room—Barbaro and Johnny Vogue.

I also heard a sad little trill that sent my heart soaring.

Peering around into the gloom, I located a rectangular wooden box in the corner on the floor. Barbaro had stuffed Brains into an old rabbit hutch and covered her over. I knelt down next to the hutch and clucked softly.

She recognised the sound of a friendly, human voice and began to purr.

I pulled off the cover and looked closer. Brains was huddled inside. No food. No water.

My blood boiled.

Galahs loathed being in the dark during daylight hours. And like most animals they didn't survive long without water.

I thought about carrying her out in the hutch then discounted the idea. It was too clunky, awkward and potentially noisy. Instead, I tucked the wrench back into my pants and unlatched the gate. She knew it was me and crawled out and onto my hand.

We bonded for a couple of seconds; me scratching, her purring. But as I stood up she panicked and fluttered from my hand onto a high stack of magazines. Trust still wasn't at the top of her agenda.

I crept forward and stretched up on my tiptoes to reach her. 'Come on, sweetie,' I whispered. 'Come to Tara.'

She lifted her foot as if to step onto my hand, then quick as a flash snaked her head forward and bit me hard.

I couldn't control my yelp of pain.

The murmur of voices in the next room stopped.

Panicking, I reached down, grabbed the cover and tried to wrap Brains up in it. She dug her feet into the paper. But as I pulled her away she dragged a magazine with her and it slipped to the floor.

The door between the two rooms flung open, then shut, and the light flicked on.

I clutched Brains harder and she started squawking in earnest.

Sam Barbaro stepped around a pile of mags and pointed a snub-nosed pistol at me.

I'd thought about physical injury a bit recently. I mean, someone—maybe this guy—had been trying to run me over. But this was different. I might die, right here, right now. I felt it, down to the sphincter at the end of my large intestine.

You never know how you'll react in extreme circumstances: paralysis; panic; incontinence; hysteria. I suddenly learned mine was uncontrollable panic channelled into spontaneous movement.

Before Barbaro could say a thing, I launched at the nearest pile of magazines with my shoulder and knocked it flying, showering him in his own porn collection. Centrefolds and lingerie crashed over him.

He fired involuntarily.

The bullet ricocheted somewhere.

Not into me. *Yesss!*

I rammed another pile at him and ran for the door.

But Barbaro was an accomplished scrambler and had me by the neck before I could turn the handle. The pistol that had pointed at my chest a moment ago now pressed into my neck, just below my earlobe.

My heart performed gigantic painful cartwheels against

my ribcage, sending my vision spotty. I tried really hard to breathe but the air just wouldn't go in.

'Back away from the door,' he ordered.

I teetered backwards still clutching Brains, who was screeching fit to bust.

'Shut the fucking thing up, or I'll break its neck,' he snarled.

'C-c-can't,' I stuttered. 'She-she's scared.'

'She'll be dead in ten seconds then, and so will you.'

I let go of the cover and Brains fell to the floor. At least she might get away if I didn't. But she promptly crawled out from underneath the rag and onto my foot.

Stupid bird! Never, NEVER work with animals.

'C-cops will know it's y-you,' I said.

'They'll never find the body,' he countered. 'They wouldn't have caught me doing that old woman's place if it hadn't been for you. What did you do with my stash?'

Stash? 'What do you mean?'

He narrowed his eyes and thrust out his jaw. 'Zach says you been followin' him. We don't like nosy bitches.'

'We? You mean Johnny Vogue?'

'I mean,' he jabbed the pistol into my ear, 'none of your fuckin' business. You shoulda got the hint when I took the bird, you—'

His term of endearment was drowned out by the motion of the door in front of me bursting open.

As Barbaro automatically swung the pistol towards the invader, I chopped at his extended arm at the elbow with every ounce of strength in my body. Barbaro gave away about six inches to me and a few kilos. He staggered. And the pistol fired again.

Not into me. *Strike two.*

I grabbed the wrench from my waistband and whacked him in the stomach while he was off balance. He doubled up and fell.

Wal Grominsky shoved a semi-auto into Barbaro's mouth before he could recover, then stamped his heel into Barbaro's hand. 'Grab it,' he ordered me.

With Brains stubbornly clinging to my foot, I stuck my wrench back in my waistband and shuffled over to Barbaro, using a magazine to pick up his pistol so I didn't get any prints on it. I was relieved I could think a little at least.

'In here.' Wal held a pouch on his belt open.

I dropped the pistol into the pouch.

'Get the cables out of the other side of my belt,' Wal instructed.

For the next few minutes I did an inexpert job of securing Barbaro's hands and feet with what looked like giant plastic rubbish-bag ties while he groaned and grunted. When Wal was finally satisfied he nodded at the internal door. 'Anyone inside here you think?'

My heart stopped for a second. Where was Vogue? Why hadn't he come to Barbaro's aid? 'Viaspa was in there,' I whispered.

Wal reached into the pocket of his trackie pants and

pulled out his own pistol. It had a long barrel and looked well used. He flicked off the safety catch with his thumb and passed it over to me. 'Keep this on him.'

I put my hands behind my back and shook my head. Tying people up was one thing but—

'Lissssten to me and do it!' Wal hissed, giving me that kind of crazy, intense look that meant, maybe, he'd shoot *me* if I didn't do as he said.

On reflex I accepted the weapon.

It felt weird holding a gun; surreal, terrible, weird.

And kinda interesting. It was heavier than I expected. My hand was sweating so much, it felt loose in my grip.

Wal manoeuvred around the magazine piles and over to the door, where he crouched down and reached up to the handle, shoving it open quickly.

'Nuthin',' he pronounced.

He stood up and came back to me, taking the pistol from my clammy fingers. 'Out.'

I hopped over to the fallen cover, grabbed it and bundled Brains up tight.

I didn't need to be told twice. I was out of the yard before Wal could put his pistol back in his pocket.

He backed out after me, stuffing the nozzle of his rifle into the kitbag that he'd dropped at the door.

By the time we reached Mona, Barbaro was yelling his head off. 'You're dead, bitch. And so's he. I know him. DEAD! Someone lemme out of this fuckin…'

I unlocked the car and dropped Brains on the back

seat. She immediately began wrestling her way free of her cloth prison.

Wal and I had an awkward moment across the boot of the car.

'What now?' I asked.

Wal twisted his mouth, suddenly uncertain. 'Tricky one.'

'I could ring the cops,' I said.

'Yeah. Tell 'em you broke into someone's house and slogged him with a wrench?'

'He stole my bird.' I bit my lip, antsy to get out of the laneway before Viaspa or someone else came.

'My phone rang. I answered it automatically. ''Lo.'

'Missy?'

I nearly collapsed with relief. 'Mr Hara. You're back!'

'OK everything?'

'Noooo,' I wailed.

'Missy, you wanna come over? We sort.'

'Yes. Yes. Right away. Can I bring someone with me?'

'Sure, sure. Mrs Hara's making minestrone.'

I hung up and stared at Wal. 'You can't stay here and I know someone who—'

The door of Barbaro's back room flung open, and four guys piled out into the yard. It didn't take one of Einstein's neurons to work out they were armed and dangerous.

Wal beat me inside Mona.

'Yeah, yeah,' he said as I spun the wheels on the gravel. 'Sounds good.'

Chapter 43

Viaspa's men fired several shots as I fishtailed down the alley and out onto the bitumen road.

Jamming the Wembley Ware between my legs to keep it from breaking, I prayed no bullets hit my car. I couldn't afford the stress of the panel beating.

'Did they get me?' I shouted at Wal as I ran a red light. 'Wal?'

But Security Chief Grominsky had done his bit for Tara Sharp Consultancy today. He was asleep, head lolling against the window.

Meanwhile, Brains had climbed her way up the seatbelt and was calmly perched on his shoulder. I clucked my tongue to soothe her and she dropped a giant dollop that ran like a small lava flow down Wal's neck. For some reason, that struck me as more funny than disgusting. I began to laugh and couldn't stop.

By the time I reached Mr Hara's cottage thirty minutes later and parked in the driveway, my nose was streaming.

I couldn't see anything for laughter tears.

Hysteria, I told myself sternly.

And started giggling all over again.

Mr Hara tapped on the car window.

My giggling became hee-haws.

He opened the door. 'Missy?'

I undid my seatbelt and fell out onto the footpath at his feet, still holding the marron plate—continuing to deliver my best hyena impression.

He left me there, and soon afterwards I felt a set of weight lifter's arms lock around me and carry me inside.

Mrs Hara plopped me on the couch in the Wembley Ware room. As she removed the marron from my grip I heard her breath catch. She placed it reverently on the sideboard alongside the plasma, drew a blanket from somewhere and tucked me up like a rolled roast.

The world didn't begin to right itself until I'd drunk half a scalding-hot cup of sugary tea and chewed my way through a plateful of minestrone thicker than pack ice.

Mrs Hara came and went from the Wembley Ware room, a worried expression on her face. Mr Hara sat opposite, fingers steepled together, legs crossed neatly, face serious, aura burning intensely.

'Bird?' I croaked at him.

'In the aviary with the cockatiels.'

Brains would probably kill them all in an hour, but I couldn't summon the words to explain.

'Wal?' I asked instead.

'In Mrs Hara's guest room, taking a nap.'

I nodded, relieved, and tried to sit up a bit straighter. My bread rolled off the tray onto the floor and under Mr Hara's chair. At the sight of it disappearing, I burst into tears and sobbed for a while.

Mrs Hara did a sweep of the room, using the handle of a feather duster to retrieve the roll. Then she dropped a box of tissues on my knees.

I snorted and blew myself back into composure.

Mr Hara laid his arms along the armrest and stretched his legs out like Buddha unwinding from the lotus position. 'Missy, tell me now?'

I nodded, and splurted the whole story out: Delgado, Viaspa, Tozzi—even the bit about the bonus.

He gave frequent little nods and his aura sped up when I got to the last part about Sam Barbaro and the shooting.

'Very serious. Very bad. Missy go to the police?'

'No,' I said hoarsely. 'No one believes me, least of all Nick Tozzi. It's only because I can see things, that I know that the mining lease document is important, and that Lupi is somehow involved. I still can't really prove any of it.' Plus there was the added problem that I'd been trespassing.

'See, see,' said Mr Hara. 'I fix it with Mr Delgado.'

'No!' I yelped. 'H-he's t-too d-dangerous, and this is m-my f-fault.'

Mr Hara jumped up and stood to his full tiny height, fixing me with a stern look. 'No, Missy, not you. Mrs

Hara has done something very bad.'

'Oh?' was all I could think to say.

The house phone trilled.

Mrs Hara answered it in the hallway. She spoke in Italian, becoming more animated by the moment.

Mr Hara listened intently to her responses. When she marched into the room her face flushed, neither of us had to read her aura to see something was wrong.

She and her diminutive husband exchanged rapid information. He wagged his finger at her and she bowed her head in guilt.

I wobbled to my feet, feeling completely at sea. 'Trouble?'

'Barbaro and Lupi are looking for you. It is safer that you stay elsewhere while Mrs Hara sorts things out.'

'Mrs Hara?' I squeaked. I mean she was scary, sure, but she didn't carry guns, or work for a crime gang.

'Mrs Hara misled Mr Viaspa and Mr Delgado. They employed you because they thought you would sleep with Mr Tozzi and learn his secrets.'

'What-at?' I gasped, my voice cracking over the word. My mind cracked a bit too. 'Why would Mrs Hara do that?'

He sighed and his aura reddened. 'I told you, Missy. My wife is a jealous woman.'

'I know she was pissed over the chocolate thing but why would she be talking to the likes of—'

'Mrs Hara is good friends with Mr Viaspa's older sister.'

I sat down again. Had all the air been sucked from the room? And here I'd been thinking the fact that Wal lived near Sam Barbaro was ridiculous.

A slamming life lesson, Tara Sharp: don't get mixed up in small-city crime.

'They went to school together.'

Well that explained, at least, Delgado's attitude towards me—looking my legs up and down. He thought I was a hooker. 'C-can Mrs Hara get Barbaro to leave me and Wal alone?'

'You lay low for a few days. Mrs Hara try and fix through her friend.'

I nodded. 'OK. I'll stay with my aunt. She's in security apartments.' I pictured Wal asleep, drooling on one of Liv's Persian rugs. 'At least, I think she'll let us stay. Can you keep the bird for a few days?'

Mr Hara nodded. 'Sure, sure. Wasser name?'

'Brains. She likes peanuts and vanilla slice.'

Chapter 44

Aunt Liv—bless her beautiful tangerine aura—was a trooper. She opened her door to Wal and me like we were invited guests, and told us we were welcome to stay as long as we needed—although she did make Wal push the fold-out bed into her sumptuous laundry. 'It's only proper,' she told him. 'In case people call in.'

Wal didn't bat an eyelid.

In fact from the moment Liv opened her door, dressed in a black silk shift with her hair piled high off her lovely pearl-encased neck, he'd acted as dopey as a newborn lamb. Even his aura changed from smoky grey to something much bluer.

I didn't think my mind or stomach could handle the way his lips were trembling, so I excused myself and had a long, cleansing shower.

Liv left a voluminous Hawaiian muumuu on the spare bed for me and I emerged clean and slightly more composed. She handed me a cup of herbal tea and curled up on the couch next to me.

'Wal?' I asked.

'I sent him to the corner shop to get wine and cheese.'

I stared at Liv in amazement. She'd always had a knack with men. And she knew a *lot of men*.

That prompted a thought. 'You've met plenty of government types through your art, haven't you Liv?'

'Don't remind me, darling,' she drawled. 'I've been to more fundraisers and white-collar do's than you've done scatterbrained things.'

I grinned. Coming from Liv it sounded like a badge of honour. From my mother it would have been a cry of despair. 'You haven't heard about anyone who might be in bed with Johnny Viaspa?'

She shook her head, but her eyes began to sparkle. 'Supremo Crimo? Ooh, but I *love* the smell of corruption.'

'This guy was overweight and wearing a suit. He acted nervous. Glancing around, hurrying.'

'You were spying on him?' She sounded quite breathless.

'Liv,' I said sternly. 'Of course not. I happened to be watching some premises and he happened to be there with Viaspa.'

'Hmmm. Well, you've just described half the politicians in the state,' she said. 'Overweight and sweaty.'

I sighed. 'That's what I thought.' I was starting to get a major headache. 'I think I'll sleep on it.'

She patted my arm. 'Good idea. You look a little peaky. There are some painkillers in the bathroom.'

I yawned and headed for the bedroom, raiding the bathroom cabinet on the way. Sleep claimed me as soon as the pills hit my stomach and my head hit the pillow.

I momentarily surfaced a while later to the sound of Led Zeppelin and clinking wine glasses, and hurriedly resuccumbed.

When I finally roused properly it was 2AM, according to the digital clock in Liv's spare room. I swallowed down some water and sat on the side of the bed listening. Everything was quiet other than Wal snoring on his bed in the laundry.

Thank the lordey-oh!

I thought about eating something, seeing as I'd slept through dinner, but I didn't have much of an appetite. Mrs Hara's minestrone was still on the way down.

I picked my phone up off the side table. Three texts and two voice messages.

The first text was from Craigo, reminding me to be at the track by 8AM.

You'll have to cancel, I told myself. Mr Hara told you to lay low.

But no one would look for me at a triathlon, I counter-reasoned, and even if they did, no one would dare do anything at such a public event. The tri would be quite safe. Besides, a whole day spent cooped up in Liv's apartment with Wal would see me back in Betsy's office, holding my hand out for a prescription.

The second text was from Edouardo—a sweet 'hi' and

looking forward to tomorrow.

Dammit! I wondered how Liv would feel about Edouardo lobbing over for dinner with Wal, her and me?

I formed a mental picture of beautiful Ed, and smiled. Liv would be fine with it.

The third text was from Tozzi. 'Tara, ring me straightaway, whatever time you get this.'

I hesitated. I was pissed with him. He thought I was a fruitloop. But even that couldn't make my fingers stay off the call-back button.

''Lo.' He wasn't asleep but he sounded muzzy.

'It's Tara.'

'Where are you?' he asked.

'Laying low,' I said. 'Some stuff cropped up.'

'I need to talk to you—in person,' he said.

'What? Now?'

'Yeah. Are you home?'

'No.' I hesitated, not wanting to bring Liv into this any more than I already had. 'I'm … err … sleeping over at a friend's place.'

'Male?'

'No. And so what if it is?'

'Just asking,' he said mildly. 'Give me an address. I'll pick you up.'

I gave him Liv's apartment block address and told him to call me when he was outside. Then I snuck into the bathroom and freshened up: face wash, some of Liv's gorgeous parfum, and a rub of toothpaste around my gums.

While I waited for him, I listened to the voice messages. The first was Lloyd Honey. 'Ms Sharp, the only connection I could find between Nick Tozzi and John Viaspa was through their grandparents. Both were born in the same village in Sicily. In fact they lived in the same street. As for Nicholas Tozzi and his wife—no. Nothing significant in the familial sense.'

Interesting.

The second message was from Mr Hara. 'Things not so good, Missy. Mrs Hara not able to help. Stay out of sight.'

I didn't have much time to think on what I would do now, because the call came in from Tozzi.

Liv's apartment was on the fifteenth floor. I stared out of her balcony window, but the only car in the spot lit by the faux door-torches was a white stretch limo.

'What colour is your car?' I whispered into the phone.

'White. Limo.'

White limos were gangster cars. My paranoia did a flip. 'You don't drive a white limo.'

'I borrowed it from a friend.'

'Why?'

'Anonymity.'

'Well. OK,' I said

I grabbed Liv's door key off the coffee table and quietly let myself out. On the ride down to the ground floor, I somehow convinced myself that meeting Nick Tozzi in a limo at 2AM fell well within the parameters of *laying low.*

I pushed opened the foyer door and did a quick reccy up and down the street. Claremont—even on a Friday night—was pretty quiet after midnight in the residential areas.

Edouardo was probably just locking up at the club, and I felt a pang of guilt about meeting Nick, in a car, in the dark. I quickly quashed it. I mean, it wasn't like Edouardo and I were *together*. One eminently suspect date did not a relationship make.

The driver hopped out of the stretch and opened the passenger door for me. I looked in and to my relief it *was* Tozzi.

But the moment my backside hit the leather I knew I should have stayed tucked up in bed. His white business shirt was unbuttoned and his smile sloppy. Nick was pissed.

''S'up?' I asked, nervously.

'Jenelle said you called. What've you been doing?'

'You know … the usual … running around.' I ran my fingers through my hair.

Bad move.

He leaned over and tugged it gently. 'Yeah, I've seen you running.' His voice was so deep that I felt like I was wading in it.

'Nick?' the driver crackled through his intercom.

'Drive,' he ordered.

The limo pulled away from the curb smoothly and headed down Victoria Avenue. I swallowed an overwhelming desire to open the door and fling myself from a moving car. I couldn't *see* Tozzi's aura but it felt like I was standing way too close to a fire.

'Are you nervous, Tara?' He dropped his fingers from my hair to the hollow of my throat. I'm sure he could feel my heart beating against my skin.

'Depends,' I said, lifting my jaw and swallowing hard. 'On what you want from me.' Sometimes a girl has to be straight up about things.

His hand fell away and I instantly missed the heat of his touch. He frowned as if I'd taken all the fun out of his game. 'Direct as ever.'

I nodded. 'Yup.'

'How come you didn't learn to play coy like all the other girls?'

Coy? All the other girls? I had a sudden rush of anger. Not only had Tozzi been sceptical—pretty much rude— about my talents, but he'd turned up drunk in the middle of the night to hit on me. Neither behaviour suggested that Mr Western Basketball was treating me with much respect. And here I'd come gambolling down to meet him like an eager puppy.

I fixed him with a hostile stare. 'Look, Nick, what do you want? I have to run in a team triathlon tomorrow.' I pressed the backlight on my phone. 'In about six hours actually.'

He stared back at me without saying a word.

'Nick?' I repeated.

He sighed. 'What would you say if I told you that I had a few drinks and wanted to see you. Nothing else. Just wanted to see you. Badly, Tara.'

I started the swallowing thing again. It would have been so easy to let him lean forward and kiss me like I knew he wanted to, but it suddenly seemed really important that he didn't.

'I-I'd say … that's nice. In fact, I'd say more than nice. One major problem though. You're married, Nick.'

Pathetic, I know. But I didn't want Antonia Falk's leftovers, or to be another notch in Nick Tozzi's belt— whichever way it worked. I thought too much of myself for that.

'My marriage isn't what it should be—'

'Jeez. Can't you do better than that?' I interrupted.

'Yes. If you let me finish.'

I waited. This should be good.

'I fell hard for Toni when we met. Bad. I mean … the way you do when you're eighteen. You've seen her, Tara. Who wouldn't? And it's not just how beautiful she is; she's so classy, and fun to be with.'

Can't say I'd seen much sign of that, but I kept that opinion to myself.

'After we got married I found out that she had a cocaine addiction. The fun side only surfaced when she was stoned. The rest of the time…'

'So you wanted out?'

'No!' he said with vehemence. 'I loved—still love her,

326

in a way. I tried to get her to go to rehab but she wouldn't do it. I tried cutting off her allowance, but she got money in other ways. She believes she's just a recreational user. First thing you learn about an addict is that they've got to want to kick the habit. For themselves. Not for anyone else.'

He went quiet for a bit.

'I'm sorry for you, Nick, but that doesn't excuse you going around hitting on other women.'

'Who says I do that?'

I looked out the window.

He swore. 'Jenelle!'

I shrugged.

'Toni won't sleep with me,' he said abruptly.

My head swivelled. *Not sleep with him. Is she mad?*

'I'm trying, Tara, trying to make my marriage work, but she doesn't seem interested. At the same time she says she doesn't want a divorce. It doesn't excuse my behaviour, you're right. But sometimes I get … lonely. And you're … you're so different to her—'

You got that right, Tozzi! But, Holy Mother, do I swallow that line, or punch him in the nose?

'Why don't you talk to her then? Tell her how much you want to make it work.' I leaned forward and pressed the intercom button. 'Back to the apartment please.'

The driver glanced into the rear-vision mirror, surprised.

Tozzi didn't object, so the driver swerved the limo around the next corner and began to loop back to Liv's.

Whether Nick's story was to gain sympathy or not, one thing was clear: his personal life was complicated.

'Thing I don't understand is, why does Johnny Vogue want to ruin you so badly? It couldn't just be a random act. Is it a vendetta or something? I know your and his family come from the same town in Sicily.'

'How do you know that?'

'I dug around.'

'Why?'

'Why? Jeez. I'm trying to understand why I'm getting shot at, and why cars are trying to run me over. You owe me some kind of explanation, Nick.'

'Shot at?' He sat up straighter.

'You first,' I said firmly.

He sighed. 'There's no vendetta. But our families do go back a long way. You've gotta understand people like him and me, Tara. Pride is everything for us. Johnny thinks I've done better than him. Married better. My business is lucrative *and* legal. He wants a piece. He's always wanted a piece. Things have been harder for me lately, and he's seen an opportunity to bring me down.'

I let that digest. 'Does it include wanting your wife?'

Had I really said all that out loud? I glanced quickly at his fists. One smack from his giant paws would likely put me in hospital for a month; one twitch of those giant fingers could strangle me in an eye-blink or two. Amazingly, though, his fists weren't clenched, or twitchy.

I summoned the courage to look back at his face. His

expression, lit by passing streetlights, was so distressed, I wanted to cry. I felt the warmth of his aura contract away from me. What had I done?

'Nick, I'm sorry!' I blurted. 'That was a stupid thing to say.'

The limo's flicker went on as it left the road and parked outside Liv's apartment.

I grabbed the door handle. 'Look, I'm out of line. I apo—'

He wrenched my hand back. 'You started this storyline, Tara,' he said hoarsely. 'Now see it through. Why did he try to rob me?'

It was a plea, hidden in a demand.

It prompted a blinding thought. Barbaro had said something odd to me. *Where's the stash?*

'What if he was only making it look like a robbery?'

'What do you mean?'

'I think that Barbaro meant to plant something. Maybe drugs. To create problems for you.'

Tozzi looked well and truly sober now. 'It would. Other than the obvious, I'm trying to get extensions on my loans. A drug offence wouldn't fill the bank with confidence in me. What made you think of that?'

'I overheard Viaspa say that he'd stick coke up your arse if he had to.'

'Why didn't you tell me?'

'Seemed like an idle threat, you know. A joke.'

He let out a breath. 'But the police didn't find drugs.'

'Did they put a sniffer dog through?'

Tozzi shook his head.

'Of course not,' I answered for him. 'They were too busy looking for what had been stolen. Maybe Barbaro panicked when your mother interrupted him, so he made it look like a robbery, tipped a few things over, and dumped the stash somewhere on the way out. He didn't have it when the police arrested him.'

We looked at each other.

'The garden!' we said simultaneously.

Tozzi leaned forward and slid open the privacy window. 'Take us to Eireen's.'

Chapter 45

Eireen didn't seem perturbed to see her son letting himself through the front door in the wee hours. She was dozing on her chair, feet tucked under a mohair rug even though it was warm, and resting on her footstool. The TV carolled an old musical.

'Who you got there, Nick?'

'It's Tara Sharp, Mama. We just need to look for something in the garden.'

'Joanna's daughter? Better than that skinny wife of yours.'

'Where's a torch?'

'Under the sink.'

He dropped a kiss on her head. 'Go back to sleep.'

She nodded.

I followed Tozzi through the house to the kitchen and out the back door. It felt weird to be standing on Eireen's back porch in the middle of the night, staring down to the back lane that I'd chased Brains along.

'So tell me what happened,' said Nick flashing the torch around.

'Barbaro came out right here. I could see him in the porch light. I was over next door, on top of the fence.'

'Show me which way he ran.' He took my arm as we walked down the steps.

I didn't resist. 'This side of the lavender bushes, I think, then straight to the gate.'

We walked the route several times without luck.

'Do you remember seeing him throw anything?'

I stopped and thought. So much had happened since that evening that the memory of it was starting to blur. 'The alarm went off and he ran straight at the gate.' I retraced to the back gate. 'He shook the gate and couldn't get it open. So he back-tracked and took a run-up.'

'Back-tracked? How far?'

I took half a dozen steps backwards and out a bit.

'Stop,' said Nick, and came over with the torchlight. He searched in a circle around me.

'Nothing,' he pronounced. He was starting to sound tired and pissed off. 'How did you talk me into doing this?'

'I didn't. You told your driver to bring us here.'

He stalked off towards the house, leaving me in the dark.

Then I remembered something. 'Nick. Bring the light back,' I called out.

He stopped, swore, and came back to me. 'Look,

Tara—'

'Shut up!' I snatched the torch from him and shone it along the fence line. One direction was lawn. The other direction was a hedge of well-clipped rose bushes.

I got down on my hands and knees near the hedge and waved the beam among the thorny stems. There it was, about halfway in and halfway down—a small packet of silver alfoil, dangling.

'I can see something,' I said, reaching towards it.

'Let me look.' Nick hunkered down next to me so quickly that his large body banged against mine, knocking me forward into the bush.

I copped a face full of thorns as my fingers closed on the foil.

'Yeeooow!' I screamed.

A giant hand grabbed my neck and hauled me backwards so that I fell on my arse.

'Tara, I'm so sorry.' Nick grabbed the torch and was peering at me. 'Oh shit. I'm sorry.'

I felt the blood trickling down my face but my attention had already moved on. With shaking hands I opened the silver packet.

Nick shone the torch at it and we stared at the pile of white powder. 'Coke,' he said.

'You'd know more than me,' I said. 'Never done anything much more than smoke pot.'

'Me neither,' he confessed. 'But I've seen Toni with it.'

We stared at each other. Dogs were barking in the

nearby yards. Next door's perimeter floodlight activated.

'I think we should go.' He shut the foil and took the drugs from me. 'I'll deal with this. You go back to the apartment and bathe your scratches.'

Suddenly my face began to hurt. I was tired. I nodded. 'Good idea.'

I slept for three hours, dreaming about Barbaro wrapping my head in barbed wire while Johnny Vogue laughed. I woke with a sore face and my mind racing over last night's conversation with Liv.

Fundraisers. FUNDRAISERS. Of course!

I rang Craigo straightaway.

'Hi Tara.' He sounded sickeningly bright and chirpy.

'Are you going by the gym on the way to the meet?'

'Yes. I'm picking up some water bottles. Why?'

'There's a newspaper cutting on the noticeboard for an over-fifties fundraiser.'

'I know the one. What about it?'

'Can you bring it with you? I need to look at it.'

'Sure,' he said.

'Don't forget, Craigo. It's important.' I let 'grave' slip into my voice.

'Everything alright?'

'I hope so,' I breathed. 'See you soon.'

I sprang out of bed, determined to bury my concerns by cooking a sumptuous breakfast.

Wal wandered out just as I reached the height of my culinary frenzy, and I plonked a plate of scrambled eggs topped with caviar in front of him. Without a word about the state of my scratched face, he sat down at Liv's petite-but-elegant wrought-iron-and-glass breakfast table, and started shovelling it down.

As I crunched my four pieces of toast and honey, and gargled on a large glass of French-vanilla milk, I watched him. In his t-shirt and dangerously worn jocks, he seemed to be slipping down on the gaunt side of healthy for a guy who was normally stocky.

'You been eating properly, Wal?'

He shrugged. 'Sometimes. If I don't fall asleep and forget. Doc's given me a prescription to help with sleepin' an' all but—'

'But?'

'Can't afford it now I'm out of work.'

'Can't afford what?' trilled Liv. She appeared from her boudoir in a floaty pantsuit and divine barely-there makeup. Her upswept hair gleamed like the crown jewels under lights. A chunky necklace finished off her outfit perfectly; slightly eccentric but *so* interesting.

Wal's fork clattered onto his plate and he just stared at her.

Liv isn't beautiful like the Antonia Falk-Tozzis of the world, but there's something utterly glamorous about her. Five years junior to Joanna, she looked twenty years younger. Her skin was many-avocado-facials lovely and her figure svelte. Mum always claimed it was because Liv'd never had children.

I could buy that.

'Tara, what on earth happened to your—'

'I'm OK, Liv. Long story. Please don't ask.'

She stared at me for a long moment then moved her inspection onto Wal's state of undress. 'Wallace, where are your pants?'

'Um—' he started.

'A gentleman never appears without pants at breakfast.' She perched herself on the breakfast bar stool and poured an orange juice from the jug I'd filled. Liv could do haughty better than anyone when she put her mind to it.

'Sorry, Lavilla,' said Wal, turning a shade of tomato.

I sucked in my cheeks, and bit on them to stop from laughing.

'Excuse me,' he added as an afterthought, then jumped up and headed to the laundry.

When we heard the toilet door close, Liv rounded on me.

'Now Tara, I let you off last night because you were clearly exhausted. But you must tell me what on earth is going on?'

I gave her the version I'd given Dad. Wal and I had been assisting the police with an investigation, things had heated up and now the cops had told us to lay low. I added the bit about the dead bird under my windscreen wiper and the blue BMW trying to run me over, just so that she knew it was serious.

Her eyes shone with excitement. 'Wallace told me he was the security executive for a private-investigation firm.'

Executive? 'Err … yeah … we're sort of … working together for the first time. He brings certain skills to the table.'

'Oh?' she raised a wicked eyebrow.

I couldn't believe it. Gorgeous, sexy, wealthy, smart, independent Aunty Liv was being flirty over psycho, down-and-out Wal. Then again, Joanna had often alluded to the questionable nature of some of Liv's past lovers. I'd thought she was just being snobby.

Take a breath.

I mean there was no doubt that Wal was completely smitten with her. But that was to be expected. Liv had laid a carpet of broken hearts and bruised egos across Australia.

I had to put a stop to this particular conquest right now. 'He's just been diagnosed with narcolepsy,' I said. 'It's making it hard for him to earn a living.'

Liv's lips twisted in sympathy. 'Truly? Poor man.'

Poor man? I picked up my toast and began swallowing it down rapidly. First, Tozzi's strange behaviour, and now Liv's; the world had gone a little tilted.

'Liv, I have to run in a team triathlon this morning,' I said, seeking safety in a change of subject.

Liv lifted one perfectly drawn-on eyebrow. 'Is that wise?'

'Quite,' I reassured her. 'Very public. I run, I come back here. No one's the wiser.'

'Well, if you say so dear.'

'I don't want to go home yet, though. You know, in case the house is being watched. Could I borrow some running gear?'

'Of course!' She clapped her hands. 'I've got *just* the thing. Used to do a spot of jogging. But what will Wallace do while you're away?'

I hadn't thought that far. In fact I had no idea what to do with Wal at all. I kinda owed him. 'Well, not a lot, I guess. Except stay quiet until the cops come through.'

'Excellent. He can help me with my shopping. We'll have a little luncheon party after your event,' she said, then disappeared back into her bedroom.

'Liv—luncheon party?'

She popped her head around the door. 'Just something casual, darling. I mean to say, you'll be pooped.'

Chapter 46

I arrived at the tri-meet just in time.

Liv had given me a lift in her Saab after we'd agreed that Mona—who was safely tucked in the basement—would be like flashing a neon billboard in a blackout for anyone on the lookout for me.

She dropped me at Perry Lakes and I threaded my way through the gathering competitors, trying to ignore the glances I was getting from all the hardened tri-nuts, and the reason why I was getting them.

'Tara?' called out Craigo. 'Over here.'

My hunky gym instructor stood in a huddle of other hunky guys near the registration tent. They stared at me open-mouthed as I approached.

'Morning,' I said, lifting my chin, trying to brazen it out. 'The cat scratched me, and I had to borrow some clothes.'

Craigo looked like he might pee his pants, but he manfully introduced me. 'Tara, meet Lewis. He's swimming for us. And James, he's support crew. And you know Petey.'

Pete was one of Craigo's more regular shags; a handsome, slim young man with blue, baby-doll eyes. Right now those eyes were popping. 'Cat scratches! Black sequins! Gold lamé!' he exclaimed. 'Outstanding.'

The four of them burst out laughing as I mumbled an explanation about not being able to get into my flat. Then I got busy filling out the rego form.

That done, I went over the route with Craigo. He'd stopped hee-hawing by then, but every now and then he bit down on his bottom lip. I'm not really sure what that meant. I didn't dwell on it.

To tell the truth, I was getting a prickly feeling on my skin that could have been pre-race nerves. Or something else. I kept glancing about, thinking I saw Sam Barbaro's face every time a dark-haired guy came my way.

'Are you listening, Tara? If you deviate from the course you'll be disqualified. They're strict on that sort of thing.'

'Relax, Craigo,' I said, tapping my head. 'Got it in here. Now, did you bring the photo?'

He reached into his backpack and produced a photocopy of the newspaper clipping. 'Is this the one?'

'Sweet,' I said, snatching it from him.

'What's so secret service?' he asked.

I stared at the photo. There he was, in the middle of the second row—my suited man. Same bulky shape, same round face. I traced my finger along the credits. 'Jensen Bridges. Who is he, Craigo?'

Craigo was staring at me. 'Tara, what's going on?'

'I'll explain after the tri, but it's really important that I find out what he does for a job. Do you know?'

'He's a minister for something or other. Most of them are politicians, or lawyers. Those two are doctors.' He pointed to two in the front row. 'They're two of my most well-heeled clients.'

'Minister for what? What's his portfolio?'

He shrugged, and I sensed his discomfort so I let it go. 'Never mind. Thanks, you've been a great help.'

'OK. Well, good luck. I'm heading down to the bike start. Lewie's a strong swimmer, I'm expecting him out of the water first.'

Bugger! They're seriously hoping to win. I opened my mouth and shut it again. It was too late to start making excuses about my lack of fitness and sleep. 'Luck,' I said.

'Back atcha.' He disappeared into the crowd and left me to it.

I climbed the stand behind the start/finish line of the run, and stood in the back row while I called Smitty.

'What do you know about a guy called Jensen Bridges?' I asked, without preamble.

She paused for a moment. Smitty took Who's Who questions very seriously. 'He's Julie Bartlett's cousin. He went to law school in the States, and then came back here to go into politics.'

'State or federal?'

'State, I think.'

'Do you know what his portfolio is, Smitts? It's important. Really.'

'Let me check with Henny. I tend to haze out when I hear the word "politics".'

I counted the flags fluttering along the back of the grandstand while I waited. There was only a light wind. Perfect conditions for running.

'Henny says he's in sport and recreation,' said Smitty, when she came back on.

'Oh,' I said, disappointed. 'Is he sure?'

'Darling, Henny's never wrong, you know that. Wait— oh, hang on … apparently Bridges only shifted there very recently, after someone retired. He used to be in mines and petroleum.'

'True?'

'*Darling!*' she said, meaningfully.

'Tell Henny I love him. I love you both.'

'Good luck with the race, T. See you after.'

I sat down and let it sink in. The minister for mining was in bed with Johnny Vogue, which meant that whatever scam they were running on assay reports had to be bigger than just Nick Tozzi's exploration lease. This was the leverage I needed to get Johnny Vogue off my case.

With trembling fingers I rang Peter Delgado.

He answered quickly, in a distracted voice. 'Yes?'

'Tell Johnny Viaspa that I know who his bent politician is. I'll keep it to myself if you back off and he shelves his plans for damaging Nick Tozzi's life.'

'Tara Sharp?'

'Yes. Tell him to leave Tozzi and me alone, or I'll blab to every newspaper in the country that he's in bed with Jensen Bridges.'

The silence on the end of the phone was protracted. 'You know who you're blackmailing, don't you?'

This was the part where I hung tough, even though my guts felt like they'd vaporised. 'Quite,' I said in a plummy voice. 'And I've made arrangements for that information to go to the police should anything happen to Nick or me. So let's just pretend we've never met.'

Another pause. 'I'll convey your message to Mr Viaspa,' he said eventually.

'Good. I'll return your retainer and hope I never see you again, Mr Delgado.'

'Don't be naive, Tara. Things don't work—' His call cut off abruptly, as if someone had grabbed his phone before he could finish the sentence.

He didn't call back. Hopefully he'd fallen down a hole, or driven into the back of a bus.

Still trembling, I lay down along the bench seat. Had I really just played hard ball with the bad guys? I *was* nuts.

Suddenly, I felt tired. I tried napping for a while, but the bench was too hard, and my nerves were jangling. Eventually, I gave up and checked my messages.

There was a text from Bok wishing me luck and saying he'd see me later today *wen we cn toast unemplymt & blisters.*

The blisters would be mine, the unemployment his. Poor Bok still hadn't found his celebrity spread.

There were also several missed calls from JoBob.

I called back, preparing to hang up if Mum or Dad answered. Thankfully it went to message bank.

'Just letting you know that I'm picking Brains up from the vet's on Monday. She's fine but none of us can visit her because she's … in quarantine until then,' I said.

Most pathetic lie in the history of pathetic lies, but they could cross-examine me later.

I thought about ringing Fiona Bligh and telling her everything, but I'd dug myself in too deep to do that.

Instead, I stuck my phone in the strap of my crop top, climbed back down to the pen and began stretching out amid all the other competitors doing the same. I kept my cap pulled low and tried to distract myself with the chat around me.

The tri had attracted over a hundred teams—not bad for a small city comp. Somewhere in the melee there was bound to be someone I knew. Yet, in Liv's gold lamé running shorts with the black sequined love heart on the butt and velvet crop top, I could do without the recognition.

'Tara Sharp! Who did you mug?'

Crap. I peeked up from under my cap. *Worse than crap*. Jenny Munro, a basketballer turned ironwoman and my sporting nemesis. What was she doing slumming it in a team tri?

'Hi Jenny. Got your braces off at last, I see.'

OK. That was straight-up nasty, but you gotta understand, Munro broke my nose in the crossover semi-final of the state championships one year. It was a deliberate elbow to put me out of the game, without so much as an accompanying 'oops!'. We beat them anyway.

She'd quit playing after that and gone across to ironwoman events. Talent scouted by the Institute, apparently. She was tough as tits and could run like a devil.

I hated her.

She looked me up and down, baring her sizeable chompers in a fake grin. 'Looking a bit out of condition, Sharp. Not to mention the fashion statement.'

I eyed her ridiculously lean, fit frame. 'Yeah, well, I have a life.'

'Oh, that's right,' she grasped one perfect ankle and stretched one perfect quad. 'I hear you're seeing Greg Whitehead—on the quiet of course.'

'Wha-at!' I spluttered. 'Who told you that load of—'

My expletive was drowned by the roar of the crowd as the first bikes entered the straight towards the transition area.

The mood among the runners changed instantly. Everyone was on their toes, wired to take off when their team cyclist reached them. I began to run on the spot. I couldn't possibly beat Jenny Munro but I'd give it a fucking good go.

And my fucking good go was just about to begin because Craigo was bearing down on me, leading the bike leg by a couple of hundred metres.

He wheeled into the T-area as if it was the start of a velodrome sprint, not the end of an endurance race, and tagged me.

I was off at a cracking pace, putting as much distance between myself and Jenny, as possible. My only hope was to force her to chase me and keep her from setting her own pace.

I hit the three-kilometre mark before the first rush of adrenaline and anger had waned. A quick glance behind told me I was only ahead by fifty now. Jenny was bearing down on me, cap low, arms pumping comfortably. Another hundred behind her was a group of about five, all pushing each other in spurts. The rest I couldn't see. There was something to be said for being at the front of the pack. YAY, Craigo!

I tried to concentrate on working through the growing fatigue, and the pain that was starting to stab just below my right knee. My running shoes weren't exactly new, and the cushioning was struggling to compensate for the extra pounds I'd put on.

I'd always managed the fatigue barrier pretty well when competing, but pain was a different thing. My mind began to wander and I caught myself gazing into the crowd instead of focusing ahead.

As I grabbed a cup of water from the first line of

volunteers, Jenny thundered past me. I coughed the drink water down and tried to put on a burst, but my lack of conditioning started to bite.

Breath burning.

Legs burning.

Feet burning.

Everything told me to stop, catch my breath. I tried to spurt again but my body just wouldn't respond. Nothing left in the tank with just over four kilometres to go and the next group a few strides behind me.

As I reached the last line of water volunteers, the group behind me converged. I caught an elbow in the ribs and someone kicked my ankle, taking me down.

I rolled on the ground, grabbing at my leg. The volunteers called out to me but I waved them off. Interference would mean disqualification. I got up and stood, bent over, grabbing my knees, sucking it in.

Then something made me turn my head; a distortion that didn't seem to fit with the blur of auras that I accepted as a common background when there was a crowd. Behind the water volunteers, standing among a random group of spectators leaning on the barricade, was Sam Barbaro. And he was reaching inside his leather coat for something.

I wasn't going to wait to see what.

An adrenaline rush sent me scooting after the group. Safety in numbers. Fear brought energy, and I caught up and hung with that group, keeping myself in the centre of them.

Periodic glances into the crowd told me that someone was running behind the first line of spectators trying to keep pace with us. I didn't know that it was Barbaro. I didn't know that it wasn't.

A web of panic engulfed me. What if he was waiting for me at the end of the race? He couldn't accost me in public. I should be able to just walk away. What if he pulled his gun on me? He wouldn't do that. Would he?

Shouts from the crowd drew me back to the present. One kilometre to go and I'd unwittingly pulled ahead of the group as I hit my second wind. Suddenly, I found myself strung out halfway between Jenny and the group.

Jenny was entering the stadium straight.

I glanced to the sideline crowd again. They'd thinned out; everyone was inside near the finish.

I saw Barbaro. He waved and pointed to the opposite side of the track.

Head swivel.

Zach Lupi was on the other side running abreast with us.

If I veered off now one of them would follow me. *Finish the race. Escape them in the confusion,* I told myself. *Run!*

But brakes squealed and things went arse-shaped. I glanced back. The blue BMW had crashed the barricade a hundred metres behind me and was on the track. My running group scattered as it fishtailed straight through the centre of them.

All I could see of the driver was a cap pulled low and a collar pulled high.

This time my adrenaline spike was more like an overdose of crack. I bolted into the stadium, towards the finishing line and the safety of the stadium seating. A dozen terror-fuelled strides brought me abreast with Jenny.

She was losing speed, eyeballing behind, checking out the furore. 'What the—'

I didn't waste a second of breath in explanation. But a blare of sirens told me that a cop car had careened onto the track after the BMW.

I hung my tongue out the side of my mouth and forced my arms to pump faster. My peripheral vision told me too many things were happening.

Craigo and the boys were shrieking on the sidelines, jumping up and down, hooting for me. Bok and Smitty as well. Edouardo would be there too but I couldn't see him.

Barbaro was ahead of me cutting towards the line, but the crowd had slowed him. Lupi was having the same problem on the other side.

I heard a growling grunt in my ear, and Jenny surged again.

'No way, Sharp,' she spat.

Literally.

I copped a gob of her spittle, courtesy of the gusty wind.

But Jenny didn't have a car trying to run her down and two thugs chasing her. We pounded the last ten, neck and neck, and that's where I got her. She was aiming for the line. I was aiming for the stadium seats twenty metres beyond it. She slowed in her last step and I ran straight on through.

And kept going.

The crowd scattered as the BMW and the cop car finished next, narrowly missing Jenny who was screaming at the top of her lungs.

I crossed the grassed area and dived over the steel railing. Once I'd righted myself I took the stairs three at a time until I finally tripped and fell over near the top. I banged my knee hard and began to roll back down until I latched onto the pole base of a seat—and a wad of recently applied chewing gum—and hung on.

Errk.

I looked down at the oval.

The BMW was spinning its wheels and blowing smoke in the long-jump sand trap. With any luck it would bog right in.

A moment later, though, it burst free, heading straight for the stadium seats, and me. Out of control. The driver jumped out at the last second, leaving her car to nosedive into the railing.

Her?

Jeans, collared tight shirt, heels. Definitely female.

Hot on its tail, the cop car cut a swathe into the stadium's pristine grass running track and slid to a stop, door swinging open.

Fiona Bligh flung off her seatbelt and left the car at a run. She tackled the woman as she climbed the fence and brought her down with a quality knee grab. Bligh had slapped the cuffs on her before I could stand up and shout hooray!

Bill Barnes joined them and bundled the cuffed woman into the car.

Bligh looked up and gave me a wave.

I hobbled down the steps to meet her. My knee wasn't bleeding but had started to swell.

She helped me over the fence.

'You OK, Sharp?' Her uniform was covered in grass, buttons missing, and there were dirt smears on her face. 'Jesus. Did you fall over?'

'Cat scratches,' I said automatically. 'Who is it?' I was suddenly thirsty as hell and feeling dizzy. 'June Whitehead?'

'No, it's Carlotta Delgado, the dodgy lawyer's wife. You know her?'

Delgado! 'Met her once, for like, an eye-blink.'

Bligh nodded wearily. 'Seems she got it into her head you were seeing her husband and started following you.'

Tears sprang to my eyes. Relief or sentiment, I wasn't sure. 'You sound like you knew.'

She nodded again. 'She's a hard case. Nearly had her once for assaulting her hired help. Never pulled a stunt like this before, though. Whitey recognised her when she tried to get you outside your house. We confirmed it with the plate number you left.'

I remembered the panicked look on Whitey's face.

Bligh stared at the finish line. The crowd was being held at bay by Cravich and Blake, who were already interviewing spectators.

I scanned the sea of faces for Lupi and Barbaro but the police presence would have sent them scuttling.

I tried to refocus on Bligh, but I felt sick all of a sudden and for some reason she looked like a dot picture. 'Think I need to...'

Chapter 47

I woke up a short time later in the back of an ambulance, hooked up to a saline drip.

Bligh was sitting next to the paramedic, writing in her notebook. I stared at her, trying to remember how I got there.

'Just a bit of dehydration, Sharp. You should drink more water before an event.'

I had to wet my parched lips to speak. 'I'll keep it in mind.' I had a sudden thought that had me jerking upright, craning my neck to see the seat behind my stretcher. 'Where is she?'

'Constable Barnes is with Mrs Delgado in the other ambulance,' said Bligh.

I settled back.

'Now, there are a few things we need to talk about.'

'Now?' I croaked.

She glanced at the paramedic, who was leafing through a copy of *Sports Illustrated*. 'It can wait until we're at the hospital,' she said.

That was it between us, until the ambulance had offloaded us into a pokey ED room, the drip had done its thing, and the duty doctor prescribed a shower, rest and a good night's sleep.

Left alone, finally, Bligh pulled her chair up close to the bed. 'I just had a call from Bill. Carlotta says her husband's secretary, Francine, told her you were having an affair with Peter Delgado.'

Giggler! I wanted to tell Bligh how I'd overheard Francine talking about her affair with Delgado, but that meant explaining other things. Like why I was at his office. So I kept quiet.

'Carlotta searched your flat and found her husband's private number on a card. She also says you live like a pig, and that she'd try to run you over again.'

'Did she trash my car?'

Bligh shrugged. 'She hasn't admitted to it so far, but I'll check it out.'

I felt sick. 'Remember that day you called on me? Someone had been in there while I was out. Must have been her.'

She wrote that in her notebook. 'You should lock your door. What were you doing with Delgado's card?'

'My accountant gave it to me. He used to work in the same building as Positoni & Kizzick. He recommended them if I ever needed a lawyer. Never followed up on it, though.'

Take that, Garth Wilmot!

Bligh kept writing.

I sighed. 'Is that it, Fiona?'

'Cravich and Blake have gone to pick up a guy named Zach Lupi.'

'Oh?' My heart fluttered.

'You know him?'

'No,' I lied.

'Nicholas Tozzi's shown us evidence today that Lupi falsified a mineral assay report. Seems that Lupi is buddies with Sam Barbaro, who broke into Eireen Tozzi's home.'

'Evidence?' I said, wide-eyed.

'Mr Tozzi got an independent assay done in Sydney showing completely different results to the one the SUP labs supplied. Lupi signed off on the report. We're getting a third assay done but Lupi's arse is on the line. We know he and Barbaro are both working under direction from John Viaspa but there's no direct connection, nothing to hang him on.'

I gulped this time; really, truly gulped. 'When did Nick call you?'

'This morning, first thing. That's the only reason we were close by when Carlotta popped her cork. We were coming to talk to you. Your dad said you were running in the triathlon.'

'My dad?' I squeaked. Bligh had been to JoBob's.

'A source saw your Monaro near Barbaro's boarding house yesterday.' Her eyes suddenly developed the intensity of a six-inch drill bit about to do its work. 'If you've got anything that could connect Viaspa to Barbaro or Lupi, we need it.'

I reached for a glass of water to give myself time to think. I couldn't tell Bligh about the shooting; they could nab me for trespassing, not to mention aiding and abetting an armed crazy man. I couldn't tell her about the warehouse either, because that'd be trespassing too, and there was Edouardo to consider.

My phone began to vibrate on the bedside cabinet. 'Excuse me one minute,' I said and grabbed it.

'Missy?'

'Hoshi?'

'Mrs Hara has a message for you from her friend. Mr Viaspa says that all is good, as long as you don't mention names. You understand?'

'Are you sure?'

'Yes. Yes. He says his dogs have been called off.'

Dogs? He meant Barbaro and Lupi.

'Thank you,' I said. 'I'll collect the bird soon.'

I hung up and smiled at Bligh. 'My boss has our family bird. You remember Brains?'

Her eyes narrowed. 'Sharp?'

'Where's Barbaro's boarding house?'

'East Park,' she said. 'Near the corner of George Street.'

'Oh,' I said, mustering a relieved expression. 'Must be a coincidence. I was picking up my aunt's boyfriend so he could move in with her. He can't drive anymore. He has a medical condition. He lives on George Street.'

'Can he verify that?'

'I expect so.'

'What's his name?'

'Wallace Grominsky.'

'GROMINSKY!' she snarled at me. 'What little game are you playing at, Sharp?'

I gave her my best innocent expression, which was a fucking genius effort, since every muscle in my body ached and I was busting to pee on account of the drip. 'I introduced them. No accounting for love's taste.'

'Neighbours reported gunshots,' said Bligh.

'Really? I'm glad Wal's moved out then. Bad area.'

She grunted and scribbled in her book. 'Where is he now?'

I gave her Liv's address.

The nurse poked her head around the curtain. 'Are you nearly finished, Constable? I'm having trouble holding back the hordes.'

Bligh sighed and stood up. 'We'll be talking again soon, Sharp.'

I sat up straighter. 'Fiona?'

'Yes.'

'Thanks for today. I mean, you know I wasn't seeing Peter behind her back. Carlotta really must be nuts.'

'*That*,' said Bligh, 'I believe. His secretary owned up to being the other woman under a little bit of pressure from Cravich and Blake.'

I should have felt sorry for Giggler but I didn't.

She left and within a second the curtain was flung open, and the cubicle teemed with excited people: Craigo and the boys, Bok and Smitty, and Edouardo.

I introduced them all to each other, and Smitty pinned Edouardo to the wall, while the boys immediately began to chat up Bok.

Craigo leaned over to give me a hug and pushed an envelope into my hand.

'What's that?' I asked.

He gave me a delirious smile. 'We won the tri. The organisers decided that the car debacle didn't influence the final placings and awarded the first prize anyway. The whole thing got such great media coverage they're happy for the publicity. And the gym is already getting membership calls.'

I opened the envelope and peered in: a cheque for three thousand dollars.

'Split three ways,' he said.

'Of course.'

'Now tell me, Tara, *who was* that crazy woman?'

A wave of elation swept over me. 'I'll tell you all about it at lunch. Everyone's invited back to Aunt Liv's for a celebration. Let's go!' I thrust back the covers and leaped out of bed.

Perhaps a little ambitious. Edouardo grabbed me as I started to wobble. With his arm tight around my waist we all headed out of the ED. The others went to the waiting room while I handled my own discharge. When it was done, I went to find them but ran straight into Nick Tozzi carrying an enormous bunch of flowers.

The heat of his glare at Edouardo was enough to melt the vinyl off the seats in the waiting room.

Bok covered the awkward moment by having a fan boy attack. While he took over introducing himself and everyone else to Nick, I read the card on the bouquet. *Tara. You were right. What can I do to thank you?* N.T.

I looked at him standing there, a gorgeous giant attracting attention from everyone in the waiting room, and had an idea.

'Bok,' I said, cutting across their babble. 'Do you still need a celebrity interview and photo spread?'

Bok's eyes lit as he caught my line of thought. 'You *know* I do.'

'Nick would be happy to do a celebrity interview for your mag. Wouldn't you Nick?'

All eyes swivelled to Nick.

Tozzi's aura radiated with the intensity of an impending supernova. For a moment I thought he would refuse. But I waved the card at him and smiled sweetly. 'Martin is one of my best friends and he needs this interview.'

Nick took a deep breath and smiled at Bok. 'I don't normally do publicity, Martin, but I have a new investor in the team, and some plans to expand, so it might be time for an announcement. Sure thing.'

'Photos?' asked Bok.

'Why not?'

'Nick's just moved into a new house,' I added. 'I'm sure he'd love to show it off.'

Bok gave a little crow of delight and got straight onto his phone to start arrangements.

'A quick word, Tara, if I may?' said Nick.

I eased Edouardo's hand off my waist. 'See you all outside in a second. Just got some business to sort,' I told them.

Edouardo looked doubtful, but Smitty dragged him along. 'Come on, Edouardo, this might be the only time I get you to myself.'

Blessed Smitty.

'I'll be right outside, waiting.' Edouardo told me, looking straight at Nick.

Chapter 48

As they passed through the automatic doors, Nick helped me over to an empty set of chairs screened from the main waiting room by a row of large potted palms.

'You were right about a connection between Viaspa and the exploration lease,' he said, as we sat down.

'What do you mean?'

'The statute of limitations state that if you don't commence mining within five years, you lose your permit. I was about to let the permit lapse because the assay report had said it was worthless. Your suspicions made me have a second assay done in Sydney. The lease is actually gold rich.'

My mouth dropped open. 'Gold? Truly?'

'Shh,' he warned. 'It's not something I want to advertise. Anyway, I think Viaspa has had Lupi pulling this scam for a while. Lupi falsifies an assay report then Vogue acquires the lease under a different name, trucks his mobile plant up there and rips the mineral out of the ground. The industry's been so buoyant these last few years that small mines have been springing up everywhere—so it's been a perfect time to go undetected.'

'So now what?'

'I've told the police about the false report. They're questioning Lupi but I don't know that an association with Viaspa will be found. You're the only person who saw Lupi at the warehouse; the only person who could connect them.'

Nick bent closer until his breath was hot on my lips. The damn cord appeared, and started pulsing between us, chest to chest. 'What do you want to do, Tara? Will you go to the police?'

'What do you want me to do?' I asked. He looked so concerned and caring that I almost melted onto the floor.

'Whatever you can live with. I'm worried for you. If Vogue knows you can pin Lupi to his warehouse then he might try and...'

'Run me over?' I ate up his concern like a starving person falling on a piece of pork roast and salt crackle. 'Actually, that wasn't him. Turned out to be Delgado's crazy wife.'

He raised his eyebrows. 'Carlotta Delgado?'

'You've had the pleasure?'

'It was no pleasure. The woman's spiteful. She tried to hit Toni one time at a charity fashion parade.'

'If only she'd tried to punch me,' I lamented, 'I could have taken her. Anyway, I've just spoken to the police.

They've got nothing on Johnny Vogue. They're pushing for something. Anything. But I've found a way to make Vogue leave us both alone without involving them.'

Nick stared hard at me. 'Seriously?'

I met his look without blinking. 'Deadly.'

'I won't ask.'

'Don't. But I promise he won't be bothering you.'

'So you're happy to leave it at that then? Lupi goes down, Vogue walks?'

I sighed. 'Not really. Viaspa deserves jail and more, but I'm just getting a business started. I'm broke.' I gave a weak smile. 'I don't want to spend the next five years in a witness protection program. Does that sound pathetic?'

'No. It sounds practical.'

'But what about you, and Antonia and…?'

His face closed over, the warmth fading from it, his aura listing like a damaged ship. 'The estimated value of the lease gives me a new asset. It'll keep the bank happy and get me over my short-term money issues. Thanks to you we've avoided the drug plant. I've employed security for the new house. Toni and I will be fine.' He smiled. 'Means I can keep the Reventon. I'd offer you a drive but—'

'You don't trust me.' I smiled back. 'Look, I didn't mean to be—'

He took my hand. 'I know, you didn't, but I can manage my marriage.'

Fair enough. 'Well that's that then?'

A silent moment.

'Umm, we're going off to celebrate our win. Would you like to come with us?' I asked politely.

'Maybe another time. But I won't forget what you did to help me. I'll never forget.' His voice deepened and his expression changed again. This time he seemed emotional. 'Tara, I—look, there's something—'

The cord of energy between us brightened and tightened, as though it was pulling us together, and I felt my lips parting in preparation for what he might say.

'Tara!' Edouardo's voice.

It cut through the moment, and I drew back. He was looking for me on the other side of the line of palms.

I smiled at Nick and stood up. As I'd just told him, I didn't need complications in my life right now. 'Maybe another time,' I said.

Chapter 49

I rang Liv on the drive home to warn her and Wal about Bligh, and the impending numbers for lunch. She took both things in her stride, and asked me to pick up extra bread rolls and a cooked chicken.

Then I rang Mr Hara and JoBob and asked them to join us as well.

Safety in numbers, I decided, was the best strategy where my parents were concerned. JoBob would never make a scene.

Bligh and Bill Barnes stepped out of the lift as we crowded into the foyer of Liv's apartment block. Bligh nodded at me as we passed. I knew better than to think that she would let things lie. The woman had a touch of pit bull in her and she wanted Viaspa.

I just wanted him to leave me alone.

Wal answered Liv's door wearing chinos and an open-necked shirt.

It took me almost a whole bottle of champagne and half a bacon quiche to get over the shock.

We sat on Liv's balcony and drank, and ate, and laughed until well after dark, when Craigo and the boys headed off to a party, and Bok ran Smitty home.

'Darling,' Smitty said, with good old alcohol-fuelled affection. 'You never, never disappoint me. Oh, I do love you.'

'You too, Smitts,' I said. 'Make her drink water all the way home,' I hissed at Bok. 'Henny will gut me for sending her home in this state.'

Bok hugged me. 'Thanks for saving my arse, T. All the national magazines have been trying to nail Tozzi for an interview for years. They've offered me a bonus if I get pics of him and Antonia together.'

'You're welcome,' I grinned, ignoring the little sore spot in my heart.

I shut the door after them and leaned against it.

Edouardo left the balcony and came inside. He gave me the most bewitching smile. 'Your friends and family are nice, Tara.'

I looked out at Mr and Mrs Hara, JoBob, and Liv and Wal playing Pictionary, and squeezed his hand. 'They're lame, actually. And I wish they'd all leave so you can give me that foot rub.'

'Just your feet?' he said wistfully.

'It's kind of crowded here at the moment, Ed,' I said softly. 'Wal's staying as well.'

'You want to come back to my place?'

I thought about it. But the elation had worn off, and the champagne and food had left me feeling kind of woozy and tired. I wanted to lie down and sleep, even more than I wanted to lie down next to the gorgeous Edouardo.

He must have caught my mood because he propelled me over to an armchair and sat himself on the footstool. Before I could argue, he picked up my bare foot and began to rub it.

I sank back into the chair and gave a little moan of pleasure. 'Where did you learn to do that?'

'It's hereditary,' he said. 'I come from a long line of masseurs.'

'Really?'

'No.'

I sighed, feeling mellow and happy, and contemplated how close this foot rub was to heaven.

My phone rang. I pulled it from my jeans pocket.

'Tara speaking?'

'Ms Sharp?'

I recognised the voice right away. 'Mr Honey?' I sat up a little straighter. 'Is everything alright?'

'Wonderful, Ms Sharp. Was the information useful?'

'Thank you, yes. How is your fiancée?'

'We've set a date.'

I relaxed again and smiled into the phone. 'I'm glad.'

'The reason for my call is that I have a friend who'd like to hire you. I've explained the nature of your ...

expertise and they're willing to double your rate if you'll take the job.'

I got a funny feeling in my stomach—but that could have been the olives mixing with the chocolate cake. 'What's the job?'

'It's a little delicate, you see. That's why I've rung you first. To ... sound you out. My friend runs ... a very superior escort agency. They want you to coach their ... employees on the art of reading body language. To enhance their clients' experience.'

'A brothel, Mr Honey?'

Edouardo's head jerked up from his task of pulling gently on my toes, his eyes widening.

Mr Honey cleared his throat. 'Ahem ... yes ... if you like.'

Maybe it was the alcohol, or the foot rub, or the whole craziness that had become my recent life, but I didn't even hesitate. I wiggled my toes at Edouardo for more and smiled. 'Why not?' I said. 'Bring it on.'

About the Author

Marianne Delacourt is the pseudonym of a successful Australian sci-fi fantasy author who is sold throughout the world. Sharp Shooter is set in Perth, where the author grew up. The next book in the Tara Sharp series is Sharp Turn. Marianne now lives in Brisbane with her husband and two galahs.

http://www.tarasharp.com.au

Acknowledgements

Many thanks go to: Alisa Krasnostein, Katharine Stubbs and all at Twelfth Planet Press for allowing Tara to spread her wings. It's been a pleasure working with you.

Sharp Turn

Also by Marianne Delacourt
Book 2 in the Tara Sharp series
Coming 2016!

Tara Sharp's unorthodox PI business is starting to attract customers—though not necessarily of the kind she envisaged… Working at Madame Vine's luxurious brothel teaching the 'girls' to 'read' their clients better isn't exactly what she had in mind when she started out…

So it's a relief when the man of Tara's dreams, Nick Tozzi, lines her up with a lucrative job. Something is rotten in the local motor racing industry and an associate of Nick's wants Tara to suss things out.

It's not long before Tara finds herself in all kinds of danger, with a murder at Madam Vine's followed by the discovery of a bloated corpse in the Swan River.

Chapter 1

My mother is an expert guilt-maker. Joanna Sharp, the Rani of Reproach, the Shazadi of Shame. When she turned her talent on me, it was usually about the fact that I didn't date the right sort of guy. Unfortunately, my mother's idea of a suitable male was someone like Phillip Dewar: privileged and pasty (and permanently plastered). But, since I'd moved back home, due to loss of employment and a spot of pennilessness, Joanna had broadened her guilt trip to include my latest career venture.

'Why can't you just get a good job in the government, darling? Or let your father help you find work?' she asked me regularly.

My reaction was consistently emphatic: 'I can look after myself, Mum!'

Of course that meant that I had to come good on my statement, which meant earning money, which explained why I was currently on my way to a meeting with a brothel madam.

'It's all good. It's ALL good!' I chanted as my 1980s' Holden Monaro—aka Mona—took the sharp left-hander onto Stirling Highway with only the faintest squeal of her wheels.

I've always been a great believer in affirmations. I CAN eat less chocolate. I CAN do more exercise. I CAN meet a perfect man. No, scrap that last one. I don't believe in perfect men.

That said, my current date, the gorgeous Edouardo, came close. He was a model, a good egg and he seemed to like me—all of which made me very uneasy. The fact was, he was just too good to be true. My track record was dotted with unfaithful Lotharios and even a furniture-stealer (my last boyfriend cleaned out my flat while I was having a massage), which made it almost impossible for me to just enjoy Edouardo's attention and not try to second-guess the whole thing.

But Second-Guess is my middle name. Tara Second-Guess Sharp.

Not just about men, about everything: a legacy from the fact that I have an unusual gift. I can see auras around people, and sometimes around objects. Occasionally, I even smell or feel things or see energy trails.

I'd been to the shrink about my gift and, instead of whacking me onto an antipsychotic, she'd sent me off to Hoshi Hara's Paralanguage School. Betsy, my psych, was an old family friend and turned out to be more alternative than I'd ever expected for a woman who favoured Brendan O'Keefe glasses.

The end result of getting to know Mr Hara was that my gift didn't go away, it got stronger. Now I was a fully accredited reader of paralanguage and kinesics with my own business, and I was starting to get jobs that used my skills. Like the one I was going to now.

One of my previous clients had recommended me to Madame Vine, the brothel's owner. It seemed the madam was a forward-thinking entrepreneur who needed my skills. In return, I hoped she'd bolster my almost-bust bank account and we'd all be happy. She wasn't exactly the kind of customer I'd expected to attract when I set up my own business, and certainly not the kind of work I'd be telling my mother about, but I wasn't about to knock back a funds infusion because of my mother's delicate western suburbs sensibilities.

IT'S ALL GOOD!

I cruised up a tiny side street in Leederville that was crammed with red-brick, Federation-style semi-detacheds, and pulled up outside number nine. It didn't look like a house of ill repute. In fact, with its minimalist garden and locked letterbox, it was much tidier than its neighbours. There was no red light or gaudy lace curtains in the windows. Madame Vine ran an upper-crusty establishment that didn't accommodate riffraff—at least that's what my Google search had told me.

I parked Mona and reached down to my bag, sighing

at the sight of the sequinned palm tree decorating its side. I'd given my favourite imitation Marc Jacobs handbag to a teenager in one of Perth's more dubious suburbs for doing me a favour, and bartered my beloved backup Mandarina Duck in a second-hand shop. That left me with my old beach bag. Hopefully this job for Madame Vine would bring me enough cash to buy something halfway respectable.

I scrabbled down the bottom of the bag for my hairbrush and then glanced in the rear-view mirror: shoulder-length brown (at the moment) hair, broad-featured, decent-enough face and a slightly wild-eyed look that was becoming a permanent fixture. Too much adrenaline and too little sleep.

IT'S ALL GOOD.

I forced my legs out of the car and told myself I was being stupid for feeling nervous. They were normal women, just like me.

Actually, considering I hadn't had sex in several months, probably NOT just like me (my new guy, Ed, and I hadn't done the wild thing yet on account of me being once bitten, twice shy).

My nervousness had nothing to do with moral judgments about ladies of the night. As far as I was concerned, you did what you had to in life; I saved the kick in the nuts for the bad guys. No, my angst was more about what they would think of me, Tara Sharp, western suburbs private-school girl with the posh voice. Maybe the sequinned beach bag wasn't such a bad look after all.

The woman who answered the door was dressed in an elegant black suit, sheer stockings and to-die-for black heels. She could have been thirty or fifty, depending on how closely you looked. I had the advantage of being able to see her aura. It was a nice sunny-day blue with the faintly fuzzy edge that older people tended to get, which inclined me to think she was closer to fifty.

'Madame Vine? I'm Tara Sharp.'

The woman frowned, sucked in her cheeks and stepped back to let me inside, then clip-clopped off down the polished wood corridor at an impressive pace considering the height of her heels. I followed more slowly, trying not to gawk at the plush lounge area or through the open doorways into the equally opulent bedrooms. This was no tenner-a-trick joint.

Ms Clippety-Clop halted in front of an ornate door and knocked.

'Entrée.'

'It's Ms Sharp, Madame Vine,' my guide announced, in a voice plummier than Joanna Lumley's. She ushered me in, shut the door behind us and waited. My guide, it seemed, was merely the PA.

I stared at the woman seated behind a large, decoratively carved cedar desk. Madame Vine was round-ish, with her hair cut in a bouncy blonde bob. From what I could see from this side of the desk, she was dressed in a silk caftan and a LOT of bling; fingers, neck, wrists, ears. Old style, though. No piercings. If I didn't know better, I'd have picked her to be in real estate.

'Ms Sharp?' she said.

'Madame Vine,' I squeaked.

The two women exchanged a look, then Madame Vine smiled at me the way an animal handler might at a new, frightened zoo inmate. 'Why don't you sit down? Thank you, Audrey.'

Audrey nodded, and walked into an adjoining room. As she passed Madame Vine's desk, the two women's auras blended snugly together. There was something more than the usual work relationship going on there.

I plopped into the brown leather armchair and cleared my throat. Time to be a businesswoman. 'Err … Lloyd Honey said you wished to discuss some potential work.'

'Aaah, Lloyd. Dear man.' Madame Vine slipped one outrageously long, diamanté-studded fingernail between her lips and sucked on it, then removed it to stroke an equally ridiculously long eyelash. 'He claims you have a unique ability to read situations. Is that so, Ms Sharp?'

'Tara, please. And yes,' I said, 'my business is reading paralanguage and kinesics. I usually lean towards investigative jobs but I do consider other things. What did you have in mind?'

Madame Vine got up from her chair and moved around to stand directly under the airconditioning vent. She couldn't have been much over five feet tall and her shrewd, plump face was shiny with moisture. A red aura punctuated with blue flashes fanned her ample frame. I mentally reviewed the aura colour code Mr Hara had taught me. People with red auras tended to be materialistic and pragmatic. The brilliant turquoise flashes signified energy and influence. This woman could probably move mountains if she set her mind to it.

'I run a superior business, Tara, and I'm always looking for ways to improve the quality of the service we give. And to be honest, the global financial crisis hasn't been kind to the more … expensive establishments like us.'

I nodded encouragingly and she went on.

'I sense some … problems amongst my girls but haven't been able to get to the bottom of it.'

'What kind of problems?' I asked.

She hesitated. 'Someone in my employ is disgruntled. Dead animals on the doorstep, threatening text messages, that sort of thing. I wondered if you might be able to work with them for a few days, maybe a week, and see what you can learn.'

'Work with?' What the hell did that mean?

Madame Vine picked up a long, thin, ivory-handled envelope knife. 'The girls get together regularly in the client lounge. I can introduce you as a new employee—that way they'll be relaxed about your presence.'

'Let me get this right. You're suggesting that I pretend to be one of your … workers?'

She gave me a keen smile. 'You wouldn't need to take on any clients. Just participate in the mingling part. The remuneration would be substantial.'

I clutched my sequinned beach bag, trying to ignore the thought of my mother's reaction if she heard about me 'mingling' in a brothel. My sweat snap-froze on my skin. It suddenly felt hard to breathe.

'I-I'm not sure this is really my line of work. And frankly, Madame Vine, I'm sure your girls would see through me in a heartbeat,' I managed to gasp out.

'I can see my proposal has taken you by surprise. Perhaps you should think on it and we can talk again?' she said.

I nodded and sprang up eager to be on my way.

Madame Vine pressed her intercom. 'Audrey. Please see Ms Sharp out.'

Audrey appeared, taking care not to trip over the fringe of the silk floor rug. Her eyebrows lifted slightly and her aura surged towards Madame Vine's. I felt a slight snap of a mild electric shock as their energies met, before she led me out into the corridor. These two definitely had it going on.

As I passed the archway that opened into the front lounge area, I couldn't resist a peek inside.

Two men sat at the small bar. One, his sharp-looking Zegna suit not quite hiding a middle-aged paunch, was skimming a newspaper. He glanced at me then kept on with his reading.

The other was drinking from a bottle of Coke while he pored over paperwork of some kind. And, God save me, I knew him.

My mouth fell open. 'Whitey?'

His head jerked up, a pie halfway to his mouth. 'Sharp?'

It was a bit hard to know where to go from there.

I knew Greg Whitehead—Whitey—at school. After graduation he'd asked me out on a date and, to my utter disappointment, had turned out to be a horny toad. I'd avoided him ever since. But Whitey became a cop, and not so long ago he turned up to a crime scene I'd accidentally stumbled upon. Short story; long outcome. A photo of Whitey and me appeared in the local paper that made his jealous wife, June, furious.

Now it looked like Whitey had found another way to well and truly piss her off. And, as usual, I happened to be in the right place at the wrong time to see it.

'It's only ten in the morning! Can't you keep your fly zipped until after lunch?' The words fell out of my mouth before I could stop them.

Mr Zegna suit sank down further behind his newspaper.

'Are you offering your services?' Whitey fired back.

'Not if you were the last shag on earth.' Ignoring Audrey's disapproving look, I flounced out the front door on enough indignation to float a hot air balloon.

Also from *deadlines**

Deadlines is the crime imprint of the award-winning Twelfth Planet Press specialty small press. We aim to promote quality, fun writing in fresh, exciting projects that seeks to raise the awareness of women's voices, and demonstrate the depth and breadth of Australian fiction to a broader audience.

TARA SHARP 2016

Sharp Shooter

Sharp Turn

Too Sharp

Sharp Edge

CAFÉ LA FEMME
by Livia Day

A Trifle Dead

The Blackmail Blend

Drowned Vanilla

Keep Calm & Kill the Chef (coming soon!)

A TRIFLE DEAD

Book 1 in *The Café La Femme* series
Livia Day

Availiable in paperback and ebook

Tabitha Darling has always had a dab hand for pastry and a knack for getting into trouble. Which was fine when she was a tearaway teen, but not so useful now she's trying to run a hipster urban cafe, invent the perfect trendy dessert, and stop feeding the many (oh so unfashionable) policemen in her life.

When a dead muso is found in the flat upstairs, Tabitha does her best (honestly) not to interfere with the investigation, despite the cute Scottish blogger who keeps angling for her help. Her superpower is gossip, not solving murder mysteries, and those are totally not the same thing, right?

But as that strange death turns into a string of random crimes across the city of Hobart, Tabitha can't shake the unsettling feeling that maybe, for once, it really is ALL ABOUT HER.

And maybe she's figured out the deadly truth a trifle late…

Shortlisted for Best Debut Book, Davitt Award for Australian Women's Crime Writing

Killer Nashville Silver Falchion Finalist